Olaya's voice, this time full of concern, made me turn around. "That's Jackie's car," she said to Consuelo and Martina. She took a step toward it. "Is she . . ."

"Sitting in it," Consuelo finished. Instantly, the three sisters started across the parking lot, headed for the silver sedan parked smack in the middle. It was in one of the darker areas, away from the light of the street lamps.

The police officers had Randy Russell handcuffed and in the back of their cruiser, and were now talking to Miguel Baptista. He stood firmly rooted to the ground, his arms folded over his chest, hands pressed flat beneath his armpits. All that had changed about him was the fact that he'd grown from the attractive young man he'd been in high school to the ruggedly good-looking man who'd just single-handedly saved the day.

My heart went from clenching to fluttering and I kicked myself. Getting involved with Miguel Baptista again was *not* going to happen. And yet—

A blood-curdling scream broke through my thoughts.

"Jackie!" Consuelo's voice was raw and fragile.

Even in the dark, I could see Olaya make the sign of the cross, touching her fingers to her forehead, the center of her chest, her left shoulder, and then her right. *¡Dios mio!*

At the first scream, Miguel was running toward the women and Jackie's car, the two police officers right behind him.

Martina had backed away from the sedan. Consuelo had buckled over, looking like she was hyperventilating. Only Olaya seemed to have kept herself under control. "She's dead," I heard her say. "It's Jackie. I think she's . . . yes . . . she's dead."

Books by Winnie Archer

Kneaded to Death

Kneaded to Death

Winnie Archer

KENSINGTON PUBLISHING CORP.
http://www.kensingtonbooks.com

KENSINGTON BOOKS are published by

Kensington Publishing Corp.
119 West 40th Street
New York, NY 10018

All Kensington Titles, Imprints, and Distributed Lines are available at special quantity discounts for bulk purchases for sales promotions, premiums, fund-raising, and educational or institutional use. Special book excerpts or customized printings can also be created to fit specific needs. For details, write or phone the office of the Kensington special sales manager: Kensington Publishing Corp., 119 West 40th Street, New York, NY 10018, attn: Special Sales Department, Phone: 1-800-221-2647.

Kensington and the K logo Reg. U.S. Pat & TM Off.

ISBN-13: 978-1-4967-0772-7
ISBN-10: 1-4967-0772-9
First Kensington Mass Market Edition: March 2017

eISBN-13: 978-1-4967-0773-4
eISBN-10: 1-4967-0773-7
First Kensington Electronic Edition: March 2017

10 9 8 7 6 5 4 3 2 1

Printed in the United States of America

Chapter One

Santa Sofia is a magical town, nestled between the Santa Lucia Mountain Range and the Pacific Ocean on California's Central Coast. I've always seen it as the perfect place. Not too big, not too small. Historic and true to its commitment to remain a family-oriented place to live. The town accomplished this goal by having more bikes than people, concerts in the park, and a near perfect seventy degrees almost year-round.

I had been gone from my hometown since college but had come back when a horrible accident destroyed our lives as we knew them, taking my mother far too young and leaving my father, my brother, and me bereft and empty. We were still struggling to make sense of what had happened and how a nondescript sedan had backed right into her as she walked behind it in the parking lot at the high school where she'd taught.

"No one saw anything. It was a hit-and-run," my best friend, Emmaline, had told me sadly. "She never saw it coming, and the doctors say she didn't suffer."

That made no sense to me. She was run over by a car. There had to have been pain and suffering, even if it was brief. I relived what I imagined were my mother's last moments. The split second when she saw the truck backing up, realizing that it was coming too fast and that she couldn't get out of the way in time; the impact when it first made contact, hurling her back against the asphalt; the force of the vehicle as it rolled over her. I caught my breath, swallowing the agony I knew she'd felt.

The final result of the tragedy was the emptiness of being back in Santa Sofia without her. The place where I was born and raised no longer filled me with the comfort it used to. Things were different now; six months later, I was still trying to pick up the pieces.

Since I was a little girl, taking photographs had always been my saving grace. Capturing the beauty or heartbreak or pure, unbridled emotions in the world around me showed me how small I was in the scheme of things. At the same time, it allowed me to revel in the moments I captured, treasuring each one as a work of art in and of itself. My mother had given me a camera when I was nine years old and constantly in her hair. "It'll keep you busy," she'd told me, and it had. I had picked up that camera and had never put it down again. Now I had a degree in design and photography. I'd started a photography blog to keep my creative juices flowing, posting a picture a day. I'd had a vibrant business in

Austin. But I was floundering. Since I lost my mother, finding inspiration had become a challenge. My voice had been silenced, it seemed, and I had nothing more to say with the images through the lens.

This lack of direction and the loss of my creative vision are what led me to Yeast of Eden, the bread shop in Santa Sofia. I might be able to end my dry spell if I could find inspiration somewhere. Somehow. But now, as I stood at the doorway, one hand on the handle, I wondered what in the hell I'd been thinking. Baking? A pan of brownies from a boxed mix? Sure. A batch of chocolate chip cookies, courtesy of the recipe on the back of the Nestlé package? Definitely. But from-scratch bread? Not in my wheelhouse. Baking was a far cry from finding beauty through the lens of a camera. The mere thought that I was even contemplating this bit of craziness clearly meant that I was under duress.

True, I'd been to the local bread shop every day since I'd moved back to Santa Sofia. Truth be told, the place was becoming my home away from home, but that did not give me the right to think I could actually make the stuff. And it certainly didn't mean baking would solve my problems. Grief had to run its course. I knew this, but the reality was that I'd never *not* feel the emptiness inside.

An image of my dad popped into my head. "What did you bring today?" he regularly asked me. It was becoming almost a joke, because I'd already cycled through nearly everything Yeast of Eden had to offer . . . twice. Baguettes. Sourdough. Croissants. Rye. Wheat pumpernickel. Focaccia.

Check.

Check.

Check.

Check.

Check.

And check.

There were so many choices, and I loved them all. But I did have my favorites. The flaky, buttery croissant in the morning or a crusty sourdough roll at lunch—these were the staples. On a sunny day, the pumpernickel with sliced turkey and cheese hit the spot. When it was rainy, I bought a round loaf of French bread, turned it into a bread bowl, and filled it with homemade chowder.

But this time I wasn't here to buy bread; I was here to get my hands dirty, so to speak. To plunge them into a bowl of dough and knead, knead, knead. And somehow, despite logic and despite reason, I knew that it was going to be life changing. I had no idea how . . . or why, but as sure as I was standing on the cobbled sidewalk in Santa Sofia, and as sure as the breeze off the Pacific Ocean blew through me, I was 100 percent certain that the bread-baking class at Yeast of Eden was going to send me on a new trajectory.

But was I ready?

Before I had the chance to answer that question in my head, the door opened, and a woman in a colorful caftan and red clogs, hands firmly on her hips, emerged. Her iron-gray hair was cropped short and loose, playful curls danced over her head. Her green eyes, heavily flecked with gold, stared me down. "*Ven aqui, m'ija,*" she said to me in Spanish, as if I could understand her. Which I could not. "You have to come inside to change your life."

I jumped, startled. "To change my . . . what? I'm sorry. What?"

"You don't think I recognize you? You, *mi amor*, are here every day. You have discovered the magic of this place, and now you want more." She smiled, her eyebrows lifting in a quick movement that seemed to say "I see this every day." "Come in. We're all waiting."

"You're all . . . ?" I stared. "Who's waiting?"

This time the woman laughed. She threw her head back and gave a hearty guffaw that made me take a step back. Of course, I recognized her, too. Her daily authoritative presence had made it easy to deduce that the woman owned Yeast of Eden. "The rest of the bakers, *por supuesto.*"

Her laughter seeped into me, and despite myself, I felt a smile tilt my lips upward, but I bit down to stop it from being fully realized. Being happy was simply not okay. How could it be when I'd lost my mother just a few short months ago, and when my dad, my brother, and I were hanging on to each other just to get by? My grief had become part of me. It was embedded in my soul. Trapped in my pores. Smiling felt like a betrayal of my sorrow. A betrayal of my mother.

The woman watched me with a gaze that seemed to burrow through every bit of me. Her voice softened. "It will be all right, you know."

A flurry of goose bumps danced over my skin. I'd spoken to this woman no more than a handful of times, and the interactions were always superficial and cursory, and yet somehow she seemed to know exactly what I was feeling. I tried to school my expression. I tended to show every one of my emotions on my face the very second I felt them; I was working on that particular problem.

"I don't know what you mean," I said, my voice a little more indignant than I'd intended it to be.

She considered me again and then gave a succinct nod. "*Está bien, m'ija.* Come in then." She held the door open, letting me pass. "It is time to bake some bread."

"I'm not . . . I've never . . . I don't cook, you know," I said, already apologizing for the future failure I was afraid might happen once I got into the kitchen.

"Perhaps not yet, but you will . . . ," she said, letting the words trail away, and just like that, I felt as if I really might be able to do the impossible and learn this new, tantalizing skill.

She flipped the sign hanging in the window to show CLOSED and locked the door. I followed her deeper into the bread shop, the scent of fresh-baked bread swirling around me and enveloping me like a cocoon. As I breathed in, letting it soak into me for just a moment, I felt the grief that was always with me soften around the edges. For the first time since I could remember, it ebbed and I felt my lungs open up.

I followed her flowing caftan–clad body through the swinging doors, which led to the back room. "*La cocina*," she said, gesturing wide with her arms. "This is my favorite place in the world. Settle in, *m'ija. This* is where you belong."

I didn't know if she was right about that, but I let the comment go, instead looking at the other women gathered around the room. They had been chattering excitedly, but their voices had tapered off as we walked in.

"It's about time," one of the women said, her gaze trained on the bread shop owner. "At long last. *Lista?* Are you finally ready?"

"Keep your *pantalones* on, Consuelo." The iron-haired woman wagged a finger at the one called Consuelo, and I noticed how alike they looked. Sisters. They had to be. Consuelo was a few inches taller and her hair was dyed a deep brown, but they had the same eyes, the same nose, slightly curved down at the end, and the same hollowed cheek-bones.

The other women in the kitchen were of varying ages. I placed the owner—I still didn't know her name—in her early sixties; Consuelo, a few years younger; and another woman, who was wearing wide-legged black pants, a T-shirt with a cardigan over it, and slip-on sandals, somewhere in her late fifties. Three others were closer to my age.

I stepped forward and gave a little wave. "I'm Ivy Culpepper."

The owner's eyebrows flicked up again, as if something she'd thought had just been validated. "And I'm Olaya," she said. "Olaya Solis. This is my shop. Bread baked the way it used to be made back in Mexico."

The comfort I'd felt when I'd walked into the shop and breathed in the scent of bread deepened. It almost seemed as if we were connected somehow, this woman and me. But the moment I thought it, I shook the thought away. It was ridiculous. I'd been away from Santa Sofia for nearly a decade, and before I started coming to Yeast of Eden, I'd never laid eyes on Olaya Solis.

But still . . .

Olaya stepped up so that she was even with me, and started pointing. "Consuelo is my sister. *Y tambien . . .* so is Martina."

The woman in the cardigan, Martina, lifted her chin and gave a slight smile and a shy wave.

"Martina is the quiet one in the family," Consuelo said, her own voice booming.

Consuelo definitely was *not* the quiet one. They were three sisters who might be different from one another, but they *had* each other. I had a brother, and while we were close, it wasn't the same as what I imagined having a sister would be like.

"I'm Jolie," one of the younger women said. She looked to be in her mid- to late twenties, maybe not around the corner from my own thirty-six years, but relatively close. She had long, straight black hair, which she'd pulled back into a careless ponytail. I inadvertently touched my own mop of curly ginger locks. I looked just like my mom, which I was grateful for, but as a result, I generally appear just a touch disheveled and not nearly as effortlessly put together as Jolie appeared. My hair looked like it had been shampooed with liquid paprika and made my green eyes sparkle like shiny emeralds. I'd pulled it up, wrapped it around and around, and tied it with a hair band.

My whole childhood, I'd longed for the sleek look that Jolie had, instead of the free spirit presence that I'd inherited from my mother. I waited for that old, familiar feeling of envy to seep in . . . but it didn't. Jolie was a beauty, but for the first time, I consciously realized that while I wasn't gorgeous like she was, I was okay with who I was. More than okay. I loved looking in the mirror and catching a glimpse of where I came from. Of *who* I came from.

"Nice to meet you," I said.

"There was a teacher—Mrs. Culpepper—at the high school. English, I think. Are you . . . ?"

"She was my mother," I said, glancing away.

"Wasn't she . . . was she . . . ," Jolie began, but she trailed off.

One of the other young women finished for her. "There was a hit-and-run at the school a few months ago."

"It was a horrible accident." I managed to keep my voice from quavering.

"Oh!" Jolie's jaw dropped. "I'm sorry."

Olaya placed her hand on my back, a comforting gesture. "Let's get to our baking," she said, sensing that I didn't want to talk about my mother's death. She introduced the other two young women as Sally and Becky. They each lifted their hands in a quick wave, and we all found our spaces at the counter. Each station had a name tag with a name neatly printed on it. Next to the name was a drawing of an apron. From what I could see, each apron was unique. As Olaya directed me to my station, I saw that even I had a name tag.

I spun around to look at her, raising my eyebrows in puzzlement. "How . . . ?"

"I knew you'd be coming," she answered.

I couldn't fathom how she'd known with such certainty that I'd come to this baking class when I hadn't even known for sure. But there was my name, my station, a lovely petit four, and an apron, all waiting for me. Each baking station had been equipped with a large mixing bowl, a container of flour, a jar of yeast, and the other essential ingredients for bread making, as well as a glass of ice water for our own hydration. I immediately took a deep sip, steadying my nerves. Only one empty station—water and petit four untouched—remained. Everyone else seemed to have eaten their sweet treat. I followed suit and nibbled mine.

Olaya took her place behind the stainless-steel

center island and began talking. I'd detected a slight accent when she first met me at the door to Yeast of Eden, but now, as she spoke about the history of bread making in Mexico, it became more pronounced. "I know what you are thinking," she said. "Tortillas, yes? The bread of Mexico has always been tortillas. And yes, I make and sell Mexico's traditional fare once in a while. But bread . . ." She gestured toward the swinging doors, which led back to the front of the now closed shop and the display cases that were littered with what was left of the day's baked goods. "I have been baking bread since I was a little girl. Once I started, I never stopped."

I listened, enthralled. Her words seeped into me, and I understood completely. It was all about passion. Mine was photography. I had left California to go to college in Texas and had stayed there for many years, building my business. Circumstances had brought me back, I was starting over, and turning to the lens was the only thing I knew how to do. I imagined the display cases in Yeast of Eden overflowing with the day's offerings every morning, and I had a sudden hankering to photograph them. I made a mental note to myself to bring my camera in the morning and take a few shots, excited to see how the light would be and thinking about how best to capture the delicacy of the bread.

As Olaya continued filling us in on her history as a bread maker, the back door opened and a woman in a knee-length jean skirt and a floral blouse breezed in. "Sorry I'm late!"

"Late?" Olaya said, not missing a beat. "Jackie, five more minutes and I would have locked the door. You would have been stuck outside, with not an ounce of bread. You would have been . . . How do you say it?" She drew a finger across her neck. "Out of luck."

Clearly, Olaya didn't like tardiness with her classes. Duly noted. But I'd detected a light touch in her voice, and there was the faintest hint of a smile on her lips. I suspected that Jackie wasn't often on time and that Olaya had learned to accept this about her.

Jackie looked around and frowned, but Olaya ushered her to her workstation. She grabbed an apron off a hook and handed it to her. "But you are here now. You might as well stay."

"I had my own class to wrap up. Not as meaningful as baking bread, of course, but my livelihood." Her eyes glinted mischievously as she pushed her name tag aside, tied on her apron, took a drink from her ice water, and bit into her petit four. "Did I miss the talk about you baking bread as a child in Mexico?"

"She was just finishing," Consuelo said, and the two women's gazes met.

Jackie mouthed, "Phew!" and a knowing grin crossed each of their faces. Evidently, they had both taken the bread-making classes before and had heard Olaya's stories.

Olaya ignored her sister and her friend. She scanned Jackie up and down, and her gaze settled on the wedge heels. "Very nice shoes you are wearing," she said. "Perfect for baking."

Jackie burst out laughing and boisterously kicked up one leg behind her in an old Hollywood starlet manner. "That's exactly what I thought. You know my philosophy. One should always look her best, and shoes are the instant wardrobe definer." She fluttered her hand. "Carry on, Olaya."

I stood back as the women chattered, taking it all in, absorbing the energy in the kitchen. Memories of being in my childhood kitchen with my mom settled over me like a layer of gauze cloaking me. We'd cooked. We'd baked. She'd taught me everything I knew about being independent, about being strong, about being a woman. The memory slipped and cracked, and once again sorrow leached through me.

I drew in a deep breath, stilling my racing heartbeat, tucking the memory of my mom and me in her kitchen into a back corner of my mind. I wouldn't think about it right now.

Olaya reached her hand into a large plastic bin and let a handful of flour cascade through her fingers. "Baking bread is an art," she was saying. "I come in at four thirty every morning, and I produce top-quality breads on a daily basis. Consistency is key. When you bake, you get one shot. You don't know for certain if the bread is going to turn out the way it should until it comes out of the oven. It must look right. It must taste right. There are no additives. There are no shortcuts. My goal is for it always to be perfect, and that takes time. That is the payoff."

My heart beat a little faster, a niggling worry about producing a flawless loaf of bread working its way through me. This was supposed to be fun, not stressful.

Olaya must have sensed the pressure building in the room, because she smiled and patted the air with her hands, as if to calm us down. "You will learn to let your experience guide you. You will learn what to look for, what to feel for, and how to work the dough until you produce bread to be proud of."

I closed my eyes and let Olaya's words and voice float around me. Let my anxiety fade away. If my bread didn't turn out quite right, well, I'd be okay with that. I was doing something new. Doing something I wanted to do. Doing something challenging. And I was excited about the prospect.

Olaya continued. "Do you know my sisters and I come from a long line of *brujas*? Witches," she explained when Jolie asked what that meant. "Family legend has it that a *bruja*, many generations past, had been wronged by a man—"

"What else is new?" Jackie snarked.

"Is there any other way?" Consuelo added. She winked at Jackie.

Martina, the quiet one, piped up. "*Cállate*, both of you. You choose badly, so what do you expect?"

Consuelo and Jackie sniggered to each other, and Olaya continued as if there hadn't been an interruption at all. "To protect the future women in her line, the *bruja* in our *familia* made it so that mothers and daughters, *abuelitas* and *nietas*, aunts and nieces, *madrinas* and *comadres*—these relationships would last and sustain themselves better than any other. She blessed the women in my line with the ability to cook. To bake. And that is how this tradition started in my family."

She continued, "Me? I have no choice. I must bake bread. You?" She pointed at each of us. "You are each here for your own reasons. I will be your guide. I will show you how to create your own bread, and you will form your own traditions. You will come to understand the power of bread. No. The power of *baking*. Of creating with your hands. Your mind. Your *soul*. We women are strong, and bread is healing. It can give you strength you did not know you had."

I didn't know what to make of the Solis women, the magic they put into bread making, and the fact that they thought they came from an ancient line of witches. But I went with it. There was something about them. I liked them all, especially Olaya, and being in her kitchen . . . in her *cocina* . . . gave me a sense of peace I hadn't felt since my mother died.

We spent the next hour measuring and mixing the ingredients for *conchas*.

"Mexican sweet bread is an easy way to start the bread-making process," Olaya said.

We went through the lesson by mixing the yeast

and warm water, adding the milk, sugar, butter, eggs, and flour, and finally kneading the mixture until a soft, pliable dough formed.

"Much of the bread I make here is to be long cultured," she continued. "Forty-eight hours or more, to get the best rise and flavor possible. But the sweet bread, the *conchas*, can rise much more quickly."

We left the dough in our greased bowls covered with a thin dishcloth and went to the front of the shop, where Olaya walked us through the different breads still remaining in the display cases, telling us the history of her experiences making sourdough loaves, French baguettes, boules, brioche, *tartine* country bread, challah, festive breads, and so much more. Part way through the bread tour, Jackie's cell phone rang, sounding like the harsh ring of an old-fashioned phone from twenty years ago. Jackie answered, avoiding Olaya's disapproving glare.

"I can't," she whispered into the smartphone. "I'm in the middle of a class."

Whoever was on the other end of the line said something that caused the color to drain from Jackie's face. She turned a ghostly white and glanced around, her spooked gaze skittering over each of us. Turning her back to us again, she cupped her hand over the phone and lowered her voice even more. "No. She's not. It was my decision. My life, not yours."

She talked for another minute, but her words were muted. Unintelligible.

Finally, she pressed the OFF button and shoved her phone into her pocket. The next instant, her phone rang again. "Kids," she said when she'd looked at the caller ID. "I told you, I'm busy, Jasmine," she said, but she looked at Olaya, rolled her eyes, and pushed through the swinging doors, disappearing back into the kitchen.

The three sisters gave each other some sort of knowing look, as if they knew something about Jackie's phone calls from Jasmine that gave them all pause, but Olaya picked up right where she'd left off in her talk.

"Artisan bread is handcrafted. They are hearth-baked loaves, and now I am going to tell you the secret. Are you ready?" she asked, a twinkle in her eyes.

We all nodded. I'd heard the stories about Yeast of Eden and the magic in the bread here. If you had a cold, people around Santa Sofia said that a loaf of traditional French bread from Yeast of Eden could cure it. If you'd had too little sleep, the five-grain bread was sure to wake you up. Heartbroken? Choose the sundried tomato and black olive or the fig and almond loaf. Either would mend the sadness. I wanted to know the secret to Olaya's magic as much as everyone else did, but part of me wondered if knowing would lessen the impact the bread could have or, worse, somehow take away altogether the magic it held. My daily visits had helped me cope with losing my mother; I didn't want that to stop.

Olaya forged on. "The secret," she said, her voice low and conspiratorial, "is wet dough."

I laughed spontaneously. I'd been expecting some mystical truth, but Olaya, although she might well be a *bruja*, was a realist. Wet dough. Okay, then.

"But the *conchas* dough wasn't wet," Becky, one of the younger class members, said.

Olaya nodded. "True. *Bueno.* That is a good observation. *Conchas* are lovely sweet breads, but they are not artisan breads. I do not want to scare you away too fast. You must learn the basics first, and then slowly you can increase your repertoire."

After another few minutes, we took a ten-minute bathroom break and then followed Olaya back into the kitchen and resumed our places at our stations with our bowls of sweet bread dough. Mine was a creamy white and had doubled, the previously dense dough now light and airy.

Olaya stood at the island, and we all looked at the mirror that was positioned above it, angled so that we could see exactly what she was doing. She'd told us how she'd had the mirror installed the previous year so she could teach others the art of bread making. As I watched her reflection mix the topping ingredients for the *conchas*, I could honestly say that the mirror was a great tool. We could all see everything she was doing so clearly, and we effortlessly followed her every move.

I followed her directions, step by step, beating the sugar and butter, stirring in flour until the mixture was the consistency of a thick paste, and then mixing in cinnamon.

Next, she turned her *conchas* dough out onto her stainless-steel counter. I followed suit, then rolled the dough into a log and cut it into twelve even pieces. After rolling the pieces into balls, I placed them onto the greased cookie sheet I'd already prepared. Olaya led us as we divided the topping paste into balls, then flattened each one, placed one on top of each of the *conchas* balls, and patted each one down lightly with our open palms.

"The last step," she said, "is to take your knife and cut grooves into the topping. Like a clamshell," she added. "*Y lista*. It is ready. Now it must rise again for about forty-five minutes, and we will bake."

It was at that moment that Consuelo looked around and asked, "Where's Jackie?"

I turned to Jackie's baking station. She wasn't there. I'd been so wrapped up in the baking process that I hadn't noticed. Neither, apparently, had anyone else.

"*Hijo de la chingada*. Of course it is Jasmine," Olaya said. "Now she wants to talk, and Jackie jumps. The girl cannot have it both ways."

"She is her daughter," Martina said softly. She definitely was the quiet sister, as Consuelo had said, but if she had an opinion, she seemed more than willing to share it.

A bowl crashed to the floor, breaking the tension.

"Sorry," Becky said.

Jolie dropped to her knees to pick up the ceramic fragments. "No, no. It was my fault."

But no one paid either of them any mind. Olaya and Consuelo headed out the back door of the kitchen. It had grown dark while we'd been baking, but the typically peaceful beach sounds of Santa Sofia weren't what we heard. Instead, the sound of male voices floated in the air. And then, like rolling thunder in the sky, at first distant, but growing louder, familiar yet at the same time ominous, an old, familiar voice crept into my consciousness. Memories from high school. Memories of my broken heart being torn apart and stomped on. Memories of the face behind all that old pain.

My heart seized. It was Miguel Baptista . . . and he was still right here in Santa Sofia.

Chapter Two

After stepping outside with the other women in the bread-making class, I saw trouble with a capital *T*. Miguel Baptista and I had dated during my junior year (his senior year). I'd fallen head over heels, and I'd thought Miguel had, too, but his desire to get out of Santa Sofia had been greater than whatever he'd felt for me. He had graduated from high school and had taken the next bus out of town. I didn't think he'd ever looked back. I'd been nothing but a blip in his love life, but I'd always wondered if he was the one that got away.

Except here he was, arguing with a man I didn't know in the parking lot behind Yeast of Eden, their figures illuminated by the old-fashioned streetlights around the perimeter of the lot.

Seeing him reaffirmed something for me. He was the one I'd never fully gotten out of my system.

"Is that Randy Russell?" Sally asked, peering at the man Miguel was arguing with.

"What's he got in his hand?" Becky drew in a sharp breath and took a step backward. "Oh my God. It's a gun!"

A shot of panic surged through my veins. A gun?

There was a burst of lavender and hydrangeas in the planter beds on either side of the door, and we all instantly dodged behind them, trampling the columbine, bellflower, coralbells, and daisies that were also planted there. Of course, I realized too late that the fronds and flowers of these pretty planter beds wouldn't actually do anything to stop a stray bullet that might happen to come our way.

I peered through the lacy flowers and saw a man waving what looked like an old pistol. The light was dim, but the streetlights illuminated the scene well enough. I could see that his cheeks were ruddy, the color creeping up from his neck. "Who is he?" I said under my breath to the other women hiding beside me in the flower bushes.

"Randy co-owns the antique store across the street with Gus Makers," Jolie whispered.

Sally pulled apart two enormous hydrangea blooms to peer more closely. "What is wrong with him?"

I couldn't hear what Miguel and Randy were saying to each other, but Randy's voice was raised. He was definitely upset about something. Miguel patted the air with his open palms, working to calm him down. We all recoiled as Randy waved his arms around. Something seemed off. I peered into the waning light, trying to get a better look at the weapon in his hand. Realization struck me.

"It's not a gun." I heaved a relieved sigh and repeated, "It's not a gun."

In fact, it looked more like an antique billy club. How any of us could have mistaken the short brown club for a gun, I was not sure. All I knew was that I heaved an enormous sigh of relief.

Olaya seemed to realize the same thing. She muttered something in Spanish, blew out a loud breath, and suddenly charged forward. "Enough. Randy Russell. *Qué pasó?* What are you doing?"

Randy stopped and slowly turned around. "Back off, Olaya," he said with a hiss.

"I will not, Randy. You interrupt my class, and you act like a crazy person."

He flung his head this way and that, as if he were looking for someone. Then he raised his hand, the billy club clenched tight.

I and the women flanking me in the flower beds gasped in unison.

"Oh my God," Jolie said.

"What's he going to do?" Becky muttered.

Sally suddenly clasped her hand on my shoulder.

I willed them all to relax, and at the same time, I willed Olaya to back away and not bait him anymore. Even though it wasn't a gun, a lot of damage could be done with a club. Unfortunately, I didn't have the magical ability to communicate telepathically with her. Instead of retreating, as I'd hoped, she advanced on him.

"Randy Russell, you hothead, you need to put that stick away, go home, and sober up. Gus and Jackie are not your business. They are old news," she told him.

Behind him, Miguel seemed to make eye contact with Olaya. She continued to distract Randy Russell, and as I watched, Miguel crept forward like a panther. In one lightning quick move, he threw one arm around him and grabbed his wrist with his other hand. "You don't want to do this, pal," he said, and the next thing I knew, Miguel had yanked the man's hand down until it was behind his back and the club was no longer in his grip. In ten seconds flat, Miguel had disarmed the lunatic, a siren blared and grew deafening as a police cruiser skidded into the parking lot, and Randy Russell broke free and took off running. Stumbling. Running.

A female officer jettisoned out of the police car before it even stopped, and took up chase. Moments later, she tackled Randy Russell and it was over.

Just as we had made a collective gasp a minute before, the four of us in the bushes let out the breaths we'd been holding, releasing sighs of relief.

"Did you think the lavender would protect you if he'd actually had a gun?" a voice said.

I looked up to see Olaya staring down at me and the other wannabe bakers still crouched behind the flowers. The white apron she'd had on all evening still covered her clothing.

"I already realized the folly," I said, "but hiding was instinct. This was the best we could do."

"Let us hope your baking talent is better than your self-preservation skills," she said. We unfurled ourselves from our crouched positions, and she ushered us out from behind the hydrangeas and lavender.

"Miguel Baptista," I muttered, sneaking another look at the boy—now the man—who'd broken my heart once upon a time. He looked the same, yet somehow completely different. A little bit weathered. Experienced. Intense. Six feet, dark hair, swarthy skin, end-of-the-day stubble, and elongated creases that ran from the side of his mouth to his chin, like exaggerated dimples. Miguel Baptista made my heart contract in my chest.

Olaya paused, considering me once again. "You know him?"

"We went to school together," I said, leaving it at that. I already felt as if Olaya could see right through me; she didn't need to know the heartbreak of my youth.

"He knows how to handle himself, doesn't he?" Jolie said, a smitten expression on her face, and I felt an unreasonable and wholly unwarranted stab of jealousy. Where had *that* come from? I had no claim on Miguel Baptista. Less than none.

"Ten years in the military will do that for a man," Olaya said. "So yes, he can handle himself quite well." She patted her iron-gray hair and looked around, frowning, and I remembered that we'd come outside in the first place to look for Jackie.

Olaya's voice, this time full of concern, made me turn around. "That's Jackie's car," she said to Consuelo and Martina. She took a step toward it. "Is she . . . ?"

"Sitting in it?" Consuelo said, finishing the question. Instantly, the three sisters started across the parking lot, headed for the silver sedan parked smack in the middle. It was in one of the darker areas, away from the light of the street lamps.

The police officers had Randy Russell handcuffed and in the back of their cruiser and were now talking to Miguel Baptista. He stood firmly rooted to the ground, his arms folded over his chest, hands pressed flat beneath his armpits. All that had changed about him was the fact that he'd grown from the attractive young man he'd been in high school into the ruggedly good-looking man who'd just single-handedly saved the day.

My heart went from clenching to fluttering, and I kicked myself. Getting involved with Miguel Baptista again was *not* going to happen. And yet—

A bloodcurdling scream broke through my thoughts.

"Jackie!" Consuelo's voice was raw and fragile.

Even in the dark, I could see Olaya make the sign of the cross, touching her fingers to her forehead, the center of her chest, her left shoulder, and then her right. *"Dios mio!"*

At the first scream, Miguel was running toward the women and Jackie's car, the two police officers right behind him.

Martina had backed away from the sedan. Consuelo had buckled over, looking like she was hyperventilating. Only Olaya seemed to have kept herself under control.

"She's dead," I heard her say. "It's Jackie. I think she's . . . Yes . . . she's dead."

Chapter Three

The town of Santa Sofia would always be part of me, the memory of my mom firmly rooted in every part of the town, every corner I turned, every street I walked down. It was a curse and a blessing. Eventually, I hoped I'd be able to let go of the sadness and revel only in the memories.

My dad and my brother, Billy, would do anything for me, and I felt the same about them. Family was everything, and they were mine. Then there was Agatha. About eighteen pounds and cute as a button, she was my little pug. I'd rescued her back in Texas just after my divorce, and she was my little shadow. We'd helped each other in our times of need, and now she was my greatest comfort.

But in the years I'd been away from Santa Sofia, Emmaline Davis had been my other constant. Emmaline had graduated college with a degree in criminal justice and had become a deputy sheriff in Santa Sofia. When I'd first heard about her position, I'd wondered if Santa Sofia even needed a deputy sheriff. Did anything criminal ever happen here?

I hadn't thought so, but the night before I'd been proven dead wrong. Jackie Makers, the woman in the jean skirt and wedge heels, was dead. And according to the officers at the site, not only was she dead, but she also quite possibly had been killed.

As in murdered.

I'd met a woman, albeit briefly, whose life had been suddenly, and purposefully, ripped from her.

And Emmaline Davis was going to be central to bringing the woman's murderer to justice.

My thoughts went back to Miguel and the scene I'd witnessed the night before. Even if he held a long petrified place in my heart, I didn't pine for him. If I'd never seen him again, I'd have been fine with that. I'd moved on. So seeing him right here in the back parking lot of Yeast of Eden, facing down a man on the proverbial ledge, had sent my blood pressure skyrocketing and now sent me straight to the phone to call Emmaline.

"Miguel Baptista lives in Santa Sofia," I said, clutching the phone between my ear and shoulder as I whipped off my ball cap, tucked my hair back behind my ears, and jammed the cap back on my head.

I heard the *tap-tap-tap* of Emmaline's fingers on her computer keyboard. She was a pro at multi-tasking. I imagined her digging into the murder of Jackie Makers. Maybe they'd already charged Randy Russell. He'd been in the right place at the right time, after all, and he might not have had a gun, but he'd had a few screws loose in his head. He seemed to be the perfect suspect.

"Why is he back here?" I asked, back to Miguel.

"His dad passed away about a year ago. He came back to take over the restaurant. His mom was in no shape," Emmaline said, distracted.

"I can't believe you never told me he was back," I said, feeling irrationally hurt.

"You and Miguel are such old news. I didn't think you'd care."

"We are," I said. "And you're right, I don't." Did I?

The death of Mr. Baptista explained it all. Miguel might have had some wild oats to sow way back when, but he came from good stock, and he knew that family was at the heart of everything good and dear. His mama had needed him, and it didn't take much to deduce that he'd done the right thing by her, coming home to save the restaurant named after the family. And none of it had even the remotest thing to do with me.

I told myself that, but Emmaline read between the lines. "Ivy Culpepper, you should just march on over there to Baptista's and say your hellos. You know you want to."

I mustered up a good dose of indignant dismay. "I most certainly do not. . . ."

The typing stopped abruptly. "You most certainly do, and don't you deny it. That man has been a thorn in your side ever since he left you, hasn't he? He probably ruined your marriage to what's-his-name—"

"My marriage was ruined by what's-his-name's lack of backbone and immature infidelity," I interrupted.

She didn't miss a beat. "And it's been forever. Get him out of your system once and for all so some other worthy man can steal your heart."

"Been there, done that. I'm destined to be single. Which I'm fine with."

"You're still pining for Miguel," she said.

"Ha! No. I'm not. And don't even talk to me about pining for someone, Em. Talk about the pot calling the kettle black. You don't have a leg to stand on." She and my brother, Billy, had been on and off again for years, had been flirting for even more years, and had each been in long-term relationships with other people but had never gotten to the commitment stage of their own affair.

"I'm black, he's white, and—" she began, as if the simple statement was meant to explain why she would have an unrequited love for the rest of her life.

"And this is California, and it's the twenty-first century, not nineteen fifty Mississippi. If you and Billy love each other, you should be together. Period."

"I know," she said from her end of the phone line, but she sounded dejected. "But you know how hard it is to cross a huge ravine without a bridge."

"You're making a ravine where there is none, Em," I said, "and even if there was some uncrossable canyon between you two, Billy would *be* the bridge. He loves you. He always has."

My brother hadn't ever confided in me about how he felt about Emmaline, but I'd seen the way he looked at her, the lovesick expression in his eyes whenever she entered the room, and their star-crossed lover thing had been going on for years. I was 100 percent sure that he'd lay down his life for her, so why they both felt circumstances had conspired against them and their love was baffling.

"So, about Miguel," Emmaline said in a not so subtle change of subject. Maybe this was why she and Billy had never really got together and stayed together. Neither one of them could stand to get serious and have the hard conversation.

"There's nothing to say. I'm back. He's here. That's all I wanted to tell you. You could have mentioned it, is all."

"You just stay away from him, then," she said, playing devil's advocate. If only her staying away from Billy, or Billy from her, made a bit of difference in how they actually felt, I might have taken her seriously. As it was, I let the pink elephant in the room quietly slip out.

"So what's the story with Jackie Makers?" I asked. This time I was the one who was not so subtly changing the subject. After discovering the body, Olaya had abruptly canceled the baking class. The police had come in, and the bread shop's kitchen had become a crime scene. They'd taken pictures and, I presumed, collected evidence. After they'd gone, I'd stayed behind and helped Martina and Consuelo dump the *conchas* dough in the garbage. But since then I'd been on edge, wondering what had happened to Jackie. Who in the world could have killed her?

The tap-tap-tapping on the other end of the line stopped, and suddenly I had Emmaline's full attention. "You tell me. You saw her before she died, right?"

"Yes," I answered, wishing anything I could tell her would actually make a difference in her investigation. "But she got to Yeast of Eden late, and then we started baking right away."

"Since when do you bake bread?" she asked.

"Since this big hole in my heart appeared."

Silence. I hadn't meant to snap at her, but the death of my mother brought a constant array of different emotions out in me, and sometimes I couldn't control them. "Yeah. Makes sense," she said.

"So, Jackie Makers?" I nudged her back to a subject I was more comfortable with. Anything not to think about how much I missed my mom.

"Randy Russell is no longer a suspect," she said. "We released him this morning."

I drew in a startled breath. "But the club in his hand, and his ranting—"

"He knew the victim, but we have no evidence pointing to a motive. He was on a bender, and it's common knowledge that he has a lot of pent-up resentment toward Jackie. She was the woman who hurt his best friend so badly," she explained. "But she was definitely *not* beaten to death, and he didn't seem to know she was there."

"Okay," I conceded. "So do you have a different suspect? Surely not Miguel . . . ?"

"No. Relax. As far as I can tell, Miguel didn't even know the woman. Right now we're sort of nowhere. We have a few people of possible interest. The bread shop owner. Her sisters. All the women in the class, in fact. Except you, of course."

My heart felt like it stopped cold in my chest. "You think one of the Solis sisters might have killed their friend? No way," I said. "Impossible."

"How are you so sure?" she asked, and I imagined her eyebrows pulling together as she waited for my response.

"I was with them all evening. We were baking bread. We listened to a talk about the history of bread in Mexico—" I broke off, drawing in another breath, but this time it was sharp and sudden.

"What?" Emmaline prompted.

"No, nothing," I answered. "How did she die?" It certainly hadn't been obvious to me as a bystander.

"There'll be an autopsy. There was no visible wound, so the logical assumption is poison of some sort. It'll be a month, maybe more, before we know for sure."

A month or more? That seemed like forever. Real life certainly didn't work like "life" did on TV. I went with Emmaline's logic and thought about Jackie being poisoned. Could it have happened while she was at Yeast of Eden? Did poison act that quickly?

I thought about the possibilities. Jackie hadn't been at the bread shop for very long, but I had one distinct recollection. We'd each had a glass of water at our stations. Olaya had directed Jackie to her baking station, and Jackie had taken a good long drink. But I didn't tell Emmaline this. I couldn't. It might have been misguided, but I couldn't stand the thought that I could have so drastically misjudged a person. Olaya Solis couldn't have killed her friend Jackie.

Could she?

Chapter Four

The Historic Society of Santa Sofia was a political hotbed on par with . . . with . . . with the worst of the presidential elections in the United States. Or at least that was how I saw things now that I was back in my hometown. My dad was the city manager and oversaw the historic society. It mostly seemed like this particular department was full of infighting and petty battles, but he loved it, and now I was walking alongside him as he took stock of a renovation project on Maple Street, in the historic district.

My dad and I walked down the sidewalk, my fawn pug, Agatha, trotting beside me in her tiny harness. Her ears were back, and her tail was curled happily. She'd been the last dog surrendered by a backyard breeder. From sitting on the couch, trembling, to scampering about in joy, she'd come a long way.

We stopped in front of a sunny yellow clapboard house. Agatha instantly sat beside me, waiting as I took in the details of the house. The front porch was adorned with a hanging bench on one side, a ceramic planter draped with green ivy, and two red Adirondack chairs. "It's so cute," I said. "What's the problem?"

My dad pinched his thumb and index finger together, pressed them against the space above his upper lip, and stroked his mustache. "Stupidity. The problem, Ivy, is pure stupidity."

Every house on the street was at least fifty years old, and some, like the one under renovation, was closer to a hundred, at least.

"How so?"

"The Mastersons, over there," he said, pointing to the pale and worn pink house next to the one being renovated, "pretty much want to destroy the Rabels."

"The Rabels own the yellow house?"

My dad stroked his mustache again and nodded. "The house was falling apart when they bought it. Was literally falling apart right in front of our eyes. It was actually sinking. Only the fireplace in the center was holding it in place. They bought it and had to rebuild the foundation and lift everything up. It's been years, and they're still working on it. From what I can see and know of them, it's been a labor of love for them."

I looked at the house while he continued, admiring the unassuming design. It was a simple square. The front door had a glass center, allowing for a clear view through to the back. A staircase on the left led upstairs, a hallway led straight back, and the main living space appeared to be on the right. "It's beautiful." I crouched down and scratched my dog's head. "We could live in a place like this, couldn't we, Agatha?"

Agatha glanced up at me with her giant, bulbous eyes. Her upper lip was caught on her top teeth. It looked like a grimace, but I called it a smile. An old home full of history and charm was exactly the type of place I envisioned myself in. Someday. My years in Austin, Texas, and the derailment of my marriage had taken a mental and financial toll. I'd been saving, but I wasn't quite there. Yet.

For now I'd just have to dream.

"So the Rabels fixed a house that was falling apart. I don't get what the problem is."

"Meet the Mastersons," he said, and he looked pointedly at the house next door to the Rabels'.

"But why? The renovations have only made the Rabels' house better, right? They'd rather have an eyesore?"

My dad cupped one hand over his eyes to block the sun. "That's logical, Ivy. Too bad the Mastersons aren't subject to using logic. They're . . . How should I put this? They have a few screws loose. They cause a lot of trouble for the city, always complaining and issuing ultimatums."

We stood side by side for another minute, and then turned to head back to my Dad's Silverado just as the door to the house behind us opened and an elderly woman stepped onto the porch. "Hallo!" she called. Her voice was surprisingly robust. Or maybe I was just expecting a halting, wavering sound, given the snow white of her hair and the map of wrinkles on her face.

My dad lifted his hand in greeting. "Afternoon, Mrs. Branford. You're looking lovely today."

She dismissed his comment with a wave of her hand, but she gave an embarrassed smile, and the thin skin of her cheeks tinged pink. "Oh, pshaw. Mr. Culpepper, how you do go on."

I had to agree with my dad. Mrs. Branford, in her lavender velour sweat suit, looked spritely and hip. She had to be eighty-five if she was a day, and although she held the handle of a cane in one hand, she wasn't leaning on it, which made me wonder how much she really needed it.

"Mrs. Branford, do you remember my daughter, Ivy?" He put his hand on my back and ushered Agatha and me forward.

An equally good question was whether I remembered Mrs. Branford. Truthfully, I had a vague recollection of having met her once or twice, but my memories didn't go any deeper than that.

"Oh yes, of course, but you were a little girl. Or maybe a teenager last time I saw you."

I smiled, my mind pretty much blank. Santa Sofia was home to almost sixty-three thousand people, plus the barrage of tourists who descended throughout the year. The fact that Mrs. Branford and I had not crossed paths in the last twenty years or so wasn't terribly surprising.

Together my dad and I walked up the uneven brick pathway toward the elderly woman. Agatha brought up the rear. As we approached, I noticed the tilt of the porch. The slope was so pronounced that if I dropped a ball on one end, it would roll right to the other end, gathering speed as it went.

"Nice to meet you . . . or see you again, I guess, ma'am," I said.

She looked at me with a twinkle in her eye and said, "Enough of the ma'am stuff. You just call me Penny. I taught school for a million years, but not anymore. My days of ma'am are long gone." She paused, taking in my hair, my eyes, my face. "You are the spitting image of your mother," she said.

Speechlessness was not usually one of my traits, but at this moment I could, quite literally, not think of anything to say. My mind felt slack. It was not that I hadn't heard the sentiment before. I knew I looked like my mom, and I treasured that. But somehow Penny Branford expressing it cut something loose inside me.

My dad came to the rescue. He cleared his throat and ran his fingers over his mustache. "She got all of Anna's best qualities," he said. I didn't think most people would be able to detect it, but I heard the faint quiver in his voice. It had been nearly six months since my mom had died, and my dad was stoic, but the veneer cracked every now and then. This was one of those moments.

I was stoic, too. Most of the time, anyway. I got that from my dad. He didn't cry, and neither did I. Losing Mom had left a hole in both of our hearts, but we stuffed the empty space with bread and music and walks in the historic district, but deep down nothing could really shore up the hollowness we both felt. So, like I said, I was a tough cookie, managing my emotions on an expert level so that nobody would even know I'd lost my mom, who'd also been my best friend. But this elderly woman . . . this Mrs. Penny Branford . . . Her eight simple words had sliced into me like a blade, opening my grief like an old wound until the ache and sorrow spilled out like sand from an overturned bucket.

"How did you know my mother?" I asked, my voice far more shaky than my dad's had been.

Mrs. Branford lifted her cane and pointed it at me. "How did I know her? Owen, does she know nothing?" My dad just shrugged, and she continued. "I taught your mother when she was knee high to a grasshopper, and when she went on to become a teacher herself? Why, I took that as a personal compliment." She pressed one gnarled hand against her chest. "I am entirely sure that I am the reason she went into education, you see."

"What grade did you teach?" I asked, the hole inside me growing wider, a craving for information taking over. If I were pregnant, surely I'd be wanting pickles and ice cream, the feeling was that strong.

"Ha. What grade *didn't* I teach? That would be a better question, I reckon. But what you're really asking is what grade did I teach when your mother was a girl. Am I right about that?"

I gave a little laugh. "Yes, ma'am, er, Mrs. Branford, you are."

"Polite young woman," she said, nodding with approval. She turned to my dad. "You and Anna did good with this one. Oh, don't get me wrong. Billy's a fine young man, too, but a sweet and polite young woman is a treasure. Anna's smiling down this very minute. Of that I'm sure."

My smile faltered as each of her words fell over me like a blanket. I wasn't sure if I felt stifled or comforted that this old woman, this Mrs. Branford, praised my parents' raising of me and felt my mother was watching down on me. I crossed my arms, letting my right hand spread on my chest, as if it were pressing my beating heart back into submission. Mrs. Branford had stirred up emotions I'd successfully kept at bay, and I wasn't sure I was ready to face them yet. The six months my mom had been gone felt like an eternity in some ways, but in others it felt as if it had been mere seconds, and I still couldn't make sense of a world without her in it.

"Your mother was beautiful. You look just like her. More importantly, she was the top student in my tenth grade honors English class," Mrs. Branford said. "I convinced her to join the newspaper staff, which, of course, she did, and she went on to be the best staff photographer we had, and during her senior year, she was editor in chief. She could have been an investigative reporter, you know, as she was that good. A nose like a bloodhound's, I'd venture to say."

"I can't picture her as a sixteen-year-old." My voice got a little dreamy, as I was trying to imagine her running around the high school, taking pictures, her ginger hair pulled up into a ponytail, her green eyes clear and excited, her skin freckled and fair. Sensing the emotion coursing through me, Agatha rubbed against my leg. "She was beautiful," people said every time they told me I looked just like her. I had never internalized that sentence quite the way I had when Penny Branford said it.

"She was smart as a whip and as strong willed a young woman as you'd ever meet. Girls from her generation, why, they had the good fortune of growing up after the sexual revolution, you know. Women's equality had a good foothold, and she took advantage of it. Went to college. First in her family, if I remember correctly."

"That's right," my dad said. I could tell he was choked up. His eyes glistened, and his chin quivered slightly. This was a conversation I knew he wanted to have. If he didn't, he'd have already made up some excuse and we'd have been out of here. But wanting to hear what Mrs. Branford had to say didn't mean it was easy. I knew he felt the loss just as keenly as I did. More so. They'd shared a life for almost forty years. "She wasn't supposed to go first," my dad had told me through his tears after she died. "She wasn't supposed to go first."

"Now you," Mrs. Branford said, pointing her cane directly at me. "You went to college, right? Your mother told me as much, but with this old mind, I'm not sure if I'm remembering that right."

"Yes, ma'am, that's right. University of Texas in Austin, but I'm back home now."

"Penny," she scolded, and I felt myself blush.

"Penny." I said the name, but it felt wrong. Presumptuous. Intimate. This woman had life experience. Wisdom. I needed the formality of her surname. She was Mrs. Branford, plain and simple.

"And what are you doing now that you're back in Santa Sofia? Because let me tell you something. It doesn't do you a whip of good to come back here and wallow in your sorrow. Your mother would not have wanted that. Would she have, Owen?" She dropped the end of her cane back to the ground, the rubber-cupped base making a loud thump on the porch, and looked at my dad.

"No. Mrs. Branford, you have that exactly right. She wouldn't want any of us to wallow." He wrapped his arm around me and pulled me next to him. "But I'm awful glad to have Ivy home, even if it is because Anna's gone from us now."

His voice quavered, sinking into the deepest part of me, and just like that, a tear dislodged from where it had been tucked away for half a year. It fell down my cheek, a lone symbol of the love I would always have for my mom and of the sadness that seeped through me.

"What's going on with the Rabels' house, Mrs. Branford?" My dad's change of subject was the opposite of subtle, but it worked, and I squeezed his hand. Our emotions were raw and on the surface, and we'd both had enough for today.

Mrs. Branford turned her body slowly, like a music box dancer whose tune was coming to a halt, until she faced the yellow house under construction across the street. "Nothing's changed, Owen. As long as that Buck Masterson is next door, the

Rabels are going to suffer. He's done it to everyone on the street, one by one by one."

"Done what?" I asked, curious about the historic district gossip and politics.

"Buck Masterson is a piece of work," Mrs. Branford said. "Think of him like a virus, slowly infiltrating until he takes hold and knocks you flat on your back. He's alienated most of the people of the neighborhood with his reports to the city. His own house is a mess, but he holds everyone else to some impossible standard, proclaiming himself to be the king of the street. The ones he hasn't alienated are just like him. Oh, he starts out as Mr. Jovial, all peaches and cream. But underneath that smile— and it's a smarmy smile, if you ask me—there's arsenic. Goes with all that old lace in that eyesore of a house of his. Ha! Arsenic and old lace. That about sums it up."

My dad and I turned to look at the Mastersons' house, and I found myself agreeing with Mrs. Branford's assessment. It *was* a bit of an eyesore. Old, yes. But well kept and appealing? Not so much. The faded pink color looked like watered-down Pepto-Bismol. The paint was peeling along the windowsills, and scaffolding balanced precariously on the upper-story roofline. From the looks of it, the Mastersons complaining about the Rabels' renovation was definitely irony at its finest.

I looked up and down the street. The sunlight beamed down on the old historic houses. No cars passed by, and the green canopies of trees rustled in the light breeze. I was struck by what it must have been like to live here when the street was young and new. This was the type of street I wanted to live on. Maybe even *this* street specifically. It was the place I belonged.

"I hear you were at the bread shop when Jackie Makers died," Mrs. Branford said. She clearly wasn't one to beat around the bush. I liked that about her and immediately thought that Olaya Solis and Penny Branford needed to meet. They were two peas in a pod.

"I was," I said, nodding my confirmation.

"I heard it was"—she lowered her voice to an ominous whisper—"murder."

"That's what I heard, too." I looked over my shoulder, as if someone might be there listening. Someone like the murderer.

Next to me, Agatha pulled on her leash. She growled, recoiled, and then let out a high-pitched bark. She scooted back slightly, drew in a hoarse breath, then let loose a barrage of barks aimed at the street.

"Speak of the devil," Mrs. Branford said, notching her chin in the direction of Agatha's attention. I turned all the way around and saw a square-faced, stocky man standing in the middle of his yard, blatantly staring at us.

Penny Branford raised her lavender velour arm and waved. "Afternoon, Buck," she said over Agatha's yowling.

His upper lip flared in what I imagined he thought was a smile. He flipped a hand up in the barest semblance of a wave before turning and disappearing around the side of his pale pink house.

Mrs. Branford grimaced as she looked back at me and lowered her voice. "I don't know how," she said, "but *he* probably did it. *He* probably killed that poor woman."

My dad and I both stared at her. "Do you really think so?" I asked her.

Mrs. Branford tapped her cane on her slanted porch. "Most definitely," she said. "I think it is quite possible. Probable even. Quite probable."

Chapter Five

Jackie Makers's funeral took place a few days later at Liberty Methodist Church, which was down the street from the bakery and catty-corner to the old antique mini-mall. The pews were filled. Tears streamed down faces. Tissues dabbed eyes. Low sobs filled the sanctuary. It was an all too familiar scene, and one that I didn't relish reliving. But I'd felt obligated to come given that I was one of the last few people to see her alive.

"She was born and bred here," Olaya said through her own swallowed sorrow. She looked at the townspeople all around us and pointed out folks, as if she were introducing me to the who's who of Santa Sofia. My dad sat in one of the back pews. In the very front and on the opposite side of the church were Consuelo and Martina. "That's Jasmine next to Martina," Olaya said. All I could see was a close crop of black hair and a long, elegant neck with skin the color of a latte, warm and rich. "She is—was—Jackie's daughter."

Jasmine was clearly a mix of her mother's fair white skin and her father's presumably black skin. When she turned, I caught a glimpse of her profile. She was beautiful, with a refined nose and high and defined cheekbones. From the way Olaya and her sisters had reacted to the phone call Jackie had taken from her, I'd thought she was a teenager, but now, looking at her, I placed her in her early to mid-twenties. She was one of those lucky women who would age well, with beautiful, clear skin that would keep her looking young.

"They were talking on the phone during the class," I recalled, not mentioning that the conversation had seemed less than amiable.

Olaya pursed her lips. Her eyes were red rimmed, and the tip of her nose was chapped. She had cried herself out and now seemed determined to focus on anything but her grief. "They've had a strained relationship for a while now. More than a year. Jackie and I were good friends. Best friends, even. But she had not been telling me everything lately. She would never say anything against Jasmine, just that things were not good."

A stab of sorrow for Jasmine sliced my chest. No matter what their issues were about, I knew from experience that she'd never forget her last conversation with her mother. If she was anything like me, it would haunt her for the rest of her life. The last conversation I'd had with my mom wasn't bad or drama filled. On the contrary, it was banal. Ordinary. Boring, even. It had been a normal conversation, just like the one we'd had every week since I'd moved away from Santa Sofia. I'd played the last conversation over and over and over, wishing I'd been sweeter, or that I'd apologized for the teenage years. Or that I'd told her I loved her and that she was my best friend.

But I'd said none of those things, and it was a huge regret.

"Have you talked to her?" I asked Olaya.

"To Jasmine?" She shook her head. "She won't take my calls."

Before I could ask her why she thought Jackie's daughter wasn't responding, Olaya pointed to a man I recognized. "That's Randy Russell."

I'd never be able to erase Randy Russell's face from my memory. It was seared there, right along-side Miguel Baptista's, although for different reasons. "He's the one Miguel was trying to talk down the day Jackie . . . died."

She acknowledged the connection with the faintest nod and then moved on to the man next to the ruddy-cheeked Randy. He was black, his head was bald, and his build lean and muscular. "That's his business partner, Augustus Makers. They own the antique mini-mall across from the bread shop. Jackie and Gus were married for twenty-five years or so. They divorced about a year ago now. In case you haven't noticed," she added wryly, "Santa Sofia is like a soap opera. Everybody is connected to everybody."

I remembered that about the town where I'd grown up. The idea that it takes a village had taken root here long before Hillary Clinton wrote a book about it. Everyone was in everyone else's business. That was just the way it was. My mom had taken the idea to heart. As a teacher, she'd been involved in all her students' lives. As a kid, I'd been oblivious, but now I saw the benefit—and the detriment—of being too connected with your neighbors and townsfolk.

"What were Randy and Miguel fighting about the other night? Why was he even there?" I followed the first two questions with another. "I think he should be in jail, don't you?"

"Randy is just a hothead," she said, as if that explained and excused everything.

"But what was the whole thing about?" I pressed.

So far, Olaya had been pretty forthcoming, but this time she lifted her shoulders dismissively and her voice lowered. "I do not pretend to know what goes on in Randy's head. We are not exactly on good terms."

I let my voice match hers. "Why not? What happened between you?"

She looked over her shoulder, the silver spikes in her hair catching the light in the church. She dropped her voice a smidge more. "Randy is a . . . What is the word? A bodybusy?"

I grinned. "A busybody."

"Right. Yes. A busybody. He is in everybody's business, when none of it concerns him. Yeast of Eden is a strong business. Many tourists. Many local customers. A good reputation. The antique minimall, on the other hand, is hit and miss. People, especially the tourists, ask me about it when they are in the bread shop. 'Should I stop by? Do they have authentic antiques? Is it good quality?' I am always honest. I tell them that if they have time to poke around and search through the rubbish, then it is certainly worth a visit. It is consignment, so I cannot speak to the authenticity or quality of anything there. That is the truth, and that is what I say."

"And Randy got wind of that?"

"He's convinced it is a personal vendetta I have against him, which could not be further from the truth."

A thought struck me suddenly, and I drew in a sharp breath. "That night, when he was in the back parking lot, was he there to see you? Is he . . . Oh my God, Olaya. Is he off the rails? Had he come to threaten you with that billy club?"

A look of utter disbelief crossed her face. "No. No," she repeated firmly. She sounded convinced, but she trained her eyes on Randy Russell, sitting in the pews, and nodded once. "And yet . . ."

He must have felt the intensity of her stare, because he turned around in his seat, his gaze met hers, and an electric charge seemed to spark between them. And not a smoldering, romantic one. No, this was more like a battle of wills, with one powerful superhero vying for power over another.

She didn't break her gaze with him as she spoke to me. "What had he been planning?" she mused.

My question exactly. That antique club he'd been wielding came to mind again, and my first thought was, Thank God he hadn't seen Olaya. But it was my second thought that made me pause. Thank God Miguel Baptista had been passing by to stop Randy Russell from inflicting harm on anyone.

With my peripheral vision, I saw a hand come down on Olaya's shoulder. At the same time a man said, "Ms. Solis?"

The current connecting Olaya and Randy Russell was severed as Olaya jumped and turned around. I turned, too, and, speak of the devil, there stood Miguel Baptista.

"Miguel," she said. *"Cómo estás?"*

"Bien, señora. Y tu?"

"Así así," she said, waggling one hand to show how she was feeling.

He hadn't looked at me yet, and I took a step backward to avoid an awkward encounter and let him say whatever it was he needed to tell Olaya, but, damn him, he was a gentleman. Slowly, a polite and slightly crooked smile graced his face. He always had been chivalrous, even back in high school. He moved to the side as he looked at me; he hesitated, as if working to place my familiar face. Something in his expression changed, his smile dropped, and his face seemed to tighten.

"Ivy?"

My dad always said I showed every single emotion I was having on my face the moment I was feeling it. I tried hard to control it, but I was 100 percent sure that I was not successful at masking anything at that moment. "In the flesh." The response sounded far coyer than I'd wanted to, which I'd actually not wanted to sound at all. I uttered a curse under my breath before saying, "Miguel Baptista. It's been a long time."

Olaya cleared her throat, which broke Miguel's concentration. "You know each other?" She shot me a pointed look since she already knew that we did.

The left corner of Miguel's mouth quirked up into grin. "Oh, we know each other, Ms. Solis. Very well, in fact."

The way he said them made the words sound almost ominous. It wasn't as if we shared some dark, secret past, but we did *have* a past. I couldn't get a read on what he meant by his tone or what he thought. His expression was almost amused, although his leaving me the split second he'd graduated from high school, and his subsequent years in the military, were anything but amusing to me. He'd been my first real love . . . and my first utter heartbreak. And here he was, grinning at me as if it had all been one big joke to him.

"Oh yes, we know each other," I agreed. "Miguel walked out of Santa Sofia without a backward glance, if I remember correctly. And look, here you are, back again. Guess escaping wasn't all it was cracked up to be." I regretted the contemptuous tone of the comment the moment it left my lips, given what Emmaline had told me about his father passing and Miguel returning to help his mother with their restaurant. Still, he deserved my anger. He had left me high and dry, after all.

"Guess I realized what a great town Santa Sofia

is. Something I couldn't appreciate when I was eighteen years old."

"Humph," I uttered under my breath, but it came out louder than I'd intended.

"Santa Sofia isn't the only thing I didn't appreciate," he said, but before I could even process what he'd said and fully wonder if he was referring to me . . . or us . . . he turned back to Olaya. "Ma'am, I haven't had a chance to talk to you about the other night. The sheriff isn't pressing charges against Randy. That being said, I think you need to steer clear of him."

"I always do," she said.

"What does he have against Olaya?" I asked, wanting to dig a little deeper. Mrs. Branford's claim about my mother being a bloodhound crossed my mind. Like her, I always wanted to ferret out the truth. After the hit-and-run that had caused my mom's death, I had gone back to the scene, had looked for skid marks, thinking I could somehow match them to the culprit's tires. I'd been determined to bring her cowardly killer to justice. When there hadn't been any marks on the pavement, I was flummoxed. Had the driver not even bothered to slow down? Had he not seen her, or had he thought he could miss her by speeding up instead of stopping? As much as I'd searched for the truth, I couldn't get any closer to it. There were no leads, and so I'd pushed my questions about how the accident had happened aside and focused on helping my dad get through his grief.

I might never understand the details of my mother's death, but I could dig a little and figure out why Randy Russell had been in the back parking lot of Yeast of Eden.

Miguel had turned to me as I spoke, but now he looked back at Olaya. "No idea."

"He is a business rival, nothing more," Olaya said.

"He looked suspicious to me," Miguel said. "I saw him in the parking lot. Saw the club in his hand. And when I asked him what he was doing, he got pretty belligerent, said it was none of my business—"

"I know very well how he can be," Olaya said.

"I talked him down, and then you all found Ms. Makers in her car." He gave a weighty pause and then said, "Just be careful."

Olaya nodded solemnly. We stood there in an awkward silence for a few seconds. I didn't know what I might have said to Miguel if I'd had the chance, but the pastor stepped to the altar and the service began. Coming face-to-face with my past would have to wait. A look passed between us before Miguel walked away and took a seat on the left side of the church. Olaya took my hand and pulled me to the opposite side of the church.

"What is your story with him?" she whispered as soon as we were seated.

I kept my eyes on the pastor but shrugged. "No story."

She looked at me skeptically, her eyes bright with tears again. "That I do not believe. I loved a man once." Her voice became melancholy. "I thought

James was the love of my life, but there were too many years between us."

I tried to mask the surprise on my face. I didn't know why Olaya was opening up to me, but it proved that she felt the same connection to me that I felt to her. My heart swelled just a little bit. "What do you mean? He was older than you?"

"Yes. By fifteen years. I didn't care, but he was married, and, well, he loved his wife. He was a rule follower. I could never fault him for that, although I wish things had turned out differently."

"I'm sorry," I said as I tried to wrap my head around the fact that Olaya had loved a married man. I tried to lighten the situation. "Love. Who needs it?"

She grimaced and said, "You do. There's nothing more important. You feel it. You need it. You just don't want to admit it to yourself."

This gave me pause. Just like my mom, Olaya seemed to have a sixth sense about me. Given that I hardly knew her, I couldn't imagine how she had her pulse on my history and my emotions. But I realized in that moment that it wasn't worth trying to hide anything from her. I knew she'd already figured me out . . . and I hadn't even figured me out. "Miguel and I were high school sweethearts," I said, "but, you know, he left. That about sums it up."

"That I also do not believe. There has to be more to the story. You thought he was the one—"

I nodded, just once. "But he didn't," I said, finishing her sentence.

She glanced at Miguel, then at me. "I'm not so

sure about that, *m'ija*," she said, squeezing my hand. "Sometimes the one comes around again, and you have a second chance together."

My view of Miguel was of the back of his head. He looked straight ahead, listening to the pastor delivering the sermon for Jackie's funeral. Whatever Olaya had seen between us in the brief few minutes we'd spoken, I couldn't say, but all I saw was our past, and it felt just like the bridge Emmaline had said was uncrossable between her and Billy. Any connection Miguel and I had had was long gone.

I felt the unmistakable sensation of someone's eyes on me. My attention shifted and was drawn to the man next to Miguel. A chill ran down my spine. Randy Russell was looking over his shoulder, but not at me. He was staring menacingly at Olaya.

Chapter Six

I stood in the *cocina* at Yeast of Eden, ready for my second baking lesson. Olaya had postponed for a week after Jackie Makers's death, and she still didn't look ready to launch into class again. She'd wanted to cancel altogether, but I'd talked her out of it. "You're always going to miss Jackie," I'd told her, "but doing normal activities is the best thing you can do. Plus, remember you told me I belonged here. That you'd teach me the art of baking bread."

"Keep busy," she'd said in response, but her voice had been flat.

"Yes, keep busy." It was another thing I knew from experience. Going about everyday activities was the only thing that had kept me sane after my mom died. Being idle meant only that I had too much time to think, and thinking was the one thing I'd wanted not to do at the time.

Olaya had agreed, but her heart wasn't in it. If only she could eat a slice of some magical bread to mend her broken heart. But with the depth of her grief, I suspected it didn't work that way. In fact, I hoped that her sadness wasn't instead seeping into the bread she made daily, only to be passed along to her patrons.

"Do not worry," she said, as if she'd just read my mind. "Our bread is as pure as it ever was."

"What are we baking?" Sally asked.

Last time there had been a chalkboard with the word *Conchas* written in beautiful cursive, colorful drawings of the sweet breads alongside. Today the chalkboard was blank. Olaya walked into the bakery's kitchen. She stopped at the chalkboard, her back to us, and wrote on the black surface with a practiced hand. A minute later she turned around and revealed the day's task: fig and almond loaf. She'd also sketched a picture of a bâtard-shaped loaf of bread, its markings crisscrossed on the top.

"Bread is healing," she said, and a sliver of relief wove through me. She was turning to what she knew, to the comfort of her baking. Yes, she was grieving, as I was, but we'd both get through it.

"I can attest to that," a voice said.

We all turned to see who had spoken. My jaw dropped. Penny Branford, dressed in a coral velour sweat suit just like the lavender one she'd been wearing the first time I met her sashayed right into the kitchen, cane swinging, a lightness in her step. On her feet were snazzy white leather sneakers, and her snowy hair was wound into tight curls on her head. I couldn't help but smile. She was a sight to see, and I knew she was a force to be reckoned with.

As my smile lit up, Olaya's dulled. "Can I help you?" Her voice was almost accusatory.

If Mrs. Branford noticed the lack of warmth in Olaya's welcome, she didn't let on. "I'm here to bake bread. Like you said, it's healing. It's one of the things that keeps me so young and spritely." The twinkle in her eyes seemed to have extra glow going on, and I wondered if she had a personal testimonial about the healing powers Olaya had mentioned.

Despite Mrs. Branford's enthusiasm, something about Olaya's expression made me think she might turn the spritely woman away. I surged forward and took Mrs. Branford's free hand in mine. "You can be at the station next to me," I said, thankful that it wasn't the area Jackie Makers had used during the first class. I felt, as I think Olaya did, that that space needed to remain a tribute to Jackie, which meant no other baker should use it. At least for the time being.

Olaya frowned, but a moment later the grimace vanished as she got the materials ready for Mrs. Branford to join the class. "Here you go," she said, holding out a floral apron with layers of ruffles, a little smirk on her face. "You definitely want to protect that lovely sweat suit."

I flinched at the sarcasm coming from Olaya. I'd never heard that from her. Her reaction to Penny Branford's entrance had raised a red flag, but now I knew. There was some bad blood between these two. I'd bet my life on it.

Mrs. Branford's expression tightened as she started

to reach for the apron, but then she dropped her hand, gave a weighty pause, then up and marched right past Olaya. She bent to look in the drawer the apron had come from. Ten seconds later she straightened up, a triumphant smile on her face and a bright blue half apron in her hand. No frills. No ruffles. But stylishly cut and sewn, and definitely more her style than the one Olaya had initially proffered.

As Penny Branford's smile grew, Olaya's faded. This, I thought, was going to be interesting.

Olaya flung her shoulders back, stood up straighter, and headed to her workstation. I could tell that she was ready to move on and stop letting whatever existed between her and Mrs. Branford interrupt her class. "As I was saying," she said, her voice crisp, "bread is healing. Anyone who doubts it has not experienced authentic bread made by hands with the power to heal."

As if we'd been prompted by her words, all of us class members, including Penny Branford in her newly donned apron, studied our own hands, flipping them over to look at the palms, then back to contemplate the backs. My hands looked ordinary, and I doubted that I'd ever get to the point where they had the power to heal. I did, however, notice a few more wrinkles than I'd had the last time I'd taken a close look.

While I was pretty sure I'd never be a bread-making healer right out of the gate, an hour later I was also positive I'd never be a professional bread maker. We'd dusted a jelly-roll pan with cornmeal, had snipped the stems from a cup of Calimyrna figs and let them steep in boiling water, had let the yeast froth in warm water, had mixed the dough and let it rest, and had added unblanched almonds and chopped figs to the mixture. Now we were letting the dough rise in a covered bowl. None of it was particularly difficult, but the stress of exact measurements and hoping the mixture would turn into a delectable bread had worn me out. The process of baking didn't seem to come naturally to me.

Despite the conflict between my perfectionist nature and my baking struggles, I was, I admit, excited for the outcome. We went through the steps to turn the dough, a bowl of water nearby to keep the sticky mess off our hands.

"Why can't we just knead it?" Sally asked. Working side by side for two sessions now had allowed me to discover something about each of the women in the class. Sally was on the whiny side. I imagined her with her siblings, one of them catching her with an arm over her shoulders, giving her a noogie, and her struggling and saying in her best ten-year-old whine, "Stooop. Dooon't."

"We allow the dough to develop as it ferments," Olaya said. She demonstrated the process of grabbing the underside of the dough, stretching it up, and folding it back over the rest of the dough. We dipped our hands in the water after each turn. Thirty minutes later, the dough had started to puff.

"Fermentation!" Olaya's giddy expression was contagious as each of us noticed our own bowl of dough rising with air. We all looked around at each other. Martina and Consuelo nodded at each other, holding out their bowls to show the other. They each shot a glance at Jackie's empty workstation, a wash of sadness skimming both of their faces. The vacant spot in the kitchen left a heavy feeling of darkness hanging over the space.

Jolie, with her perfectly straight black hair, which was once again pulled back into a carelessly perfect ponytail, stared at her bowl, her mouth downturned. "Mine isn't doing that puffy thing. It looks flat."

Olaya strode over and stood by Jolie's side, and the two of them studied the failed almond and fig dough. After a moment, she raised her gaze to Jolie's and asked, "Did you add the yeast?"

Jolie rolled her eyes. "Of course I did," she said, her tone calling Olaya out for asking such a ridiculous question.

Olaya ignored the attitude and focused only on the bread. "No, I am quite certain you did not, actually."

"But I did." She held up the squat brown jar of yeast. "It's right he—" she started to say, but she stopped when Olaya took the jar right from her hands.

"See this depression in the lid?" Olaya ran her finger over the top. I looked at my jar of yeast, and from the corners of my eyes, I saw the other women in the kitchen do the same, each of them feeling the top of the lid.

"This is still sealed," Olaya said. "Once it's opened, this little button area is raised."

"Is your dough rising, Ivy?" Olaya asked me.

The depression in the yeast jar was not there, and my dough was fluffy. It was coated with a fine layer of tiny air bubbles. Yeast successfully added. "Rising," I confirmed.

One by one, Olaya checked each of the bakers' doughs, nodding as she looked and poked and sniffed at each station. As she approached Mrs. Branford, her expression once again tightened. "I didn't know you still baked, Penelope."

"Once you learn, you never forget. I'm eighty-six years old, but I'm not senile. Or incompetent."

"If you say so," Olaya said with a smirk. "Did your dough rise?"

"Like the sun every morning," Mrs. Branford said. She pulled her bowl forward so Olaya could see.

Olaya frowned "So it did." I got the feeling Olaya would have grinned happily if Mrs. Branford's dough had been a fail. As it was, she said, "Ladies, entertain yourselves for a moment. We have a bread emergency." She glanced at what had been Jackie Makers's workstation, a veil of sadness clouding her face. I saw her steel herself against her emotions, pushing away her grief, as she turned back to Jolie and they began the recipe from the beginning.

"Well," Mrs. Branford huffed, "this is going to take longer than a moment."

I'd thought that Olaya Solis and Penny Branford would get along, that they were two peas in a pod—both strong, smart, assertive, and accomplished. But maybe they were too much alike, because a friendship between them clearly wasn't going to happen. They had some history, these two. The bad blood I'd sensed was simmering just below the surface, and I wanted to know more.

"How do you know Olaya?" I asked.

Mrs. Branford wasn't biting. At least not at this moment. "That, my dear, is a story for another time."

"I'm holding you to that," I said, pressing. "When?"

Mrs. Branford laughed, her already wrinkled face compressing into a crisscrossed map of lines. She considered me for a moment, her hand over her chin, her fingers on one side of her mouth, tapping. "Hmmm. I do believe I could use a bit of help around the house."

I cracked a smile. "Do you, now?"

"Those cupboards in my kitchen are abnormally tall." She looked me up and down. "And you're, well, perhaps not abnormally so, but you are also tall."

I was a mere five feet eight, but that was definitely taller than her five feet five inches or so. I went with it. "I guess I am."

"Tomorrow morning, then. Eight o'clock. Don't be late, my dear."

"I wouldn't dream of it," I said, liking Mrs. Branford more and more with each passing second.

Sally strode toward us, drying her hands on a kelly-green dish towel. "Don't be late for what?"

Mrs. Branford grinned. "This lovely girl is going to help organize my kitchen tomorrow."

Judging by the frown on her face, Sally didn't seem to think that sorting through Mrs. Branford's dishes and pans sounded all that appealing.

"I take it you don't want to come along and help?" I said with a laugh, already knowing she'd decline.

"Come along where?" This time it was Becky who'd come over.

"Cleaning house," Sally said. "Not something I like to do in my own place, let alone in someone else's."

"You leave your kitchen how you like it, but you have to clean up *here*," Olaya announced, a glint in her eyes. She'd been busy with Jolie, but she was aware of absolutely everything in her kitchen. Eyes in the back of her head and all that.

A blush of pink spread from Sally's neck to her cheeks. "Oh, of course!"

Olaya winked at her, and then she turned her attention to Mrs. Branford and her expression hardened. "Penelope, it's just like you to put this poor girl to work."

"Nonsense," Mrs. Branford said. "Ivy is not a *poor* girl. She's tough, just like her mother was."

"I can hear you, you know," I said, "and I wouldn't say I'm a 'girl.'"

"I'm knocking on eighty-seven's door, my dear. You can't be more than what? Thirty-five—"

"Thirty-six," I said, correcting her. Exactly fifty years her junior, which was crazy to think about. She had instantly become my role model. I wanted to *be* her in fifty years.

"A spring chicken," Penny Branford said, a twinkle in her eye that made her seem more like the spritely young thing she was describing me as.

"I'm happy to help sort the kitchen. I'll bring my

camera, too," I said. The words came unexpectedly, but the second I spoke them, I knew I wanted nothing more than to photograph the street I'd instantly fallen in love with the moment I walked the sidewalks there. Maybe my creative voice wasn't entirely gone. "I want to take some pictures of the houses on Maple."

Mrs. Branford nodded sagely. "There is never a dull moment on Maple Street."

I suspected there was never a dull moment with Penelope Branford. "Tell me more."

This time, instead of twinkling, Mrs. Branford's eyes became hooded. "That Buck Masterson, you know, the one who lives across the street from me? He thinks he's a one-man neighborhood watch."

Ah, the intrusive Buck Masterson. I wondered if he was the only thing "going on" on Maple Street. He rubbed Mrs. Branford the wrong way—there was no doubt about that—but was her perspective entirely reliable? "Right. You said he keeps an eye on the whole street."

"A self-appointed eye, and that does not give him a green light to go into people's houses. He calls it entitlement. I call it breaking and entering."

I stared. "Wait. He went into someone's house?"

"Oh yes," Mrs. Branford said. Her voice dropped to a whisper. "He's a sneaky one. Or at least he *thinks* he is. I'm sure he thought no one was watching. But me? I. Am. *Always*. Watching. What else do I have to do, after all?"

Before I could ask whose house Mr. Masterson had snuck into, Olaya clapped her hands and brought us all back to attention. "We are nearly ready to bake bread," she announced.

We spent the next few minutes dividing our dough into two equal pieces; rounding each piece by pushing against the bottom with the sides of our hands, our palms facing up; working and shaping our fermented dough into spheres; covering the spheres and allowing them to rest, rise, and proof until they were 50 percent larger than when we'd started.

"The last step," Olaya said, "is to take your serrated knife and draw it across the center. Then make a second perpendicular slice. Not too deep, mind you. Just enough to mark it as the bread bakes."

We all followed her directions, brushed our loaves with water, and baked them for thirty minutes. By the time the loaves were lightly browned and cooked through, the kitchen and all our workstations, except for that of Jolie, who was behind in her process, were spotless and the kitchen smelled of freshly baked bread.

While Olaya and Jolie waited for her loaf to finish up, the rest of us brushed our baked loaves with melted butter and took our masterpieces home. I felt a throb of sorrow in the pit of my stomach. Though she was trying to hide it, I could feel Olaya's sadness, and Jackie Makers's absence in the baking class was palpable, her empty station like a beacon re-announcing her death.

Chapter Seven

Bright and early the next morning, Agatha and I drove from my parents' house to Maple Street, purposely parking at the east end of the block so I could walk down the sidewalk and take pictures. I stopped at each house, Agatha on her harness and leash beside me, getting the full effect and studying the rooflines, the dormers, the porches, and the other details that made each one unique. The houses were each beautiful in their own way and gave the street its historic and distinct personality. Once again the longing to live on Maple Street hit me square between the eyes. I saw myself here, felt the pull of the history, wanting so much to be part of it.

I found myself following the light, the shadows, and focusing on pieces of each house: a window here, a cornice there. When I got back to my computer, I'd upload my shots and try to see them from an objective perspective. I was hoping I'd be able to recapture some of my creative voice right here in the historic district of Santa Sofia.

One house in particular struck me. It was a red Tudor-style home that drew me closer. It was crafted of old brick, had the traditional half-timber exterior, a steep gable, and a high-pitched roofline. The wavy-edge siding at the gable peaks was a deep red, a warm and welcoming color in my world. Pulling Agatha along beside me, I crossed the street to get a closer look, loving how the tall trees softened the fairy-tale gingerbread look of the house, noting the cobbled walkway up to the arched front door, and admiring the blush of color the flower beds brought to the home.

I sighed, and after another minute I made my way up the street toward Penelope Branford's Victorian. But as I walked, I kept looking over my shoulder at the Tudor. I tossed up a wish that one day I'd live in a place just as beautiful and filled with as much character as that house.

Fifteen minutes later I was ensconced in Mrs. Branford's kitchen, a cup of tea on the table in front of me. Agatha was lying by the side of my chair, a rawhide bone I'd brought along stabilized under her front paws. She licked and chewed loudly, but happily. Mrs. Branford's house looked like it had gone through a few careful renovations over the years; the interior was compartmentalized, with a wide center hallway in the entry, which had doors leading to a library, a den, the parlor, and the dining room. French doors separated the dining room and parlor, and another pass-through was situated between the dining room and the kitchen.

"This is a beautiful house," I commented, absorbing every detail of the kitchen. Parts of the room seemed to be original, while some, like the floors and countertops, had been remodeled. On the floor were black-and-white checkerboard tiles. Instead of a traditional tile backsplash, worn, nicked beadboard lined the walls, accenting the off-white, green-specked granite countertops. Rustic green ceramic tiles added a splash of vintage color behind the old off-white ceramic stove. The avocado-green refrigerator looked like it was from another era, but it was comforting, and when taken together, the entire room was as welcoming as pot roast on a cold, blustery day. "How long have you lived here?"

Mrs. Branford glanced up to the ceiling, her lips moving she counted. "Let's see. My grandparents built this house back in eighteen ninety-nine. My mother grew up here. My parents left it to me. Jimmy—that's my husband—we moved in here forty-two years ago."

"And Jimmy . . ." I felt a memory or a thought tug at the back of my mind, but I couldn't pull it out. I let the sentence hanging there.

Her voice became tinged with sadness. "I lost my Jimmy."

"I'm sorry."

She pressed her lips together and nodded. "It's been, oh, ten years now. It's true what they say. I miss him every day, but time heals. You'll heal, too, Ivy."

I knew she was right. My sorrow would lessen, and I'd be left with memories that would fill me with a melancholy joy. "I think you brought me here under false pretenses," I said. Not a dish seemed out of place, not a speck of food littered the counter, and Mrs. Branford didn't appear to need a bit of help with anything. I'd bet my life that she was the most self-sufficient, organized, and capable eighty-six-year-old woman on the planet. In fact, if she were pitted against any woman of any age, I'd lay odds on Penelope Branford.

She grinned sheepishly. "I wanted the chance to talk to you. This seemed as good a ruse as any."

Other than meeting Mrs. Branford with my dad, I didn't remember ever laying eyes on her. I couldn't imagine what she'd want to talk with me about. Still, I felt nervous for some reason. "Oh?"

She patted the air. "Now, now. Don't panic."

"Is it about my mother?" That was the only thing we had in common . . . that I knew of, anyway. Any progress I'd made—or thought I'd made—in dealing with my grief was fleeting. Talking about my mom might be therapeutic at times, but it was also torture. At this moment, I was pretty sure the agony would outweigh any healing that might happen.

"No, dear. Your mother was a beautiful soul, but you knew her far better than I did. No, I have a . . . proposition for you."

The nerves gave way to relief. "What kind of proposition?"

"Pictures."

"Pictures," I repeated, not following.

"Photographs," she said, clarifying the matter.

She leaned forward, rested her elbows on the table. I tried not to focus on the tight curls of her snowy hair, but they were so perfect that they drew my eye. Not only was she spry, but she was stylish, too. Just looking at her made me smile.

"I'm not as young as I used to be," she began, as if I wouldn't have discerned that tidbit on my own. I covered my smile as she continued. "I can see you agree. It's well established, in fact. An eighty-six-year-old woman is no longer in her salad days, even if she still feels like she's forty inside. You know, I used to say that I felt as if I were still twenty years old. Now I see what shenanigans so many twenty-year-olds are up to that I'm grateful I'm well beyond that. My forties, yes. Now, those were good years."

I couldn't help but take her perspective to heart. I was fast approaching my forties, so to hear that I was heading toward a great decade made me feel rather happy.

She continued. "Because I'm not in my forties anymore, however, I can't always do the things I'd like to do. Like take pictures. My hands aren't as steady as they used to be. Arthritis, you know. They ache and don't bend like they should." She held her hands out for me to see the trembling.

"That would make it hard to hold a camera," I agreed, "but what do you want to take pictures of?"

She lowered her voice to a whisper, as if someone might hear us. "The neighborhood," she said.

"I'm already doing that. Such beautiful houses here," I said.

"No! That's not what I mean." She practically jumped up from her chair, went to a drawer next to the refrigerator, and returned, holding a spiral-bound journal. The cover was pale green and adorned with butterflies. As she flipped through the book, I caught a glimpse of page after page after page of lists. Finally, she found the one she was looking for and turned the notebook for me to see.

"What's this?" I asked.

"Buck Masterson's comings and goings."

She stopped talking, letting the statement hang there between us.

I tamped down my surprise—and concern—that Mrs. Branford clearly spent too much time documenting her neighbor. Was she just a busybody with excess time on her hands, or had she observed something about Buck Masterson that had given rise to a legitimate concern? As I contemplated these possibilities, I skimmed the list, noting random events dating back six months.

12:03 p.m. Left house. Returned at 2:30 p.m. Historic district committee meeting. Buck led the attack against the Rabels' construction. Inciting.

8:21 a.m. Snuck into Jackie's backyard. Exited five minutes later.

3:55 p.m. Buck and Nanette sat on porch and stared at my house until 5:03 p.m. Stared. And never looked away.

The list went on and on. "You could be a private investigator," I said.

She patted the curls of her hair. "I have often thought the same thing, my dear. I might say that I missed my calling, but I loved teaching."

I looked back at the list. "They just sat and stared at your house?"

"For more than an hour. I don't think they even blinked."

"But why would they do that?"

She slapped the table with an open hand. "Exactly my question. I want you to help me figure it out. That man has no right snooping around other people's homes, causing trouble with the historic district, and trying to intimidate people. Luckily, I'm not so easily bullied."

"No, you're not, are you?"

"He's trouble, that Buck Masterson. I just need to prove it. And I need your help."

I sighed. "I'm not a private investigator, Mrs. Branford."

Her spine straightened. "If you're anything like your mother, you have a nose for it. Why, I remember when she was back in high school, she single-handedly uncovered a cheating ring among the students. This was before computers, mind you. Some of the students would write their notes and adhere them to a water bottle. The water acted like a magnifying glass, and no one was the wiser. It was quite a scandal when your mother broke the story."

I stared. I knew she had often nosed around to

ferret out the truth of something, but my mom had never told me that story. I felt a mixture of gratefulness at learning something new about her and an odd emptiness that there were missing pieces to my mother's history, pieces that I didn't know about. Pieces I'd never know about. Knowing this about her sent my curiosity into overdrive, and a rogue thought entered my consciousness. My mother had died so suddenly, and the hit-and-run had some oddities about it. No skid marks, for example. And no witnesses. Maybe it wasn't an accident like we all thought. Was that possible?

I shook my head, dislodging the idea. Of course it wasn't possible. No one would want my mother dead.

"I can see it in your eyes. You're just like her," Mrs. Branford said. "You always get to the bottom of things, don't you?"

Her comment brought me back to Mrs. Branford's kitchen. I directed my gaze to the ceiling as I considered that question. Did I? "I guess so." I had, after all, deduced the affair my former husband had been having. He'd done a good job of hiding the evidence and operating on the down low. But secrets, I found, were meant to be discovered. An unfamiliar number on the cell phone bill, a lip gloss container on the floor of his car, late nights at work but no answer at the office when I'd called. Bit by bit, I'd pieced together the clues. And then I'd divorced his cheating ass.

"Buck Masterson is up to no good, Ivy, and I want to catch him in the act. I *will* catch him in the act."

"In the act of doing whatever it is he does—"

"Exactly."

"Like sitting on the porch and staring at your house?"

"Well, no. That wouldn't be very exciting, now, would it?" She leaned forward. "We need to do a stakeout and catch him breaking and entering."

"Breaking and entering?" This was sounding way out of my league. "Maybe we should call the police and let *them* know what he's doing. If he's breaking and entering, that *is* illegal. They'd be able to stop him. Arrest him. Something."

"He's come uninvited into my house, you know. Opened the door and waltzed right in, acting like we're old friends. He's intrusive, and it has to stop. He's got some nerve, don't you think? And, no, I don't want to go to the police. I'm perfectly capable of handling issues in my neighborhood."

Except she wasn't. She needed me to help her handle the issues in her neighborhood. And if I was being honest with myself, I was happy Penny Branford had come to me for assistance if it meant I could form a tenuous connection between myself and who my mother had been when she was a girl. Add to that that my mind was going to be more occupied than it had been in months, and I was sold, any danger in staking out Buck Masterson notwithstanding. Distraction was something I desperately needed.

"Now if Jimmy were alive, he'd have skinned Buck's hide."

The scraping of Agatha's teeth against her bone stopped, and she peered up, almost as if she'd understood and didn't like the idea of any hide being skinned.

Mrs. Branford continued. "He was a rule follower, my Jimmy. He might have teetered on the line once in a while, but he never crossed it. Buck Masterson would be thinking twice if Jimmy were still around."

At the mention of Jimmy's name, that inkling of a feeling came back. There was something . . . It hit me like a fifty-pound sack of flour. The bad blood between Penny Branford and Olaya Solis. The love of Olaya's life. Olaya had said he'd been a rule follower, just like Penny Branford's Jimmy. Jimmy and James. Could they be the same person?

The more I thought about, the more sense it made. Which led me to my next thought. Perhaps it wasn't so crazy to think I'd be able to catch Buck Masterson up to no good. Who knew? Maybe I'd even be able to figure out what had happened to Jackie Makers. After all, if I was right, I'd just identified the source of the feud between two women who otherwise would be great friends. I knew that in my heart. They were more alike than they probably realized.

I sat back, sipped my tea, and concocted a plan with Mrs. Branford to stake out Maple Street to spy on Buck Masterson. It was turning into an interesting day.

Chapter Eight

Mrs. Branford waved to me from her front door. "Can't wait for tonight," she said, beaming.

"Six thirty. See you then."

I walked down the street, stopping to let Agatha take care of business and cleaning it up with a plastic doggy bag. I took a few pictures along the way. An old freestanding red gas pump caught my eye. It stood to the side of a detached garage. I walked as close as I dared. With the camera in my hand, I doubted I'd be accused of trespassing, but walking on someone else's property felt wrong. Even though I stayed as far back as I could, I was still halfway up the driveway. I hadn't brought my best telephoto lens, but I was able to zoom in enough to capture detail without compromising stability.

My cell phone ringing made me jump. Agatha yelped, and together we hightailed it to the sidewalk.

Olaya Solis's voice filled my ear. *"Dónde estás, m'ija?"*

I had a basic knowledge of Spanish, thanks to

high school, college, and a childhood spent in California. "On Maple Street," I answered, smiling inside that Olaya didn't feel the need to make small talk or offer pleasantries. It was like we were family . . . or old friends. We were neither, but I had the feeling we'd get there sooner rather than later.

"*Qué bueno*! Great minds," she said.

"Oh?"

"I am also on Maple Street. Come join me."

I spun around, looking up and down the street, thinking she might materialize right in front of me. "You're here? Where? Why?" I asked.

"*Aquí*, Ivy, *aquí!*"

I heard her voice calling me and turned to follow the sound. Finally, I spotted her. She waved her hands over her head. "I am here!"

My jaw dropped. She stood on the front porch of the Tudor house I'd instantly fallen in love with just hours before. I checked the street for cars. The coast was clear, so I jogged across the street, Agatha keeping pace with me. "Is this your house?" I asked as I slowed to a walk on the cobbled path and joined her on the stone porch.

"No, no," she said. Her smile didn't reach her glassy eyes. "This is . . . was . . . Jackie's house."

I hadn't been expecting that, and a new wave of sadness washed over me. It was easy to see a person who'd died as simply gone. I hadn't even known Jackie Makers, and her horrible demise had shaken me. But at this moment, she became more to me than just a woman I'd briefly met who died. Looking around and into the house, I began crafting together the life she had lived. She'd picked out the furniture. She'd created this space. She'd had a daughter and friends and a job and enemies and people who felt hollow inside with the loss of her.

Jackie Makers suddenly became 1000 percent real to me, and I ached inside for Olaya. I knew what she was going through. I knew firsthand the emptiness she felt. I knew, and it made my own ache grow even stronger.

Olaya opened the door for me to follow her in, but I stopped, pointing to Agatha.

"What a sweet baby!" She crouched down and used the pads of her fingers to scratch Agatha's compact little head. Looking up at me, she asked, "Is she housebroken?"

"Completely." It had taken a good year or more for Agatha to realize that I wasn't going to abuse her. When she crossed that hurdle, she also figured out that outside was the place for pottying. It had been a tough year for both of us, but now I couldn't imagine my world without her.

"Come on, then," Olaya said, stepping aside for us to enter.

Olaya followed me and Agatha in. I gazed at the arched doorway as I passed through. I hadn't even seen the inside yet, but something about the house filled me with warmth and comfort.

"The police have finished their search," she said, answering the unspoken question in my mind as to why she was here. "Jasmine finally called. Said she wanted to start sorting through her mother's stuff and asked if I'd help."

"So here you are."

"Here I am." Her voice cracked with emotion, and her chin quivered. She swallowed hard. "It feels too soon. I cannot understand. She is gone, and Jasmine wants to forget."

"People grieve differently," I said, laying my hand on her arm in comfort. "Can I help?"

She let herself smile slightly. "Just what I was hoping you would say."

"You're boxing things?"

"Jasmine wants to sell the house." She gave me a quick tour. The master bedroom had French doors leading to the immaculate backyard. Jackie had had a knack for gardening. Flowers bloomed in abundance, and it was more of an oasis than any backyard I'd ever seen. The room itself was a pale, warm yellow and had the same arches and architectural details as the front entry.

There were two other bedrooms, a living room, and a small informal family room off the kitchen. The garage, also off the kitchen, housed two cars.

"The police towed Jackie's car back here," Olaya said. "The other one is Jasmine's old one. There are a few dents. Some chipped paint. I guess we will get them fixed and sell them, also."

"What room are you starting with?" I asked as we came back in from the garage.

"The kitchen. Jackie loved to cook. I'm the baker, but if I brought her a chicken and some vegetables, she could whip up a gourmet meal." She ran her fingers under her damp eyes. "Chicken and dumplings. That was her specialty."

The kitchen had a brick arch over the stove, with a window behind it overlooking the front yard. An island in the middle with bar stools gave it a homey look, and the pale yellow cupboards were the perfect complement to the honey-colored wood floors. An empty pink bakery box with cupcake remnants was open on the counter. Fruit flies buzzed around the rotting bananas and apples in a three-tiered rack. It was a beautiful kitchen.

"My mom loved to cook, but she always said we could and should hone our skills. 'There's nothing worse than growing old and growing lazy,'" I said, quoting her when a memory spirited into my consciousness. "She and my dad were taking lessons together. She had decided that he should finally learn to cook like a Food Network chef."

It was as if my mom had had a premonition, I realized. Maybe not that she was going to die, but that for whatever reason, my dad should learn to cook for himself.

Olaya's brows tugged together. "Did she? I wonder . . ."

I pushed the emotions of my mother's sixth sense away. "Wonder what?"

"Jackie ran a cooking school. Well Done. It's a little kitchen over on Bissonet Street. Is that where your mom and dad took their classes?"

Well Done. I repeated the name of the cooking school in my head. It didn't ring a bell, but then again my mother might never have mentioned the name of the actual business. "That would be a small world, wouldn't it?" Another way Olaya and I were connected, even if that particular thread was tenuous.

"I wouldn't be surprised. Jackie's was the best cooking school in Santa Sofia. There was competition for a while. What was that place called?" She tapped her chin with one finger, thinking. "Divine Cuisine, I think. Anyway, it went out of business, and Well Done had a corner on the market. Now I guess I'm it for cooking classes in town."

"Why did she take baking classes from you if she ran a school of her own?"

Olaya took a cookbook from one of the two black baker's rack shelves and flipped through it. It was based on the blog *Smitten Kitchen*. I'd read posts by Deb Perelman and drooled over the photos of her recipes. If Jackie had used all these cookbooks in her cooking school, no wonder it had been so successful.

Except, of course, that she'd been killed. Viciously murdered. Could her death have had anything to do with her school? I guessed there was no way to know the answer to that.

It was so tragic that Santa Sofia had lost two successful, smart, and accomplished women in Jackie Makers and my mother, Anna Culpepper, in just six short months.

"When you think of chefs," Olaya said, "they tend to specialize in something. Perhaps one is a saucier or a pantry chef or, like me, a pastry chef. Even I specialize within the realm of baking. Bread is my passion, although I am perfectly skilled at producing sublime cookies and cakes and pies and anything else dessert related. Jackie was trained at the Culinary Institute in the Napa Valley. She was a personal chef for many years. She took the required pastry classes, of course, but that was never her specialty. But when she opened up her business, she wanted to incorporate pastry and bread components into her sessions."

"But didn't that conflict with your classes?"

Olaya waved away the question. "Not one bit. What I do is magical. People like Becky and Sally may learn the fundamentals of baking, but they will never come away with the deeper understanding of how bread can change lives. You, on the other hand . . . There is something about you that makes me think you have something different inside you. Maybe because your mother taught you to cook. Or maybe because you see things through the lens of a camera. You see the details. The creativity that exists in baking. The cracks in the crust. The texture of the dough. The final crumb.

"These are things that can be taught, but you, I think, already possess them. Jolie shows promise. So does Jasmine, but then her mother was gifted, so that makes good sense. My sisters, of course, have it, although not to the degree that I do. Penelope Branford." Olaya drew in a deep breath and held it for a moment, as if she was deciding how kind to be about Mrs. Branford. "She has it."

She paused for a second, letting her angst about Mrs. Branford slip back into a corner of her mind before she continued. "Jackie didn't want to delve into baking bread like I do. She wanted to master her own skills so she could incorporate a bit of baking into her school and her catering business."

From the way Olaya spoke, I could tell there had been no competition between the two friends. People killed for all sorts of irrational reasons. A business rivalry wasn't too far-fetched as a motive. Emmaline telling me that the Solis sisters were suspects had never left my mind, so to hear Olaya dismiss any conflict was a relief for a worry I hadn't known I'd been feeling.

Once Olaya found a soft blanket for Agatha, my little pug promptly went to sleep. She and I then worked in companionable silence, starting with Jackie's cookbooks. I handed them to Olaya, and she perused them and then placed them into one of two piles: books to keep and books to donate.

"Jasmine doesn't want to go through them?" I asked after a few minutes. My brother, Billy, my dad, and I still hadn't gone through my mom's things. It was too emotional of a job, and we'd been putting it off. It was a step we needed to take, a step Jasmine Makers was taking already. If we followed suit, then maybe we could start to heal and accept my mother's death.

But it wasn't healing that Jasmine was doing, apparently.

Olaya said, "She's eighteen. She's holding on to her grudge. She won't have anything to do with any of this. She just wants it done."

How could she hang on to her anger? I wondered. What was her anger even about? Her mother was gone. For good. The complicated relationship my mother and I had had—that any mother and daughter had—had evaporated into simple grief when she died. It was a loss I could never fully accept. It had happened too quickly. Too unexpectedly. In the end, none of the rest of our ups and downs or disagreements mattered. I couldn't understand Jasmine's distance.

"So she's leaving it for you to do?"

Olaya nodded as she picked up a copy of *Joy of Cooking*. "I don't mind," she said. "We were friends for thirty years. She was with me through so much."

"Through losing James?" I asked, testing the waters.

Olaya's head snapped up. "That and more."

She handed me *Joy of Cooking*. "This is a keeper," she said.

"For Jasmine?"

"For me. Jasmine doesn't want to keep anything. Nada."

One by one, we went through the shelves of cookbooks. Olaya had commentary on about half of them, and she kept that many in her keeper pile.

"Tell me about James," I said to her after another stretch of silence.

She raised an eyebrow and shot me a suspicious glance. "Why?"

I shrugged. "Just curious. Was there never anyone else . . . after?"

Olaya picked up the next cookbook, this one a tome on vegetarian cooking. "Love is love. Sometimes things are not meant to be, that is all. I never wanted anyone else."

"But don't you think there's more than one person we can fall in love with?" I asked. An image of Miguel Baptista came to me. He was my first love, but I'd been in relationships since. I'd been married and divorced, but I didn't want to believe that my relationship failures were because Miguel was my one and only.

"For most people, yes," she said, sensing my disappointment. "It was simply not in the cards for me."

"He was older than you?"

She straightened up. "You remember everything, yes?"

I nodded, smiling. I was blessed with a good memory.

"The years, I am afraid, were significant."

They were, I agreed, but if I was right, it was more significant that he was married. "Is that why it didn't work out?" I was fishing, searching for confirmation that the love of Olaya Solis's life was also Penelope Branford's deceased husband, but Olaya waved her hand in the air, and it was clear she'd decided she was done talking about her past relationships.

"Would you go through the papers in this? Make sure there is nothing important stuck in there?" she asked me, handing me a file folder filled with recipes that looked as if they'd been printed from the Internet.

I sat on a backless wooden stool at the kitchen's

center island. The island itself was painted a warm
olive gray-green and had open shelving on either
end. Coffee cups and a few decorative cookbooks
adorned the shelves. The dark wood of the island
countertop was pristine. The buttery white of the
cabinets, complemented by wrought-iron hardware,
and the dark wood frames of the leaded windows
gave the kitchen an old-world feel reminiscent of
the 1920s or 1930s. I glanced at the wrought-iron
light fixture above the island. It was a horizontal
circle with six yellow glass tubes affixed to it. They
mimicked the look of candlelight. The light fixture
illuminated the exposed dark beams on the peaked
ceiling above. The kitchen was a place I never
wanted to leave. Cooking here would be a dream.

I opened the file folder and flipped through the
pages one by one. I read recipe after recipe, observ-
ing the notes written in neat script in the margins.
Measurements had been crossed out and adjusted.
Cooking times had been changed. Wine pairings
had been added. Jackie Makers was thorough and
looked at every aspect of her cooking, I thought.

The last few pages in the folder were not recipes.
I started skimming the first page, then paused and
started again, this time reading more slowly. It was
a photocopy of an essay, typed and double-spaced,
but there was no name on it, and no title, date, or
other identifying information. Those had all been
removed before the copy made. Still, I felt sure it
was a high school paper. The prompt was written
on a sticky note, which was paper clipped to the top
of the page.

*Write a story about a time when you taught
something to someone. What you taught could be
a song, an activity, a game, a way of figuring out
a homework problem, or something else. Be sure to
narrate an event or a series of events and to
include specific details so that the reader can
follow your story.*

I read the prompt, then went back to the essay,
all the while wondering why it was here in Jackie's
recipe folder. The essay itself was decent, well
written, even if it didn't quite address the prompt.
The author had written about teaching a lesson
rather than a skill, song, or activity. It felt cryptic
somehow, although I couldn't quite put my finger
on why or how. The whole thing was about choices
and how one decision could impact that person's
life, as well as the lives of others. There were a few
comments written in the margins. Things like *More
detail needed. What is the lesson, specifically? This touches
the surface; go deeper.* And *How do you factor into this
lesson?*

I left the folder on the counter and went back to
the cookbook shelf Olaya was still going through. "I
don't think anything much in the folder is worth
saving. They're all recipes and nothing original of
Jackie's," I said. "But," I added, "I did find this." I
handed her the essay.

She put down the book she'd been perusing and
scanned the page. She frowned and uttered a puzzled
"Huh."

"There's no name on it."

She tucked it into the oversize brown leather bag that was on the floor next to her. "I'll ask Jasmine about it. Must be hers."

I nodded. Of course. That made perfect sense. Jackie would keep her daughter's essay. Odd that it was randomly tucked into the file folder of recipes, but I often stuck things somewhere convenient rather than taking the time to put them away where they belonged. It was a bad habit and one my mother had tried to break me of. To no avail. Her propensity for organization hadn't been passed on to me. She'd organized every bit of her classroom and every corner of the house she shared with my dad. She knew where everything was, and she had a firm philosophy about loose papers and random stuff. File it, deal with it, or toss it. If you couldn't do one of those three things, your life would end up in disarray. It was true; I was living proof. I had stacks of bills and papers that stymied me. I didn't know where to begin, and so I did nothing, and the stacks grew until I was forced to tackle them in their entirety. My mother had tried to teach me, but my brain didn't work that way.

Maybe Jackie's hadn't, either.

Olaya and I spent another twenty minutes finishing the cookbooks and were just ready to move on to the first cupboard when a knock came at the front door. Olaya peered through the kitchen window, then quickly withdrew so she wouldn't be seen. I leaned over her and saw Penny Branford.

"What does she want?" Olaya demanded, as if I had invited Mrs. Branford and was personally responsible for the fact that she was now standing, stoop shouldered, on the old brick porch.

I shrugged helplessly. I liked both of these women, but it seemed evident that they were never going to like each other. I couldn't choose between them, but somehow I got the impression that this was what Olaya wanted. "I'll go see."

A minute later, I walked back into the kitchen. Mrs. Branford sauntered in behind me, the hook of her cane looped over her wrist.

"I'm sure I'm the last person you want to see, Olaya. Believe me, I feel the same. However, this is important." Olaya scoffed, but Mrs. Branford ignored her and continued. "About a week ago, Jackie stopped by—"

Olaya's head snapped up. "She stopped by to see you?"

"We were neighbors, Olaya. The fact that we were on friendly terms wasn't a betrayal of you."

Olaya's nostrils flared slightly as she drew in a deep breath. "*Por supuesto*," she said. "I know that."

"Anyway," Mrs. Branford continued, "I just remembered this morning—after you left, Ivy—that she'd been in a state."

"What does that mean, in a state?" Olaya asked.

"She was worried. She asked me if I could keep a secret, which of course I can—"

"Yes, I'm sure you can."

Mrs. Branford drew herself up, throwing her hunched shoulders back as much as she could and lifting her chin indignantly. "Look here, Olaya Solis. You . . . *you* fell in love with my husband, not the other way around." She pointed a gnarled finger at Olaya. "*I* should be angry with *you*. For many years I *have* been angry with you. But life is too short. Jimmy's gone. Jackie's gone. Everything can change in a single moment, and we need to be grateful for the things we have. The friends. The family. The love. This"—she waved her finger back and forth between the two of them—"this animosity doesn't do either of us any good."

"James stayed with you," Olaya said, her voice quiet and laced with hurt and regret. "He stayed with you."

"He was my husband. Should he have left me for you?"

"I loved him."

Mrs. Branford's expression softened. "I've no doubt you did. And I believe he probably loved you, too."

"But you were his wife," Olaya said with resignation.

"I was his wife."

A heavy moment of silence passed between them, and then Olaya said, "I never meant for it to happen, you understand." Her gaze finally met Mrs. Branford's, and a thread of understanding seemed to pass between them.

Mrs. Branford nodded solemnly. "I know, my dear. I've always known *that*. Jimmy didn't, either."

Olaya shook off the emotion flooding her, swallowing and blinking away the tears that had been pooling in her eyes. They'd had a breakthrough. I didn't know if it would last, but I was happy, for the moment, to have them in the same room without the heat of anger heavy between them.

"Have a seat," Olaya said, gesturing to the kitchen table.

Mrs. Branford plopped herself onto a cushioned chair, then leaned her cane against the distressed wood table.

"Now," Olaya continued, "what were you saying about Jackie?"

"She was upset about something that day," Mrs. Branford said. "I'd completely forgotten. My old, addled brain, you know."

"You remembered," I said, encouraging her to go on. "That's what matters."

"I haven't remembered much," she said, clarifying. "She looked over her shoulder a few times, as if someone might be following her. She was afraid. I'm sure of it now that I'm looking back on that day. She was definitely afraid."

Olaya's cheeks had tinged pink, and her hands had balled into fists. "I knew it."

"Knew what?" I asked.

"Something was going on with her. Something she would not share with me."

I sucked in a sharp breath. When I'd first met Mrs. Branford, we'd seen Buck Masterson, and she'd made an offhand remark that he probably killed Jackie Makers. Could there be truth behind that? Was Jackie afraid of her own neighbor?

"But who would she have feared?" Olaya asked, pondering aloud.

"Buck Masterson?" I offered. I looked at Mrs.

Branford. "You said he'd gone into your house un-invited." The invasion of privacy would certainly have me on edge if it had happened to me.

"He did?" Olaya asked.

Mrs. Branford nodded. "He's a menace to the neighborhood," she declared. "But," she added, "I'm not sure if that's who Jackie was afraid of. Quite possibly. She mentioned Jasmine that day."

"She and Jasmine were not getting along, but she wasn't afraid of her own daughter," Olaya said.

"No, no, that's not what I mean. I don't believe so, either," Mrs. Branford said. "But there was something going on there. Something that had her on edge."

"We could ask Jasmine," I suggested. Seemed to me that if you had a question or concern, you simply needed to go to the source.

Olaya shook her head. "I told you. She will not return my phone calls."

"I don't know her," Mrs. Branford said. "Never had her in my class, and while I've seen her around over the years, it's been a long time."

They both looked at me expectantly. "You could reach out to her," Olaya suggested.

I spit out a laugh, chagrined. Were they serious? "Are you serious?"

They both nodded.

"I've never even seen her," I said, then proceeded to rattle off other reasons why I should not be the one to contact Jasmine about her mother's murder. "She'll think I'm a freak if I just randomly show up and start asking her questions about her relationship with her mother," I paused. "I have no idea how to even find her. I'm really pretty shy," I lied. "There's no way!"

"You are the farthest thing from shy," Mrs. Branford said.

"The farthest," Olaya agreed. "And I have her home and work address."

"Of course you can't just show up and start quizzing her about her mother. But, Ivy," Mrs. Branford said, "you're your mother's daughter. You're curious. You're smart. Think about the stories your mother broke when she was in high school and on the newspaper. You just have to be creative and dig a little."

"You mean lie." I'd have to visit Jasmine Makers on some false pretense. I couldn't even imagine what that might be.

Mrs. Branford shook her head. "Not a lie, Ivy. A manipulation of the truth. You can do this."

"For Jackie." Olaya said.

I held back a scoff. Telling a lie and manipulating the truth were one and the same, but I kept my thoughts on that to myself. My shoulders sagged. Despite my misgivings, I knew I'd give in.

As I accepted what I knew would happen, it occurred to me that we still didn't know why Jackie Makers had shown up at Penny Branford's house. "What did she want that day?" I asked.

"Oh!" Mrs. Branford exclaimed. She slid a gray

canvas daypack off her back. "I don't care for purses," she said when she noticed me looking at it.

"That is quite practical," Olaya said with approval.

"It is," she agreed. She reached into her daypack and pulled out an eight-by-ten goldenrod envelope on the table between us. "She'd been having trouble with Buck Masterson." She grimaced. "Of course."

"She talked about him, this Buck Masterson," Olaya said, looking from me to Mrs. Branford and back.

"Only because he's the biggest menace to Santa Sofia and the historic district since Richard Nixon," Mrs. Branford said.

I stared. "Um, Richard Nixon?"

"Okay, forget Nixon. Buck Masterson is the biggest menace to Santa Sofia. Period."

Olaya shook her head, puzzled. "How have I never met this menace?"

Mrs. Branford patted Olaya's hand. "You're better off, my dear."

I covered my mouth with my hand, hiding my grin. I knew they were meant to be friends, and now, despite the Jimmy/James situation, their friendship destiny might be secure.

"Buck wanted Jackie to tear out the patio cover she added in her backyard. Tear it right out." Mrs. Branford slapped her hand on the table. "It probably cost Jackie ten thousand dollars. Tear it out, indeed. That man is horrible!"

"She told me about that. She said a neighborhood committee was giving her a difficult time about the work she'd done. That she did not have it approved by the historic district before she did the work."

Mrs. Branford folded her left hand on top of her right, nodding. "But her backyard work was actually done in . . . the . . . backyard. Not visible from the street. Not attached to the house. Not required to get approval by the historic district."

"What is this guy's problem? How did he even know about the work she did?" I asked.

Mrs. Branford tilted her head as she responded. "Remember I told you he'd been sneaking into houses on the street?"

I gasped. "Jackie's house? *This* house?"

She nodded solemnly. "*This* house. I saw him with my own two eyes, and let me tell you, I called Jackie right away. Of course she was in her kitchen. Buck had carte blanche to break and enter without Jackie's knowledge," she said. "But he didn't count on me," she added, shaking her head. "He could have known about the work she did only by being in the house or in the backyard. And Jackie did not give him permission."

"Let me understand this," Olaya said. "You saw him enter Jackie's house. You called Jackie to tell her. And then she came over to your house and brought this envelope?"

"Yes. Oh! Yes." Mrs. Branford flipped the goldenrod envelope over and unclasped it. "She came to find out what I'd seen. We got to talking, you know. I do miss her."

"I miss her, too," Olaya said quietly.

Mrs. Branford continued. "As I said, we got to talking. I told her that I'd seen Buck walk down the sidewalk, all nonchalant-like. He looked over his shoulder, then up and down the street. Quite suspicious, if you ask me."

Olaya and I both nodded. "Very," I said.

"We talked for a while. Just chitchat about her work, her daughter, life's mysteries." Mrs. Branford chuckled. "I have sons, so I couldn't really help her much with the issues she was having with her daughter. She said that no matter what she said, her daughter didn't understand. Couldn't understand."

Olaya frowned. "This is why I never had children."

"Hey now," I said. "Jasmine may not be daughter of the year, but some of us are pretty good kids. *I'm* a pretty good kid." I'd probably driven my parents crazy as a teenager, and moving to Texas had been hard on both of them. My divorce had taken its toll on them. But in my heart I knew that most parents thought their children were worth all the grief and frustration.

She patted my hand. "I know you are. Your parents, they are good ones."

"Yes, they were. Are." I swallowed the lump in my throat and let my fingertips touch the edge of the envelope. "Back to the mysterious envelope. She gave it to you?"

"No, no," Mrs. Branford said. "She left it behind. I confess that I looked in it." Mrs. Branford's eyes glazed, and she seemed distressed. "I snuck a peek, and then I tucked it away until I could give it back to Jackie. And then . . ." She paused, twisting her fingers around each other. "And then I forgot all about it."

Suddenly her face looked more worn than it had just a few minutes ago, her wrinkles etched deeper into her skin. She was an old woman, and it seemed she was going through the experiencing some forgetfulness, as so many elderly people did.

"It happens," Olaya said, giving Mrs. Branford a sympathetic glance. "It is nothing to be concerned about."

Mrs. Branford held up her hand, silencing any more discussion about any gaps in her memory. "I happened upon the envelope again this morning, after you left, Ivy. In the freezer, behind the gallon of ice cream, if you can believe that."

That was an unusual place for it, which was an understatement, and it raised a bit of concern. I set that worry away for another time and unclasped the envelope, slid out the papers from inside it, and took a quick glance. "They're letters to the historic district." There were six, and each one was dated within the last month and signed by someone with a Maple Street address.

"Yes! From the looks of it, Jackie was gathering ammunition to oust Buck Masterson from his seat on the council. She must have come by that day to ask me to write a letter. I'm sure that was her intent."

Olaya asked the obvious question. "But?"

"But she got a phone call. Her daughter, she said. And then she dashed off—"

"To save Jasmine from herself," Olaya said, finishing the sentence, her sarcasm heavy.

I hadn't met Jasmine yet, but if I were to describe her, *selfish* was the word that came to mind. She didn't strike me as someone I'd be inclined to hang out with.

We spread the letters across the table. One by one, Olaya and I read them, sliding them back and forth as we finished one and reached for the next.

"This one's pretty direct," I said, considering a handwritten missive from Mr. Harold Reiny. The writing was neat and precise, slanting slightly to the left. I was no handwriting analyst, but if I had to guess, I'd say Mr. Reiny was a tough old guy who didn't take any crap from anyone, least of all a devious man like Buck Masterson.

Granted, I hadn't actually met Buck Masterson, either, although I'd seen him from across the street while I'd been at Mrs. Branford's. I hadn't met a lot of the players in this crime drama in which I was living, but I was getting a good handle on many of them despite my lack of personal knowledge.

I read aloud a snippet from Mr. Reiny's letter: "Buck Masterson is single-handedly destroying Maple Street. He manages to make people think he has good intentions and only wants the old houses here cared for, but in reality, the man is power hungry and is a menace to his neighbors. He does not represent me, my house, my family, or my interests."

Each of the letters had a similar message. The

good people on Maple Street did not want Buck Masterson involved in their lives and the decisions made regarding their homes and properties.

Half an idea started to form in my mind. "Do you think Jackie initiated this letter campaign?"

Olaya considered the question. "If she did, she never told me about it, but it sounds like something she would do. She did not like that man."

"None of us do," Mrs. Branford muttered.

"But do you think . . ." I trailed off, not sure how I felt about what I was thinking.

Both the older women who were suddenly part of my life prompted me to continue. Olaya rolled her hand in the air, and Mrs. Branford patted my arm and asked, "Do we think what, dear?"

I formed the thought into words. "Do you think it's possible that Buck Masterson got wind of the letters and Jackie's campaign against him? Do you think he really could be behind her death?"

Olaya and Mrs. Branford looked at each other, looked at me, and then looked back at each other. Olaya clasped her hand over her open mouth. Mrs. Branford gasped.

"Buck Masterson, a murderer. A murderer?" Mrs. Branford said it as if she were testing the idea out to see how it sounded, then repeated it again. "Buck Masterson. A murderer."

"I do not know the man, but a killer? Jackie's killer?" Olaya leaned back, pondering.

"Someone in this town killed her," I said. "Someone who had some strong feelings against her. Why not Buck Masterson? If she was behind trying to stop his antics here on Maple Street and with the historic district, he might have seen that as a vendetta against him. Maybe he's unhinged—"

"Unhinged." Mrs. Branford tried that word on for size. "Buck Masterson, unhinged. Breaking and entering. Sneaking around. Inserting himself into other people's business. His smarmy smile." She nodded. "I'd say that he most definitely could be a trifle unhinged."

Olaya spoke up, the voice of reason. "None of those things make him a murderer."

Mrs. Branford agreed. "No, but as Ivy said, someone killed Jackie. Now we know that Buck actually has . . . had . . . a motive."

"Okay, look," I said. "We're being armchair detectives, and the truth is we aren't the ones to solve this. Why don't I take the letters to the deputy sheriff? Let her investigate Buck Masterson if she feels like it's warranted?"

After another few minutes of debate, they both agreed. Emmaline Davis would be able to determine if Buck Masterson was a killer or just a know-it-all busybody.

Chapter Nine

Easier said than done. My phone calls to Emmaline went unanswered. I had a few hours before I was to meet back up with Mrs. Branford for our stakeout, so I tucked the envelope of letters into my camera bag and headed back to my dad's house. I'd try Emmaline again before I headed back to Maple Street at dusk. Or, I thought deviously, I could give the envelope to Billy and ask him to deliver it. A little matchmaking never hurt anyone.

The house was empty when I got home. As the city manager, my dad was always busy with a million tasks. He probably wouldn't be home until after nine. Since my mom died, his hours had gotten later and later. "Nothing to come home to," he'd told Billy and me.

Agatha jumped from my car and zoomed to the gate leading to the backyard. I let her off her harness and leash, and she instantly took off at a high-speed run. She slowed, spun in happy circles, leapt straight up into the air, and then took off again like the Tasmanian Devil, cutting hard to make a tight turn, her normally curled tail elongated with the force of her run.

I let her run, tossing a tennis ball for her to chase, until she slowed down, panting, and was finally worn out. Once inside, she settled down in her bed, happily chewing on a knotted length of braid, and although the house was deathly quiet, I was glad for the solitude. I wanted to look through some of my mom's things, which I hadn't been able to bring myself to do yet. After spending the morning with Mrs. Branford and then with Olaya at Jackie's house, I felt ready. Ready to think about my mom and the life she'd led. Ready to face the raw emotions that hovered on the surface of my mind. Ready. Just ready.

I dropped my purse and camera bag on the white slipcovered couch and headed straight for the garage. My dad had carefully placed all my mom's school and classroom supplies along the left side of the garage, but no one had been able to muster up the courage to look at them since. They were obstructed by my mom's car, which also hadn't moved in the past six months.

"Should we sell it?" Billy had asked me when I first returned to Santa Sofia.

"I think it would break his heart. He needs to hold on to her."

I wasn't sure Billy understood what my dad was going through or why his emotions were tied to every little thing that my mother had touched, but

I got it. If he started to get rid of things, he'd be shedding his memories of her bit by bit. I think he saw that as a betrayal of her. That somehow, from wherever she was, she'd look down and see that he'd moved on and that she wasn't mourned anymore. It was not true, of course, but he had to grieve in his own way and at his own pace.

We all did.

I needed to start today.

I walked into the kitchen, took the only set of car keys hanging from the mounted hook there, went back to the garage, and rounded the back end of the pearl-white Fiat crossover my mom had loved. Once inside it, I started the engine. It roared to life, and seconds later I backed the car out and parked it on the driveway. I had considered a short jaunt around the block but had decided against it. Baby steps. Even sitting in the car, surrounded by the still new-smelling black interior, made me choke up.

"Big enough for grandkids," Mom had told me with a smile and a wink when she'd picked it out.

Grandkids she'd never get to meet. Babies who'd never know their grandmother. I choked back the lump that had risen in my throat. It was just a car, but remembering how carefully my mom had picked it out, how she'd envisioned driving around her grandbabies in it, and how she'd loved it made my dad's decision to keep it all the more reasonable. I didn't want him to sell it, either.

I drew in a bolstering breath as I got out of the car and went back into the garage. "Stay focused," I told myself. "Just one box."

I set up one of my dad's collapsible lawn chairs, grabbed the first box, hauled it from the stack along the wall, and sat down with it. The box was labeled CLASSROOM BOOKS, and sure enough, it was full of teaching manuals, books on instructional strategies, and games for the high school English classroom. I searched through the box, flipping through a few books in case there was anything personal tucked away, but there was nothing. This was truly just a box of books my mom had felt were important enough to own print copies of.

I overlapped the cardboard flaps, closing the box again, and retrieved the next box from the stack. This one, labeled DESK, held all the miscellaneous stuff my mom had kept in her desk drawers. Clear acrylic containers of paper clips, staples, Post-it notes, a vast collection of pens and pencils, with a heavy emphasis on colorful Paper Mate Flair pens. "They're perfect for grading papers," she'd told me once when she'd bought a jumbo pack of them. "I try to stay away from the dreaded red. Grading in purple makes me happy."

I closed up the box, set it aside, and took another one down. STUDENT WORK. Inside was a series of file folders holding students' essays. The folders were dated and organized by year and went back a decade. Each folder held anywhere from one to five essays.

I took a closer look at a few of the writing pieces. They weren't originals but had been photocopied. Just like the one I'd found in Jackie's kitchen. I got to thinking. Had my mom been Jasmine's teacher?

I ran through some possibilities in my mind and finally settled on the idea that if Jasmine *had* been in my mom's class, my mother might have created a copy of the essay because of the cryptic nature of it and given it to Jasmine's mother. What really struck me, however, was that it was quite possible that my mother had actually known Jackie Makers, that they'd been connected, even if it was only slightly. The realization gave me a chill.

I refocused on the essays. Did teachers regularly keep copies of their students' writing? Pastel-colored sticky notes adhered to many of the samples. Notes my mother had made. One said: *College admittance UCLA.* On another she'd written: *3/15 Contacted counselor and mother Re: cutting.* A third noted: *Use as exemplary next year.*

My mom had copied and kept select student writings for a variety of reasons, ranging from concern to pride. I had a faint recollection of overhearing my mom telling my dad, "Somebody was Barack Obama's teacher. Someone taught Ronald Reagan and Angelina Jolie and Johnny Depp. One of my students may go on to do great things. If they do, maybe I'll be able to say, 'Look! Here's an essay Frances wrote on Julius Caesar back in her sophomore year of high school!'"

I laughed at the memory. My mom, the dreamer. She knew she was making a difference in the lives of her students. They came to her with their problems, their failures, and their triumphs. They trusted her, and she loved them. She respected them. And right here in front of me was the proof.

I pulled out a random file from the box. It was filled with copies of several essays from the previous year. They were all literary responses to *Bless Me, Ultima; Death of a Salesman; The Grapes of Wrath;* and *The Great Gatsby,* among others. I smiled, proud. My mom knew how to challenge her students.

I spent another hour looking through her boxes, memories flooding me. How many hours had I spent helping her set up her classroom every August, and then helping pack it all up again at the end of each school year so the room could be cleaned or so she could move to a new room? Countless. As a teenager, I'd hated being asked to spend days of my summer vacation helping, but looking back now just made me smile. Those were good memories. Time with my mom that I now treasured and wouldn't trade for anything.

My cell phone beeped, bringing me back to the present. It was a text from Emmaline.

Back in the office. Call whenever.

A moment later a car door slammed, and my younger brother, Billy, strode into the garage, set down a bag he was carrying, then stooped to give me a peck on the cheek. "What's going on here?"

"Looking at some of mom's school stuff."

Billy had gotten my dad's dark brown hair and hazel eyes, as well as his tall, lean build. At thirty-three, he was an eligible bachelor in Santa Sofia. But his heart, if only he'd admit it, belonged to Emmaline Davis.

He sank to his haunches and pulled a random file from the box I still had open. "Anything interesting?"

"These are old student essays Mom kept copies of. This box goes back ten years."

He glanced at the stack of twenty-plus boxes still lining the garage wall. "She taught for what? Twenty-eight years?"

She'd gotten her teaching credentials when Billy and I were little. I couldn't remember exactly when, though. "Something like that."

He flipped through the file folder, nodding. "Wish I could have had her as my teacher. My friends always loved her. Said she really 'got' them."

"My friends said the same thing." School policy had been that, because she was our mom, we couldn't be in her class, so we'd both had Mrs. Jameson for sophomore English, then Mr. Lemon as seniors, when my mom had changed to twelfth grade English.

"She was a good teacher," Billy said.

"And an even better mom," I said.

"Are you looking for something in particular?"

I wondered if there was something that I was subconsciously hunting for, something I knew my mom had had in her classroom that I was hoping to find. I'd racked my brain, but if there was, it wasn't rising to the surface. "No, nothing. I just wanted to be close to her. I miss her," I said softly.

He moved closer and rested his hand on my back. "I do, too."

We restacked the boxes, and I pulled the car

back into the garage. Billy retrieved the bag he'd brought, and handed it to me.

"That's a lot of kiwis," I said.

He winked. "You know how Dad loves 'em."

That he did. Kiwis. Berries. Mangos. Pretty much any fruit made our dad happy.

"Could you do a favor for me?" I asked, taking a kiwi from the bag and turning the fuzzy brown sphere around in my hand.

"Sure." He didn't even ask what it was. That was my brother. He was an inherently good guy. He followed me into the house. I set the kiwis down, went to the couch, and returned to the kitchen holding out the envelope from Mrs. Branford. "Can you drop this at the sheriff's office for me?"

His hand stopped in midair. "Uh, why? What is it?"

I gave him an abbreviated version of the Maple Street saga, ending with the letter campaign initiated by Jackie Makers against Buck Masterson. I concluded by saying, "Emmaline needs to see them."

"You think this Masterson character might have had something to do with that woman's murder?"

Leave it to Billy to sum it up in one succinct sentence. I answered with Mrs. Branford's words. "Someone killed Jackie. And this guy, this Buck Masterson, he had a pretty good motive."

"And you want Emmaline to take a look at the letters."

Again, he cut to the chase.

"She's in charge of the investigation," I said by way of an answer.

Billy was nobody's fool, least of all mine. He'd seen through me the second I mentioned Emmaline's name. "Your matchmaking isn't going to work, Ivy."

"Relax, Billy. It's not a date. You're just dropping off an envelope."

"And why, exactly, can't you do it, when you need to explain the situation to her, anyway?"

It took it as a rhetorical question, so I didn't bother to answer. Instead, I went with, "You know you and Emmaline are meant to be together."

Billy closed his eyes, his eyelids fluttering with frustration. "We had our chance, Ivy. It didn't work out."

"You wouldn't let it work out. There's a difference. She cares about you. You care about her. So why can't you just do something about it? You're being stupid. Didn't losing Mom teach you anything? Life is too short. You're letting your chance at love slip right through your fingers."

My brother was a handsome man. Five feet eleven inches, a gentle wave to his dark brown hair, broad shouldered, and fit. But when he scowled, like he was doing now, he looked a little menacing. I knew when to leave well enough alone.

But he surprised me by taking the envelope. "I'll leave it with the receptionist," he growled.

"That's fine. Thanks. I'll call Em later to fill her in."

He snatched an apple from the fruit bowl and headed back out through the garage, leaving me to get ready for my stakeout with Penelope Branford.

Chapter Ten

This was my first stakeout, and I had the feeling it might be my last. Mrs. Branford was antsy in the passenger seat of my tiny car, and the potential hours we could sit here together stretched before me.

"What kind of car do you have? Maybe we should use it instead," I suggested.

"Oh no, dear. I long since stopped driving," she answered. "It's been sitting in my garage for years. Who even knows if it would start at this point?"

I sighed, wishing I had a bigger car with more legroom and interior space. As it was, my little economy car barely let me turn my body and prop my camera in the open driver's side window. If I ever did another stakeout, I'd find a different solution. Of course, I'd never have a reason to do another stakeout, so really it was a moot issue.

I considered our current situation and why we were here. Buck Masterson had a motive to want Jackie Makers out of his way. If he had anything to do with her murder, that gave me double the reason to want to catch him doing something incriminating.

I had my camera out, as well as a U-shaped bean-bag support, which I'd propped over the window frame. Thankfully, it was a temperate seventy degrees this evening. I imagined those funny graphic T-shirts geared toward people who loved to sew and their resulting self-descriptions as fabricaholics. My passion for photography meant I had more camera equipment than any reasonable person might collect. Every spare dime I saved went to Nikon gear and paraphernalia. And every dime was well spent. Fabric was to a seamstress what camera lenses were to me. My own graphic T-shirt might say IF I CAN'T BRING MY CAMERA, I'M NOT GOING or I FLASH PEOPLE.

For the stakeout tonight, I'd chosen an 85mm lens with an f-stop of f/1.4. It was the fastest lens I owned. To the layman, this meant absolutely nothing and probably filled him or her with anxiety. Given the minimal ambient light on the street, to me the specs on this lens meant the difference between a black screen with no image, a mess of movement as the camera tried to capture light in the dark, and a halfway decent shot. Getting a shot of Buck Masterson and his wrongdoings was, in theory, possible. Now we just had to wait for the subject in question.

"That's quite a setup you have," Mrs. Branford commented once I had the four-inch camera lens propped on the beanbag.

I focused and took a practice shot, examining

the digital screen to gauge the lighting and the adjustments I needed to make. "Let's hope it pays off," I said, but truth be told, I was a little doubtful. Buck Masterson would have to be a Class A idiot to do something blatantly illegal in full view of the neighborhood, and in my wildest dreams, I couldn't actually fathom what we could catch him in the act of doing, anyway. But I wanted to make Mrs. Branford happy, and who knew? Maybe we'd get lucky and bust him doing something diabolical and nefarious. Stranger things had happened.

Ninety minutes later, we'd fallen silent. My rear end was numb, my neck ached from continually looking up and down the street for evidence of Buck Masterson, I was sleepy, and my back was stiff from the way I was angled in the seat of the car.

"I say we give it another thirty minutes, then call it a night," I said grudgingly. I wanted to see what my lens could capture in the dark, but without a subject and short of sending Mrs. Branford out into the street to be a test subject for me, it seemed unlikely that I was going to get the opportunity.

Mrs. Branford's response was a snort through her nose and a burst of air blowing between her lips. I snuck a look at her—sound asleep—and stifled a grin. I didn't blame her. My eyelids were heavy with the weight of boredom. I'd fought the urge to give in to letting them close; Mrs. Branford had lost that fight.

A movement from across the street caught my attention. We were far enough away that only someone with bionic vision would be able to detect us sitting there. Still, I shrank back in my seat. We weren't doing anything wrong, but I'd rather not explain to anyone about our stakeout. I peered through the eyehole in my camera, letting my superpowerful lens do the work for me. I drew in a sharp breath as recognition hit me. Buck Masterson was actually striding down Maple Street, but he wasn't alone. Next to him was a woman with what looked to be red hair. She had a round middle and skinny legs, and her arms swung purposefully as she walked alongside Buck. Surely, *this* was Nanette, the wife and the person who'd stared intimidatingly at Mrs. Branford from the front porch.

I didn't know her, but I already didn't like her.

As they walked down the street, I depressed the shutter button on my camera, checked to make sure I was getting decent images, and waited. I continued to watch through my lens. The zoom allowed me to see their faces, gestures, and actions. Nanette Masterson turned her head and said something to her husband. He nodded and ushered her forward with a wave of his arm. She glanced over her shoulder once, then continued on at a brisker pace.

Suspicious. "Where is she going?" I muttered.

Next to me, Mrs. Branford stirred. "Where is who going?" Her words were slurred, but I caught the gist.

Buck and Nanette were on the opposite side of the street and far enough away that there was no way they could hear me, but still, I kept my voice at a stage whisper. "The Mastersons."

Mrs. Branford sat bolt upright. Or at least as upright as her hunched shoulders and back would allow her to. "They're out there?" She leaned forward to peer out the front windshield. "Where? Where are they?"

Instinctively, I shushed her, extending my arm and pointing south. "Right there. They were walking together, but Nanette said something to Buck, and then she started walking faster. They look like they're up to something, but—" I didn't have the chance to finish my thought before I knew exactly where Nanette was headed. "Jackie's house."

Mrs. Branford clapped her hands triumphantly. "I knew it! Did you get a picture?"

Oh! In my excitement to see where Nanette Masterson was heading, I'd almost forgotten. Nanette was darting across the grass, bypassing the front walkway and door in favor of the side gate leading to the backyard. The area was tangentially lit from the street lamps. I hoped it was enough light to allow for some clear images. *Click. Click. Click.* I snapped picture after picture as she snuck onto Jackie Makers's property, her husband following. But Buck didn't go all the way through the gate to the backyard. Instead, he stood sentry at the fence, what looked like a cell phone in his hand. A security light shone down from the corner of the house, illuminating the area enough for me to get some halfway decent shots.

"Got 'em," I said, taking a few more as Buck put his phone to his ear and spoke to someone.

I glanced at the front of the Tudor house as the

blinds in the front living room parted and someone stared out. Buck had probably been talking to Nanette. Testing their covert operation and alert process, I presumed. Buck was the lookout, and Nanette had done the breaking and entering.

"They could be looking for the letters," I said.

"But how would they even know about them?" Mrs. Branford mused.

"Remember that one man, Harold Reiny? He was pretty straightforward in his letter. Maybe he told Buck that his days on the historic district's council were numbered."

Mrs. Branford sat back, considering. Finally she nodded. "Yes, I think that's possible. Harold is a pistol. He doesn't mince words, and it's gotten him in trouble on more than one occasion. Buck has no boundaries, and Harold has no filter. They're like oil and water, you know. They have never gotten on."

I debated our play. We hadn't really thought about what our play would be if we actually saw the Mastersons doing something nefarious. We could continue to watch, document with pictures, and keep the incident to ourselves. After all, I hadn't seen Nanette break into Jackie's house, and although I took a picture of the cracked blinds, I knew there was no way I actually got a shot that captured her face.

For the time being, more photos of Buck Masterson were out of the question. He'd shrunk into the shadows and all but disappeared.

After a moment, I made a decision. If they had

anything to do with Jackie Makers's death, then keeping their illicit actions quiet was a mistake. I would alert someone who'd actually know what to do. With one eye still on the house, I picked up my cell phone, went to favorites, and dialed Emmaline.

"About time," she said by way of answer.

"Hello to you, too."

She ignored my sarcasm. "Thanks for the heads-up," she said. "I was *not* prepared for that."

In the distance, Buck Masterson appeared under the security light beside the fence, cell phone at his ear. I snapped another picture. It wouldn't give me any additional information, but I took it, anyway. "Prepared for what?"

"Playing dumb does not become you, Ivy Culpepper. Next time you send Billy on an errand for you, give me fair warning."

"Oh, shoot. Sorry, Em." I played contrite, but inside I was smiling. So Billy hadn't dropped the envelope of letters off with the receptionist at the sheriff's office. He'd opted to pay a personal visit to his soul mate. Explaining to Emmaline that he hadn't wanted or planned to see her, but that he'd apparently changed his mind didn't seem like the right response. Instead I repeated, "Sorry."

Mrs. Branford waved her craggy hand in front of my face. "To whom are you speaking?" she said dramatically.

Emmaline, ever the detective, promptly asked, "To whom are you speaking, indeed? Please tell me, pray tell, with whom are you spending your time, Ivy?"

I answered Mrs. Branford first. "To the deputy sheriff. Her name's Emmaline Davis."

"My question next," Emmaline said into my ear.

"I'm sitting with Mrs. Penelope Branford on Maple Street. We just observed Nanette Masterson entering Jackie Makers's house. Her husband, Buck, is standing guard at the side gate leading to the backyard."

Emmaline didn't miss a beat. "Number one, how is it that you and Mrs. Branford were able to observe this alleged breaking and entering at this time of night and in the dark? Number two, why are you so interested in Jackie Makers's death? And number three, how did you come by these letters Billy delivered for you today?"

I answered in reverse order. "Olaya Solis and I were cleaning out some of Ms. Makers's things, and Mrs. Branford stopped by. Jackie had left the envelope with the letters at Mrs. Branford's house a few weeks ago."

"Don't you dare tell her I found them in my freezer," Mrs. Branford said, still leaning forward and peering through the windshield at the Tudor house.

Emmaline cleared her throat. "You might tell her that I can actually *hear* her."

I ignored them both, moving on to Em's second question. "I'm interested in Jackie Makers's death because she was good friends with Olaya Solis and Mrs. Branford. That makes me a friend—"

"Or acquaintance—"

"By association. Plus, I guess I have a curious side."

Mrs. Branford leaned back and gave me a pointed look. "And you've got that investigative gene your mother had."

I answered Emmaline's final question. "And lastly, we are on a stakeout on Maple Street."

Emmaline interrupted me with an indignant "What? You're on a *what*?"

"A stakeout. Buck Masterson, as those letters Billy brought you explain, is in everybody's business on this street. Mrs. Branford has seen him sneaking into houses. He's threatened her and others on the street. So we've been sitting here, seeing if we could catch him in the act. Which, I might add, we did."

She covered the receiver of her phone, and I heard her say something to someone. When she came back, she let out a heavy sigh. "I have some problems with this whole thing, Ivy. I can look into the letters, of course. I'll need to talk to Mrs. Branford and Ms. Solis. So that's all fine. But you should know that curiosity killed the cat. You're staking out someone who, by all intents and purposes, appears to have had a motive to kill Jackie Makers. I'm not saying this Buck Masterson or his wife is guilty of murder, but if, by chance, they are, you're getting in their way. Whoever killed Jackie did it for a reason. He, she, they won't hesitate to do it again. And finally . . . and most importantly . . ."

Sirens blared in the distance. She'd reported the breaking and entering, I realized. The sirens, though, had also reached Buck Masterson's ears. The cell phone was glued to his face again, and a moment later Nanette joined him at the gate.

Together they raced down the street, back the way they'd come. Just as a police cruiser appeared on Maple Street, Buck and Nanette Masterson disappeared into the darkness in the distance, and presumably into their own house.

"All you've done by staking out Maple Street is alert the Mastersons that we're on to them. Which makes my job that much harder."

I let out my own exasperated sigh. "But you wouldn't be on to them if we *hadn't* staked out Maple Street," I said. "And actually," I added, bringing her down off her sheriff's high horse, "I think *you* alerted them with the sirens. A little stealth can go a long way."

Another heavy exhale. She couldn't argue with me. We'd had this conversation so many times. I had never understood why the police always announced themselves with their lights and sirens when it seemed to me that they could catch bad guys in the act if they were more subtle about their approach.

"The house is secure," Emmaline said. "You should leave the stakeouts to the professionals, Ivy."

"Tell that to Mrs. Branford."

Mrs. Branford stirred beside me when she heard her name mentioned. "Tell me what?"

"Deputy Sheriff Davis says we should hang up our private-eye hats."

Mrs. Branford, bless her, blew a raspberry through her pursed lips. "Why would we go and do a thing like that when we clearly excel at it?"

I grinned, silently agreeing with her. We'd caught

the Mastersons in the act of breaking and entering, we'd gotten photographs, although I didn't really know what good they'd do anyone, and we'd put the fear of God in them. If they had killed Jackie Makers, hopefully they wouldn't target anyone else, and if they hadn't killed her, at the very least, maybe they'd think twice before continuing their Maple Street shenanigans.

Chapter Eleven

Before dawn the next morning, I took Agatha for a long walk at Wayside Beach, my favorite stretch of sand in Santa Sofia. I yawned, struggling to get energized at that early hour. I must have been crazy to agree to meet Olaya at such an ungodly time. "What was I thinking?" I asked Agatha.

Agatha looked up at me from her lazy stride beside me. I could tell she agreed that it was far too early, even if we were walking on the beach, something that had become her very favorite thing to do since we'd moved back home. She'd been born and bred in Texas's Hill Country, so sand and ocean had been foreign concepts to her. She'd adjusted like a champ.

After our walk, I left her crated at my dad's house, then met Olaya at Yeast of Eden. The sun was barely peeking over the horizon.

"How do you do this every day?" I asked her, stifling my tenth yawn of the morning.

"Early to bed, early to rise . . . Is that not how the saying goes?"

"It *is* how the saying goes. But still . . ."

"I run a bakery. It is how the business works."

Photography wasn't much different. The best photographs happened in the wee hours of the morning, usually just after sunrise, when the light was soft, warm, and dimensional. It was, in short, magical. Shadows were long and fluid, and everything seemed more dynamic.

Which was why I was at Yeast of Eden so early. I was shooting the pictures for a new brochure for the bakery, and I wanted the best shot possible of the front facade. The striped awning, the colorful Mexican garlands strung in the windows, the old-fashioned tables and chairs, the potted plants with geraniums and pansies all added to the quaint ambiance of the bakery. Waiting until midday would have made the whole shot harsh and bright, but the magical hour after sunrise meant the colors would be warm and welcoming: exactly what we wanted to make the place look its most inviting.

Olaya and her staff had filled the window racks with the day's offerings of fresh bread, the aroma drifting out to the sidewalk and even across the street, where I stood. I'd switched out the lens from the night before, going with a 24–70mm zoom lens, all that was necessary given the short distance from across the street to the bakery. Since the sun was up, I set the ISO to 100 and the f-stop to f/5 so I had enough depth of field to keep everything in focus. I didn't want my camera to home in on any one element of the storefront; instead, I wanted to capture the whole thing in its entirety.

I walked up and down, shooting from different angles to see what would work best. I'd brought my laptop with me to upload the shots so Olaya could look at them when I was finished and I joined her inside Yeast of Eden. At that point we could decide in which direction to go and if more shots were needed.

"Wanna take some of my place?"

I jumped, spooked by the voice behind me, and then remembered Olaya's comment about my startle factor. I hadn't heard anyone approach, which meant my situational awareness was not very good at the moment. I turned to see a bald man with skin the color of dark-roast coffee. He had a fair share of wrinkles lining his face, but they didn't age him. Instead, he was rugged and good-looking. I pegged him to be somewhere in his fifties.

"Oh!" I stumbled back, widening the area between us.

He guffawed, his infectious smile reaching to his penetrating brown eyes. "Didn't mean to startle you, young lady."

I resisted correcting him on that point. Thirty-six meant I wasn't quite a young lady anymore. "It's okay."

He offered his knobby hand. "Gus Makers."

Gus Makers. As in Augustus. As in Jackie Makers's ex-husband.

"I own the antique mini-mall down the street."

Right. And he was partners with the crazy man, Randy Russell.

"Ivy Culpepper," I said. "Nice to meet you, Mr. Makers."

"Mr. Makers was my pop," he said, "and he's long gone. Call me Gus."

I smiled at how normal and pleasant he seemed. Much different from the sketchy business partner he had. "Well, nice to meet you, Gus."

"Tell me what you're up to over here. Does Olaya know you're snapping pictures of her place?"

"She does," I answered, thinking how nice it was, despite the divorce he'd been through with her best friend, that Gus was watching out for Olaya. It was the neighborly thing to do, but people didn't always act in a neighborly fashion, as Buck Masterson had so aptly proved to the people of Maple Street. "She asked me to, in fact."

"Why's that?" he asked.

He was also blatantly nosy, but I didn't mind. Turn around was fair play, after all. "She's creating a new brochure for Yeast of Eden. I'm shooting photos for the front of it."

Traffic had started to pick up on the Pacific coastal road, and the parking spaces in front of Yeast of Eden were now filled. The bread shop sold only bread, but that didn't stop people from indulging or making two stops if they also wanted doughnuts or cookies or some other bakery delicacy. "Unadulterated bread is what I offer," Olaya had told me that first day. "And it's what people want. If they wanted the tasteless stuff, they could simply get it at the supermarket. Yeast of Eden is for the connoisseurs. It's for the people who really care about their bread and what they put in their mouths."

Personally, I was a convert.

"Good for her," Gus said, nodding his approval. "We compete with the beach, and with Broadway, where all the historic downtown shops are. Olaya's reputation brings a lot of folks to our neck of the woods, though."

So, Gus liked and respected Olaya, while his partner, Randy Russell, had waved a billy club around, threatening to shoot her because she no longer referred people to the mini-mall. Randy might be a hothead, but at least he was honest about it. A little part of me wondered if Gus Makers had the same anger toward Olaya and just hid it, or if he really was as pleasant and innocuous as he seemed. Had his divorce from Jackie Makers been amicable, or did he have animosity that had spilled over onto Olaya because of her friendship with Jackie?

I figured there was no harm in digging a little to find out. After all, I didn't relish Randy Russell appearing again, and if Gus here was anything like Randy, I wanted to know.

"Doesn't Randy Russell own the mini-mall, too?" I asked innocently.

Gus's smile never dropped, but I sensed a change in him nonetheless. A slight tightening of the jaw? Or maybe it was a dulling in the eyes. "Do you know Randy?"

I shrugged and did my best to look sheepish.

"I was taking a bread-making class at Yeast of Eden when the, uh, incident happened."

"Aha."

He didn't offer any more than that quick utterance, but I pressed. After all, if Randy Russell had spotted Olaya and attacked, things could have gotten really bad really fast. Or worse, if he'd had a gun instead of a club, I could well have been caught in the cross fire. "We were all pretty unsettled."

Finally, his smile faded into a grimace. "I bet you were."

"What was that about, anyway, with the stick?"

Gus Makers shrugged. "He was having a bad day."

I tried to stop my jaw from dropping, but I didn't succeed. Having a bad day, for me, meant I was grumbly, snappy, and didn't much want to be around people. It didn't mean I went around waving a weapon and threatening people. With all the shootings in the country, the idea that this unhinged anger was okay as a response to having a bad day left me with a sour taste in my mouth. "Really? And so he came to threaten Olaya?"

Gus's whole demeanor had changed. He was deadly serious, and his anger seemed almost to ooze from his pores. "Randy's not the nicest man anymore. I admit it. That's why I try to look out for the people around here. He's basically harmless."

"Basically harmless" was not a soaring recommendation, but I let it go. The sun had risen over the buildings now, that soft morning light giving way to the more severe light of the day. I shaded my eyes. "Do you think he'll try it again?"

It took him a few moments, but he finally answered, "I can't say. I hope not."

That was not a ringing endorsement of our safety. "You think he should have been arrested?"

Gus contemplated this question. "I don't know how to answer that. We've been business partners for a long time, and friends for even longer."

"Sounds like he has some secrets, though." Randy's anger that night in the back parking lot of Yeast of Eden, and again at Jackie's funeral, was almost palpable. He had been out for blood, but who knew why? And what if he still was?

Gus grimaced, his lips twisting into an angry frown. "Doesn't everyone, Ms. Culpepper? Doesn't everyone?"

Chapter Twelve

Everywhere I went, it seemed that Miguel Baptista lurked nearby. Okay, maybe *lurked* wasn't the best word to describe his presence. Santa Sofia was a smallish town, after all. It wasn't surprising that I'd see him around. But I felt as if I were newly pregnant, and suddenly, around every corner was a woman with a baby in utero.

Of course, I saw pregnant women everywhere, too, and I was not even close to having a baby. Divorced. No boyfriend. No prospects. That meant motherhood was not in my near future, yet my biological clock was ticking. It was Murphy's Law . . . or something.

This time, it wasn't a baby bump that struck me. It was Miguel. Gus Makers had gone back toward the antiques mini-mall, and I had packed up my camera bag, my back to the street and to Yeast of Eden. I jumped at the sound of three short horn blasts, then whipped around instinctively and just barely in time to see Miguel, his hand raised in a stationary greeting, driving past.

"As if a honk and a wave wipe away you being . . . you," I muttered. I couldn't quite call him a name. It didn't fit. He'd graduated high school and left to pursue his own dreams. I couldn't really fault him for that. We had been teenagers, after all, and that had been nearly twenty years ago.

But despite the logic of my argument not to hold him leaving me against him, I held fast to my anger. And I didn't plan on letting go of it anytime soon. Miguel Baptista maintained a special place in my heart, right smack in the middle of the fissure he'd created when he broke it for the very first time.

Olaya walked up to me at that moment. "Let it go, *m'ija.*"

"I'm trying to, believe me," I said. I gathered my things and followed her across the street and into Yeast of Eden. She had a little office just off the kitchen. Off-white faux blinds covered the two large windows, which were currently pulled up. The activity in the kitchen was hectic, yet organized. The staff worked quickly, jogging from one station to another, but together they operated like a well-oiled machine.

We spent the better part of ninety minutes arranging and shooting all the different bread choices Yeast of Eden had. "What did Gus want?" Olaya asked as we set up the last shot. At my direction, she placed a single rustic sourdough round on a worn teak cutting board lightly dusted with flour.

I adjusted the aperture and shot, moving around

to get some different angles. "He was looking out for you, actually. Wondering why I was taking pictures of the bread shop."

"Hmm," she said, and it sounded like a mixture of surprise and approval.

"He was telling me a little about Randy Russell. I'm still worried about him. That he might come back."

She dismissed my concern with the wave of a hand. "He is harmless."

"That's what everyone says . . . until someone comes unhinged and shoots up a senior center . . . or a school. Then they're not so harmless anymore. What if *he* killed Jackie? What if he comes back and tries to kill *you*?"

She put the bread back on the professional-grade metal bread rack, then wiped the cutting board clean with a damp cloth. "He had no reason to kill Jackie, and he certainly has no reason to want to kill me. We don't get along. I'll give you that. But he is not a killer, Ivy."

I'd dropped the subject as we set up my laptop in her office and I uploaded the pictures. She sat in her plush black office chair, and I pulled up a smaller, less comfortable chair, then pulled up the photos.

"Gorgeous," she said as I scrolled through the shots.

"The lighting was perfect."

She went back and forth between several but finally zeroed in on one particular shot. I'd stood directly across the street and centered the storefront in my lens. With the pink awning and shutters, the quaint green table and chairs, the pots overflowing with flowers, and the bread artfully and delectably arranged in the windows, it was the perfect choice. "This is it," she said.

"It's a good one," I agreed.

We spent another hour selecting the interior brochure shots, flipping through the different bread types, evaluating the shape, size, and the overall appeal of each one. Finally, we had a solid selection, one she felt represented the vast yet traditional offerings of Yeast of Eden.

Just as I was closing the folder on my laptop screen, she put her hand on mine, stopping me. With her other hand, she pointed to a folder labeled "MapleStreet_May10." "Are those the pictures from last night?"

"Yes." I double clicked on the folder, opening it up. "I had my best lens, but it was dark. They turned out pretty grainy."

The first series was of Buck and Nanette Masterson walking down the sidewalk, then stopping to confer before they closed the distance to Jackie Makers's house.

"Nothing notable there, is there?" Olaya said.

"Not at that moment, no."

I moved on to the next series, which showed Buck standing sentry at the gate to the right of Jackie's house. I scrolled through the photos one by one, allowing enough time for Olaya to take a good look before moving on to the next shot.

"Look at the window of the house," I said, pointing to the shadowy face behind the blinds on the right side of the house.

"They actually broke into Jackie's house." Olaya's voice was incredulous. She muttered under her breath, ending with, *"Hijo de su madre.* I cannot believe they would do such a thing."

I still couldn't believe it, either. I hadn't gone by to show the pictures to Emmaline yet. I hadn't even had a chance to look at all of them myself. After the police had left the scene, I'd driven the short distance to Mrs. Branford's house, parked in the driveway, and walked her inside. I had no reason to suspect that she was in any type of danger, but I'd still wanted to be sure her house was buttoned up tightly. Back at my dad's place, I'd uploaded the pictures, then glanced at a few to confirm what I already knew. The quality was as good as I could have hoped for given the light conditions and my powerful camera lens, but they still weren't, by any definition, acceptable.

Now, with Olaya next to me, I moved through the next few frames. I'd taken multiples of each shot, so I flipped through them quickly, but once again, Olaya stopped me.

"What was that?" she asked.

I pressed the BACK button and returned to the previous frame. "What?" It was the same shot: Nanette in silhouette as she peaked through the blinds.

"No, not that one. Go forward."

A moment later, we both stared at the picture, stunned.

"Is that . . . ?"

She nodded, and a chill swept over me as she whispered, "Someone else was in the house."

Chapter Thirteen

I pointed to the upstairs window, showing Emmaline the figure Olaya had spotted in the picture.

"Wait," she said. "Go back a few frames."

I knew what she was doing. Looking at a series of pictures in a row, all of which looked basically the same, was like looking at one of those old cartoon flip books that showed a hand-drawn cartoon character going through some simple motion. Mickey Mouse spinning Minnie in a sweet dance move. Popeye downing a can of spinach and flexing his bicep. Curious George doing somersaults.

I went back to the first shot, which showed the shadowy image of Nanette Masterson peering through the downstairs window of Jackie Makers's house. Clicking the right arrow, I advanced through the next few photos one by one until we saw the change.

She stared at the screen. "Unbelievable."

In the previous frame, the upstairs window had been dark, but this frame held the clear image of a figure, backlit by ambient light from somewhere in the house. It was eerie and ghostlike, the way the upstairs window had been dark and now it was filled with a human shape.

"Male or female?" Emmaline posed the question aloud, but I knew she didn't expect me to answer. There was no way to know. Even with super crime center–enhanced imaging equipment, which I was pretty certain Santa Sofia didn't have, I didn't think there was any way to get more details from the photograph.

I scrolled through the next few pictures, stopping when the window upstairs went dark again.

"Nanette Masterson's gone, too," Emmaline commented.

Sure enough, the downstairs window was dark again, the blinds closed tight, not a speck of light coming from inside.

"I think that's when we first heard the sirens," I said, lowering my chin slightly as I looked at her to drive home my stance that in a situation like this, sirens did more harm than good.

She ignored me, instead scooting the laptop closer to her and taking over the touch pad. She went back to the beginning and scrolled through the entire collection slowly and methodically, taking notes on a pad of paper she'd pulled from her desk drawer. "So you started your stakeout around eight thirty?"

"Right. We wanted to wait until the sun went down. Mrs. Branford seemed to think the Mastersons wouldn't venture out and do anything nefarious until it was dark. We settled in a little before the sun went down."

"I guess she was right about the cover of darkness," Emmaline commented. "And you first saw them at—"

"About ten o'clock. Can I just say, as an aside, that stakeouts are not fun?"

She arched her perfectly coiffed eyebrows, tucking her thick black hair behind her ears. "You don't say."

"Watching grass grow, and all that." *Or maybe watching bread dough rise,* I thought. That was about as exciting as the stakeout had been before we hit pay dirt with the Mastersons' appearance. "I do say. I was ready to call it a night. I'd just told Mrs. Branford that we should give it thirty more minutes, then *bam!* There they were."

"And then what happened?"

I took her through the events, aligning them with the captured moments from my camera, ending with seeing Nanette and Buck Masterson make a hasty retreat from Jackie Makers's house back down the street to their own just as the police car pulled up.

"You stayed until the police left?"

"We stayed in the car, which was parked down the street. We waited a while longer after the police cruiser left, just in case the Mastersons came back."

"But they didn't," she said, still taking her notes.

"Not that I saw."

She stopped again at the photos showing the dark

shadowed figure in the upstairs window. "And you never saw anyone else enter or leave the house?"

I shook my head. "No. Either they snuck out through the back somehow or they were still inside when Mrs. Branford and I left."

"Male or female?" she asked herself again.

"It could have been her daughter," I said, realizing that Jasmine very well might have decided to end her ban on all things having to do with her mother. I filled Emmaline in on what little I knew about Jasmine and the feud she'd been in with Jackie. "She came to the funeral," I said, "but she refused to help Olaya—"

"Solis? The bread shop woman?" Emmaline asked

"Right. She refused to help her clean out Jackie's house. Maybe she had a change of heart. She'd have every right to be in the house. Except . . ."

"Except that the lights weren't on. Which means it probably wasn't Jasmine." Still, Emmaline turned the page of her notepad and wrote down Jasmine's name. "So she and her mother didn't get along. She refused to help clean up the house and pack up Ms. Makers's effects. If she changed her mind and *was* there last night—although, again, why would she remain in the dark?—she would have been surprised by someone else sneaking into the house."

"Right!" I slammed my open palm against the desk. "Which is why she would have looked out the window, so she could see if she could spot anyone. A car, another person, anything to tell her who might be in the house."

"Any other ideas, Ivy?"

Buck Masterson was the only other person I could think of who'd had it in for Jackie Makers. He was already in the mix, so beyond that, I was drawing a blank. "No. Nothing," I said.

We rehashed the events of the stakeout one more time before calling it a night. "Dinner?" she said as she shut down her computer.

"Yes." As if on cue, my stomach growled. I'd had a chocolate croissant at Yeast of Eden earlier in the day, but nothing since. And I was starving. "Where should we go? Chinese? Thai? That new sandwich shop on Acorn?"

"We can talk about it in the car," she said, already halfway out the door. "I'm driving."

I figured we'd take her civilian car, but instead she got in the driver's side of a police-issued SUV.

"What happened to your Jeep?"

"It's at home. I just drive this most weekdays and save the Jeep for the weekends."

"I didn't think you took weekends off."

"This is Santa Sofia, Ivy. Pretty much nothing all that exciting or extreme happens here that warrants weekend work. Until now, of course. I won't sleep until we find Jackie Makers's murderer."

I hadn't paid any attention to where she was driving until we pulled into the parking lot of Baptista's Cantina and Grill. I bolted upright in the passenger seat. "Oh no," I said. "We aren't having dinner here."

"It's by far the best Mexican food in town, Ivy, and I need some chips and salsa. And *queso*."

My left eye narrowed suspiciously, and I tilted my head to the side. She'd zeroed in on my weakness.

The gooey, melted deliciousness that was *chili con queso* had me salivating. It was everywhere in Texas, but not so prevalent in California. "They have *queso*?"

"They do, indeed. The best."

I harrumphed fairly indignantly. "I doubt that. I lived in Austin, remember? I don't know if anyone in California can make it as good as they do back there."

There was a glint in her eyes. "Wanna bet?"

I weighed my options. Miguel might be in there. It was his restaurant, after all. So I could refuse to go in, acting like an immature twentysomething, or I could deal with my past heartbreak and have cheese dip.

I was no fool. I held out my hand. "Winner treats."

She shook my hand rather vigorously and grinned, her teeth bright and white against the milky chocolate color of her skin. "Deal. Better bring your wallet."

Twenty minutes later, I took my wallet out of my purse and laid it on the table. Our main course hadn't arrived yet, but our large order of *queso* and the basket of tortilla chips were both gone. "You win. My treat."

She laughed. "Told you. Wait till you taste the Tacos Diablos."

We'd ordered one dinner plate to share. I was already stuffed, but when it arrived, it looked too good to pass up. Three homemade corn tortillas were cradled in a metal contraption made just to house tacos. Bacon and jalapeño-wrapped shrimp filled the bottom of each tortilla and were topped with shredded cabbage slaw and creamy lime-chipotle mayo.

I took a bite, and a bit of the sauce dribbled down my chin. My cheeks were bulging when some-one approached our table, a shadow looming over us. "Welcome to Baptista's," a familiar baritone voice said.

Miguel.

My mouth was on fire from the jalapeño. I peered up at him through my watering eyes. I quickly chewed, then swallowed in one dangerously large gulp. Before I was forced to answer his greeting, with cabbage probably still in my teeth, Emmaline spoke up.

"Delicious as always, Miguel."

He rocked back on his heels, hands in his slacks pockets, a satisfied grin on his sun-kissed face. "Glad you think so." He swiveled his gaze to me, his grin lifting on one side. "And do you agree, Ivy?"

I swallowed the last of the food in my mouth, swiped a napkin across my chin, took a sip of water, and finally attempted a smile. "Definitely. Very good stuff."

Good stuff? I cringed at the lame comment on his restaurant's food.

His gaze found the empty bowl on our table. "Liked the *queso*, too, I see."

"Apparently, *queso* is Ivy's favorite," Emmaline said. "A result of living in Texas. She was skeptical, but yours passed muster."

I remembered Miguel as having one of those

faces that was hard to read. He had never put his feelings out there on his sleeve for everyone to see. He masked his expressions, making it impossible to know what he was really thinking behind a smirk. Looking at him now, I could see he hadn't changed in that respect. The mildly cocky grin was still there, but what was churning in his mind behind it was anybody's guess.

"Glad to hear it," he said. "I wouldn't want you to be disappointed in the *queso*, Ivy."

My eyes narrowed involuntarily. I couldn't tell if he was being facetious or sincere. "Mmm-hmm," I said noncommittally.

"Take a load off, Señor Baptista." Emmaline scooted over, making room for Miguel on her side of the booth.

I tilted my head. "*Señor* Baptista?" I mouthed, eyebrows raised.

"Ah, he knows I'm just messing with him, don't you, Miguel?"

"I'd expect nothing less, Em."

Em? How well did these two know each other? The world had turned topsy-turvy.

They continued chatting, and it was clear that they were comfortable with each other. No, more than comfortable, they were downright friendly. I didn't know if I should feel betrayed by Emmaline for her friendliness with Miguel or if I was being hypersensitive about a man I had no business being sensitive about. Still, for a brief second I wondered if the reason Emmaline was still resisting Billy might be Miguel. But after a few minutes Miguel rested his forearms on the table, his attention fully focused on me.

"How long are you in Santa Sofia for, Ivy?"

Inside my stomach was in knots. I couldn't deny it; Miguel Baptista still had a hold on me. But outside I played it cool. Or at least I tried. "Cut right to the chase, why don't you, *Señor Baptista.*"

"It's all the military training, I bet," Emmaline interjected. "No time for small talk when you're in a ditch, fighting for freedom."

"Guess not," he said with a chuckle, but his eyes never left me. "So?"

"I'm here to stay."

Emmaline dropped her fork with a clang. "You are?" she said at the same time Miguel said, "Hmm."

I could have sworn I'd told Emmaline about my plans to stay in town, but now that I thought about it more carefully, I realized I'd only intended to tell her. I hadn't ever actually gotten around to it.

"I want to be here for my dad," I said.

Miguel dipped his chin in a single nod, and I knew we had some common ground. He understood.

From across the table, Emmaline grabbed my hand. "Texas's loss, but our gain."

"I mean, don't get me wrong. I'll miss Austin. It's a great city. But—"

"But since you found *queso* here," Miguel said, "you'll be fine in Santa Sofia."

"That's right," I said with a coy smile. "*Queso* and the bread shop."

Emmaline and Miguel both nodded in agreement.

"Olaya Solis is a master," Miguel said reverently.

"For a little while, Em thought she might be capable of murder."

"What?" Miguel's spine went stiff as he sat bolt upright. "No way. That woman helps people. She doesn't kill them."

"I have to agree," Emmaline said. "I've been digging all day, and I have zilch for a motive. I'm still looking at the other Solis sisters, but I haven't been able to find anything on them, either."

Miguel whistled softly and shook his head. "Hard to believe there's a murderer walking around Santa Sofia."

Just as I was wondering how good a friendship Emmaline and Miguel had, and if Em would reveal the theory we'd tossed around about Jackie Makers's daughter, Jasmine, having a motive, her cell phone rang. She glanced at the screen, instantly muttering something unintelligible under her breath and holding up one finger. "I have to take this."

She answered with a curt "Davis," then listened. A moment later she had hung up and was gathering her bag, shoving her phone inside it, and sliding toward the booth's exit. "I gotta go, guys."

Miguel stood to let her slip out. I slung my purse strap over my shoulder, ready to join her, but Emmaline held out her hand, palm facing out, stopping me. But instead of talking to me, she turned to Miguel.

"Hate to ask, but would you take Ivy back to her car? It's at the station."

"Uh, no. Don't worry about it, Miguel," I said. "I'll just go with Em."

But Emmaline was already heading to the door. "Can't. There's a . . . a situation. I'm heading in the opposite direction. No time, really. Sorry. Talk tomorrow, Ivy."

"Sure," I muttered, but she was already gone.

"I won't bite," Miguel said, sliding back into the booth. He pushed the plate of Tacos Diablos toward my side of the table. "Enjoy. They're on me."

What the hell. Em had abandoned me, so it wasn't as if I had much choice. I didn't have to sacrifice my dinner just to hurry up and be free of Miguel's company.

"The *queso*, too?" I asked.

He laughed. "The *queso*, too."

A silence descended for an awkward minute before he spoke again. "I was really sorry about what happened to your mom."

The bite of shrimp in my mouth turned into a tasteless lump. "Thanks. I heard about your dad, too."

"Yeah. It was pretty sudden. My mom's still having a rough time of it."

"My dad, too. He tries to be stoic and strong, but it's hard."

Another awkward silence filled the space between

us. I took the time to look more closely at the man Miguel Baptista had become. With his six feet, broad shoulders, and lean physique, courtesy of years of military training, no doubt, he was definitely someone you'd want on your side in a dark alley. His already normal olive skin was tanned from hours in the sun, his hair was shorn close to the scalp, and faint smile lines on either side of his mouth softened his hard jawline. But it was those massive dimples that weren't exactly dimples curving around his mouth that clinched the deal. He was still the most attractive man this side of, well, anywhere. He was a cross between Mark Harmon and Enrique Iglesias. An odd combination, I knew, but there it was.

And, damn it, I still found him sexy and appealing.

As if he'd read my mind, he said, "You look good, Ivy."

I gave a self-deprecating laugh. "Divorce and death will do that."

"Yeah, I heard about the divorce, too."

"Good news travels fast in Santa Sofia, eh?"

He shrugged. "I run into Billy every now and then."

I silently cursed my brother for sharing my business with the man who was supposed to have been my soul mate. But I had to check myself. After all, I shared his business with his soul mate.

"You never settled down?" I cringed at how the question sounded as it left my lips. It might as well have been Mrs. Branford asking, it had sounded so dull and middle-aged.

The corner of his mouth rose in a half grin. "No, I never settled down. I still have a few good years in me."

I tried to play off my ineptitude at small talk. "Of course you do. Lots of time."

"You, however, had better hurry." He tapped the face of his watch with his finger. "Tick tock."

I felt my eyes narrow, my glare piercing. "Tick tock? Seriously?"

He chuckled. "Yes, Ivy. Seriously. You're thirty-six," he said, his voice laced with sarcasm. "Practically over the hill."

I breathed in, holding in the rash response hovering on my tongue. Clearly, I still harbored a good amount of anger at Miguel. I was ready to pounce and take him down, but the glint in his eyes and the tone of his voice helped me check myself. He was pushing my buttons, something he had always been good at and had done in flirtatious fun. It looked like he was channeling the old days. Once again, I spoke without thinking. "Since we're both past our salad days, we might as well commit to each other right here, right now."

His grin morphed into something smoldering. "Done. We can meet at the top of the Transamerica Pyramid in the city on New Year's Eve five years from now."

My jaw dropped, and words failed me. He knew about Cary Grant and Deborah Kerr in *An Affair to Remember*? Or maybe he knew about Tom Hanks and Meg Ryan in *Sleepless in Seattle*. Whichever movie he'd connected with, the romantic gesture was unmistakable, and I didn't know what had just happened. But before I could even begin to formulate a response, three women bounded up to the table. Jolie, Becky, and Sally from Yeast of Eden's bread-making class stood there, all teeth and smiles.

"Ivy!" Jolie clutched her cross-body purse, barely containing her excitement. "I thought that was you. I told the girls here that it was, and Sally was like, 'No, that's not her,' but I swore it was, and, look, it is!"

I blinked, switching gears from the cryptic conversation I'd been having with Miguel to Jolie's "train of thought" speech. "Different setting, right? We're not covered in flour—"

"And Olaya isn't on your back." Sally's grimace seemed to be in commiseration with Jolie, although I didn't get the sense that Jolie herself was displeased with Olaya.

"Sal, she wasn't on my back," Jolie said. "I forgot the yeast. She was helping me fix the *conchas.*"

I'd already pegged Sally as whiny, but now I amended my earlier assessment. She was whiny by proxy. It didn't have to be her own issue she complained about, and it also didn't seem to matter whether the so-called wronged person was actually upset. Interesting. I filed the information away, thinking it might help me understand her even better at some point.

Becky, the quiet one of the group, cleared her throat.

Jolie instantly picked up on the cue, shot a glance at Miguel, and raised her eyebrows suggestively. "Who's this?"

Inside I cringed. My mother's death had sealed my heart. Introducing Miguel to the Yeast of Eden baking group felt too intimate somehow, as if I was opening up some part of my past to this bevy of strangers.

Miguel saved the day. "Miguel Baptista," he said, nodding at them collectively.

Jolie tucked a loose strand of her jet-black hair behind her ear and tilted her head coyly. "Hold the phone. Baptista? As in this restaurant, Baptista's?"

He smiled, and if I'd had to qualify it, I'd have said his smile was almost modest. "Family owned," he confirmed. Modesty. It was a side of Miguel that I hadn't seen, one he had developed in his adult years.

Jolie had a slew of questions, some about the restaurant and others that skirted around flirtation. She didn't come right out and ask about it, but she was fishing for information about Miguel's availability. "And Mrs. Baptista," she finally said when Miguel didn't take the bait. "Does she work here, too?"

This time Miguel's smile lifted on one side. It was a flirtatious look I knew too well, and the fact that it was directed toward Jolie sent a tiny sliver of jealousy through me. Irrational, I knew, but there it was.

"She does, as a matter of fact," he said. "Occasionally."

I did a double take. "She does?" Inside I formulated a different question. There was a Mrs. Baptista?

His brow furrowed, his head tilted to one side,

and I got the sense he was trying to communicate something to me.

"Ah, oh, yes, she does. Of course she does!" I said, the truth of his statement hitting me like a ton of bricks. The only Mrs. Baptista in Miguel's life was his mother.

Before Jolie could inquire more about Señora Baptista, Sally swatted Jolie with the back of her hand, and this was followed quickly by the same knock against Becky's arm. "Isn't that the crazy guy from the antique store? The guy with the stick from that night that lady Jackie died?"

We all turned to follow her gaze. Sure enough, Randy Russell had sauntered into Baptista's. At that moment he looked around and spotted Miguel.

The three women seemed to stiffen in unison, their spines practically crackling with instant nerves.

"What's he doing here?" Sally asked under her breath, her voice thready with anxiety. She drew in a sharp breath. "Oh my God, he's coming over here. Why is he coming over here?"

It was true. Randy Russell was heading right toward us.

"Be cool, girls." Jolie seemed to have taken on the role of queen bee in this little group, and like any leader, she knew what to say to calm her followers. "He's not here to see us."

They stepped aside, making space for Randy Russell as he sauntered right up to the table. He glanced at the three of them, one at a time, glared at Jolie for an extra beat, gave me a cursory look, and then directed his attention to Miguel. "We need to talk."

The softness that had been in Miguel's expression a minute ago had been replaced with hard edges and lines, but he nodded. "What's up, Randy?"

Randy looked at us again, his eyes clouded with doubt. "Privately."

Jolie read between the lines and cleared her throat. "We'll just go now. Good to see you, Ivy. Nice to meet you, Miguel." She turned to her friends, gestured with a quick nod of her head, and off they went. Randy watched them go, waiting. Sally sent a nervous backward glance over her shoulder, but as the young women left the restaurant, Randy turned back to Miguel.

Miguel folded his hands on the table. "Anything you want to say to me, you can say in front of Ivy. She's one of my oldest friends."

Randy hesitated, seemed to consider this, then finally drew in a deep breath through his flared nostrils. Up close he was more weathered than I'd realized.

"That night . . . in the parking lot?" Randy began. "At Yeast of Eden?"

"What about it?" Miguel asked.

"I'd gone to the Broken Horse before I headed to the bread shop."

Miguel grimaced. "Yeah, I smelled the booze on you."

"Nothing wrong with a drink," Randy said, a defensive tone seeping in. I wasn't sure if he actually believed what he was saying, or if it was just what he told himself to get by.

"Nothing wrong with it," Miguel agreed.

I melted into the shadow of the booth, wishing I could be invisible so maybe Randy would get to his point a little sooner.

He must have read my mind, because the next second, he blurted out, "Someone else was there."

Instead of hiding under the invisibility cloak I'd wished for a split second before, I sat bolt upright, leaning eagerly over the table. Maybe he was talking about Jackie's murderer. "When? You saw someone in the parking lot?"

I really think Randy had forgotten that I was there. He took a wobbly step backward, and I wondered if he'd stopped by the Broken Horse for a shot of courage before coming to Baptista's tonight. But he gave a deep nod and said, "Yes. With Jackie."

I waved my hands, trying to process what he was saying. "Back up a second," I said. "You got to the parking lot of Yeast of Eden. Kind of belligerent, I might add. You were heading to what? Have it out with Olaya Solis for some reason?"

Randy dipped his head in a solitary nod. "She's screwing with my livelihood."

I didn't want to touch that can of worms. Whatever issues he had with Olaya had to be dealt with by her. As long as she wasn't in imminent danger from Randy Russell, I was more than happy to let her handle him herself. I redirected the conversation.

"So you got there and what happened? What did you see?"

"I didn't know what I saw," he said. "Not then, anyway."

Talking to Randy felt like pulling teeth. "But now you do?" I asked.

He hesitated again, as if he were weighing his options. Should he tell us, or should he not? Finally, he made up his mind. "Jackie was in her car . . . with a man."

I stared. "Wait. What?"

"You're saying someone was in the car with her?" Miguel asked.

"I saw him, sure as you two are sitting here. He was right beside her. I musta blinked or turned around, 'cause when I looked back, he was gone."

"When did you get there? To the parking lot?" Miguel demanded.

Randy drew back, thinking. "I didn't check the time, dude. I'm just telling you, she was with someone."

That niggle of doubt about Miguel being involved in Jackie's murder taunted me again. Surely he'd had nothing to do with it. I couldn't imagine him involved in anything criminal. But he was a man, and suddenly he'd been there to fend off Randy and his billy club.

I turned to Miguel, and for my own peace of mind, I asked the question that had been in the back of my mind since I saw him in that parking lot. "Why were you there?"

His eyebrows angled together, and I got the distinct impression that he knew why I was asking. He answered, anyway. "I was dropping off my weekend order. Nobody makes *pan dulce* and *tres leches* cake like Olaya."

"*Tres leches* cake? But she bakes bread."

"She makes it special just for Baptista's," he said patiently, as if explaining himself to an old girlfriend and giving his alibi for the time of a murder were second nature. "I was hoping she had a leftover sourdough from the day," he added, "but I never did get the chance to ask."

Randy slapped his hand against the tabletop, bringing our attention back to him. "As I was saying. Someone was in her car. I couldn't see clearly, but someone was there."

"You didn't tell the police?" I asked. Telling Emmaline what Randy saw was the first thing I was going to do. She needed to know there was a suspect who had been right there and had slipped away. My mind went straight to Buck Masterson.

"With the chaos and the fight, and then hearing that Jackie was dead . . . I just . . . I don't know. Forgot? That doesn't sound right. Doesn't sound possible." He sucked in a bolstering breath. "But it's the truth, man. Someone was there with her."

He got the implausible part right. How could you forget you'd seen a man in the car in which your best friend's ex-wife was just found dead?

"Maybe I had more than one drink at the Broken Horse," he said reluctantly.

Miguel and I shared a knowing look. Like three or four or five drinks, maybe. That many might blur the senses enough.

"And you just remembered?" I prompted. I didn't want to alienate him, but I also wanted to get as much information as he was able to give.

"He was on the tall side," Randy said by way of answering. "Brown hair. A jacket. Maybe blue. Or black. Hard to say." His voice cracked, the first sign of emotion I'd seen from him, his anger notwithstanding. Truthfully, I was glad for it. He had to have known Jackie for years and years. A little sorrow at her death seemed in order.

From what I'd gathered, Randy had lived in Santa Sofia for a long time. So had Buck Masterson. Surely they'd crossed paths at one point or another. The description was a little vague and generic, but it *could* fit the man from Maple Street. I'd seen him only from a distance, and he didn't seem inordinately tall to me, but then again, Randy looked to be about my height. So to a man who stood five feet eight inches, someone five-eleven might seem tall.

"Have you ever seen this man around town?" I asked.

Randy shrugged heavily. "Nah. Maybe. I don't know."

"You need to tell the police," Miguel said.

Randy lifted his upper lip revealing an expanse of pink gums. "I reckoned if you saw the guy, too, then it wouldn't look so bad that I didn't say nothin'," he said.

Miguel shook his head. "Sorry, man. I saw you talking to yourself, walking in circles, and then heading toward the back door of Yeast of Eden. If there was someone else in the parking lot, he was gone before I got there."

Randy nodded, looking resigned. "I'll call the deputy in the morning. That man—maybe he killed Jackie."

Maybe. Except that from what Emmaline had said, the theory was that Jackie had been poisoned. It seemed improbable to me that she could have met up with someone in her car and been poisoned with something that killed almost instantaneously. But what did I know? Anything was possible.

A little while later, I sat in Miguel's truck in the parking lot of the police station, where I'd left my car. I was still processing what Randy Russell had said, wondering if he really would call Emmaline Davis in the morning. There was no sign of her cruiser, and the light in her office was off. Either she was still at the crime scene that had pulled her away from our dinner or she had wrapped it all up and had gone home for the night.

"It was good to see you tonight, Ivy." Miguel's voice was low and sincere, and it hung there between us like a warm blanket.

I had my hand on the door handle. Being here with him felt like old times, and I had a fleeting thought that he might lean over and kiss me.

He didn't.

I waited, maybe a second too long, and an awkward silence replaced the warmth I'd thought I felt. Finally, I opened the door. "Yeah," I said, going for nonchalant but sounding impetuous. "You too, Miguel."

Chapter Fourteen

Randy Russell's confession the night before at Baptista's had stuck with me. Who had the mysterious person in Jackie Makers's car been, and did he have anything to do with her murder? I couldn't shake the feeling that he did.

But more than that, I had a niggling thought about something else. When I'd gone through my mother's boxes in the garage, she'd had photocopied essays—just like the one I'd found in Jackie's kitchen. Clearly, they'd known each other, at least on a cursory level. I also thought about my conversation with Olaya about Jackie's cooking school and the classes my mother and father had taken. I finally put into words the thought that had been circling my mind. Could my mother's death be connected to Jackie's? It didn't make a single bit of sense to me, but then again, nothing seemed to these days.

After walking Agatha along the beachfront, I headed straight to Yeast of Eden. I'd asked Penny

Branford to meet me there, and I summoned Olaya outside. The three of us sat at one of the bistro tables under the awning. The morning sun was just beginning to peak over the mountains to the east, the dappled light softening the morning. It was too early for the street to be busy with tourists, but a few locals strolled along the sidewalk. Agatha was not a barker. She stared at passersby but stuck close to me. Her tail curled when she was happy, but she was a skittish thing, and the activity on the street had her on edge. Her tail was currently hanging down stick straight. Something was making her nervous.

"Shhh, shhh, shhh, *perrita*." Olaya ran her hand over Agatha's shiny hair, calming her. To me, she said, "She is a wary one."

"Being wary can get a person far in this world," Mrs. Branford said. "Leaping in headfirst and without a plan can mean disaster."

I definitely agreed with that. Agatha would never run away from me or go willingly with a stranger. She stuck to me like glue, and I was absolutely fine with that. "I rescued her. She was the last dog surrendered from a backyard breeder in Texas. I never could find out the full story, but I was pretty sure she was abused."

We all looked lovingly at sweet Agatha. Her tail curved a little, and I sat back. I wanted to talk about my mother and Jackie, but I couldn't quite do it. Instead, I went with the other thing on my mind. "I saw Randy Russell last night," I said, and I spilled the whole story.

Olaya stared at me, then beyond the businesses across the street to the blue of the ocean. After a few minutes, she looked back at me. "He is sure someone else was with Jackie in her car?"

So she couldn't corroborate Randy's story. "You didn't see anyone?" I asked her. It hadn't occurred to me the night before, but on top of nobody seeing anyone in the car with Jackie, and no one seeing a person leaving the parking lot, no one had heard a car door slam. Maybe Randy Russell had had more at the Broken Horse than he'd conveyed and those drinks had had him seeing things.

She shook her head. "No one. I was thinking only of Randy and Miguel. That fight. It was not until later that we saw Jackie in her car. And she was alone."

Mrs. Branford grimaced. "And she was dead."

At first, the comment struck me as a bit heartless, but Mrs. Branford's expression was anything but. She was simply stating the sad fact that had led us to this conversation.

Olaya's eyes glassed over. Her tough facade had cracked for a moment, the idea of the killer made more real by Randy's assertion.

"It could have been Buck Masterson," Mrs. Branford said.

"My thought exactly, but how do we find out?" I mused. We'd already done a stakeout, and all it had shown us was that Masterson and his wife had broken into Jackie Makers's house. The why was still an unknown, but aside from following the man,

I couldn't think of a way to figure out what he was up to.

Olaya's face lit up. "What if Mrs. Masterson wins a free baking class? We'd have her in the kitchen with us for a few hours and maybe—"

"She'd spill all her husband's secrets without even knowing what she was doing." Mrs. Branford clapped her hands with glee. "Brilliant!"

"Assuming she takes the bait and shows up," I said, the voice of reason. It was a good idea, but Nanette Masterson was an unknown, in my opinion.

"Then we need to make it irresistible," Olaya said. "We will create a certificate—"

"I can do that," I said, getting on board with the idea.

We brainstormed ideas and finally settled on the concept of Yeast of Eden reaching out to members of the Santa Sofia community and offering free bread-making classes as a way to attract new customers and thank existing ones.

We moved from the bistro table in front of the bakery to Olaya's office. We gathered around the desk, me at the keyboard, and set to work on a Yeast of Eden "free baking class" certificate. An hour later the three of us sat back to admire our handiwork.

"I might incorporate this idea into the business," Olaya said, holding the printed document.

"It does look good," I said. We'd used the Yeast of Eden logo, which was a simple oval with "Yeast of Eden" prominently written in a typed font, and "Artisan Bread Shop" beneath it in a readable cursive. It was classic and accessible, like Olaya herself.

"How are we going to explain how she won it?" Mrs. Branford had asked midway through the production.

"The accompanying letter," I'd said.

Now Olaya directed me on opening up the letterhead for the bread shop, and I started typing. A short while later, I printed the letter and read it aloud to them.

> *Dear Friend,*
>   *Yeast of Eden has been part of the Santa Sofia community for more than fifteen years. Our bread is a testament to the artisan practice of bread making the old-fashioned way, and we've been fortunate enough to do what we love for many years. Our continued success is due, in great part, to people like you. If you're an existing customer, we'd like to say thank you. If we're unfamiliar to you, we'd like to introduce ourselves. We're offering you free registration in our exclusive bread-making classes. Learn how to make some of your favorites in la cocina, the bread shop's kitchen. Please call to register. Hurry! Spaces are filling up fast.*
>   *With appreciation,*
>   *Olaya Solis*

Mrs. Branford clapped her hands. "Perfect! You have a way with words, Ivy, just like your mother did."

I waited for the tug of sorrow I'd grown accustomed to feeling whenever my mom was mentioned, but for the first time it didn't come. Instead, I felt pride. It started as a sliver of a feeling in my heart and spread outward, giving each of my limbs a pleasant sensation of warmth.

"Thank you," I said, smiling, savoring the connection Mrs. Branford had shared.

Olaya put her hand on my shoulder, and I recognized the gesture as a sign of her gratitude. She wasn't effusive; I'd already learned that about her. But she managed to show her appreciation with a single touch. I laid my hand on top of hers, and in that instant the connection between us grew. I understood suddenly what the Grinch must have felt as his heart grew three sizes. I was filled with what I could describe only as love, both from and for these two women. It wouldn't ever replace the relationship and connection I'd had with my mother, but it was the next best thing. There was something about a bond between women that fed the soul. I'd been missing that since I'd been back in Santa Sofia, and since my mother's death. But now it was rekindled, both with Emmaline Davis, my oldest friend, and now with Penny Branford and Olaya Solis.

The moment faded, but the feeling of contentment remained. Olaya handed me an envelope, Mrs. Branford rattled off the Mastersons' address, and I folded the letter and the certificate, then slipped them inside the envelope. We stamped it, and minutes later, Agatha and I were walking down the street toward the post office to mail the summons to Nanette Masterson.

Chapter Fifteen

"She never called to register," Olaya said a few days later. I'd picked up Mrs. Branford on my way to class, and we'd arrived at Yeast of Eden, ready to bake.

"I tried to run into her in the neighborhood," Mrs. Branford said, "but she's been in hiding or something. Nary a sight or sound from that house all week." She shrugged. "Truly, I thought about calling someone to check on them. But I didn't. I'm nosy, but I'm not *that* nosy."

"I guess we'll see," I said.

I tied my floral apron on and then tied the back of Mrs. Branford's utilitarian number for her, and we set to inspecting the ingredients at our stations. I photographed the canisters of flour and sugar that sat on the counter, grouping and arranging them artistically, framing them in the lens to capture interesting angles and portions of the bags and clear plastic containers, spoons, and measuring cups.

I had reactivated my blog and had been posting

more regularly. Most of my photographs lately had been of food, and more specifically bread. I had a good sprinkling of coastal images I'd taken on my morning walks with Agatha, and I'd started capturing the birds I saw around town, too. But the *cocina* at Yeast of Eden was chock-full of interesting things that I was loving photographing. Bit by bit, I was recapturing my creativity and was feeling more like myself.

The other class participants began trickling in. Sally, Consuelo, and Becky came in first, and then a few minutes later Martina showed up. Jolie trailed in last, just as Olaya was getting under way with the class.

No Nanette Masterson.

"*Bienvenidos a todos*," she said, a chipper quality to her voice, which I was pretty sure was manufactured. She was just as anxious about Nanette coming as Mrs. Branford and I were. We all hoped she'd hold some vital key to figuring out what had happened to Jackie Makers, most importantly if her husband had been with Jackie in her car just before she died.

I listened as Olaya talked about the baguettes we'd be making. "Baguettes are a French staple. The flour is the absolute key ingredient. Sixty percent of the bread by weight is flour. We use only the best quality," she said, pointing to the canister at her station. "It is ambitious to be making baguettes at this point in our adventure together, but why not, as they say, go for the gold? Baguettes are just flour, yeast, water, and salt. And time. Always time."

"Why is it so complicated when it seems so easy?" Jolie asked.

Olaya smiled. "As I said, it comes down to time. All of us, we are too impatient. Cell phones. Social media. Work. We want to rush, rush, rush, but with the baguette, we cannot rush. We will wait while the flour and water and salt do their work in the bowl. It is magical. We will knead, we will let the dough rest, and we will let it rise. We will wait and let time work its magic with the dough."

Sally piped up. "But we're not here all night to do that. I have to help my mom later. I have other things to do."

Once again Olaya smiled. "*No problema, señorita.* I have the different steps of the process completed for you. We will work in stages."

We started by mixing together the flour, water, and a pinch of yeast. We each mixed our concoction and set it aside.

"Ivy," Olaya said. "*Ven aqui. Ayúdame.*"

I stared at her, trying to piece together the three words she'd spoken to figure out what she wanted me to do.

"She wants you to help her," someone said from the doorway.

I turned, as we all did, to see Nanette Masterson walking in.

"Nanette!" Penny Branford lunged forward, an enormous smile on her face. She clasped her neighbor's hand ardently. I didn't know how well Nanette Masterson knew Mrs. Branford, but it seemed obvious to me that her enthusiasm was overexaggerated.

"Oh, uh, hi. Hi there, Mrs. Branford," she said, taking a step back.

Mrs. Branford didn't let up. "How wonderful to see you here! I didn't know you were a baker."

I stifled a laugh. Those were pretty much the same words Olaya had said to Mrs. Branford when she'd shown up at Yeast of Eden.

Nanette Masterson held out the certificate we'd so carefully created. "I don't bake. Much. I got this in the mail, so I thought I'd . . . check it out." Her gaze found Olaya's. "I meant to call ahead, but—"

Olaya waved her hand, dismissing Nanette's excuse before she had time to utter it. "We happen to have room in this particular class."

I met Olaya's eyes and grinned. Inside I did a silent cheer. Our ruse had worked! Olaya sent me a look that said to take it slow and not spook Nanette. I nodded, completely agreeing. If Nanette knew anything that could be helpful about Jackie Makers's murder, she wasn't going to just blurt it out. And if she or her husband *was* involved, then she'd work triple hard to keep her mouth shut. Which meant Olaya, Mrs. Branford, and I had to play this carefully.

"What did you need help with?" I asked Olaya.

She beckoned me to the back counter near the large walk-in refrigerator. We were too visible for us to have any sort of private conversation, but we shared another satisfied glance. Bowl after bowl was laid out across the stainless steel, each one filled with an odd bubbly white goop.

"Take one of these to each baker," Olaya instructed.

"Ew. What is it?" Sally asked, wrinkling her nose and taking a tentative sniff after I handed a bowl to her.

"That," Olaya said, "is the starter. What you just created with the flour, yeast, and water will turn to this after many hours. We are speeding things up. I made these early this morning. This, *mis estudiantes*, is what yeast looks like when it starts growing. It is exactly what we want. *Exactamente.*"

I passed out the rest of the bowls before going back to my own station, giving Mrs. Branford a wink as I went by.

She waggled her eyebrows in response, and I stifled a laugh. She was not the subtlest person, but I doubted Nanette Masterson would equate Mrs. Branford and her wiggly salt-and-pepper brows with the subterfuge we were in the middle of.

Olaya showed Nanette to the station next to mine, then handed her an apron and a bowl of starter. "It is Mrs. Masterson. Is that correct?" she asked, feigning ignorance. She did it quite well, I had to admit.

"Nanette's fine."

Olaya clasped her hands together. "*Qué bueno.* And this is Ivy Culpepper. Ivy, *mi amor*, will you help Nanette if she needs it?"

"Oh, sure," I said, hoping my innocent act was as convincing as Olaya's. Of course we'd planned the whole thing in advance. Olaya had reconfigured the stations, moving Jolie to Jackie Makers's spot and sliding Mrs. Branford over one. This had left the space next to me open and ready for Nanette . . . if she showed up.

Which she had.

I felt slightly diabolical and thought about rubbing my hands together, throwing my head back like Maleficent, and letting out a twisted "mwahahaha."

Instead, I smiled at Nanette.

Working with the starter as our base, we added flour and salt to our mixers, then put warm water into the starter bowl to loosen up all the little tidbits of goop stuck to the sides of the bowl. "You want every last bit," Olaya said, demonstrating how to scrape the bowl with a spatula. The water turned slightly opaque, the starter bits floating around in it. Next, we added another dose of yeast to the milky water and stirred to mix it in.

"Like this?" Nanette asked me.

I glanced over at her handiwork. "Looks right to me." I held up my camera. "Do you mind?"

Her mouth pulled down on both sides in a heavy frown. "Uh, no, thank you. I don't want a photo taken of me."

"Oh, no. I was talking about the yeast concoction."

"Why not take it of your own?" she asked, glancing at the mixer on my counter.

"You can take a picture of mine," Jolie said. She took the stainless-steel bowl from her mixer and held it in front of her. I had to admit, I thought it

would make an excellent picture. She had on a
white and red apron with a red- and white-checked
gingham ruffle and succulent-looking cherries as
the fabric's main pattern. She clasped the bowl on
either side with her hands, her fingernails painted
red, grinning at her handiwork.

I aimed, focused my lens, and shot, focusing on
the contents in the bowl only and blurring the rest.
"That's actually perfect, Jolie. Thanks."

Olaya directed us to add water and the starter
mixture to the ingredients already in our mixers
and let the beaters do their magic, churning just
until the dough formed a cohesive ball. "Now, at
this point," she said, "we could switch to a dough
hook and let the mixer do the work, but we are not
going to do that."

Sally grimaced at the sticky mess in her stainless
bowl. "We're not?"

"We are most certainly not," Olaya confirmed.

Consuelo piped up from her corner station. "My
sister likes to make us work harder than we actually
need to. We're going to knead this dough by hand."

Martina smiled, nodding. "Always. When we
were little girls back in Mexico, she would make us
sit under the single tree in our yard, mix water with
dirt, and make mud pies. If we did not do it right,
we had to start again."

"*Otra vez,*" Consuelo said with a laugh. "*Otra vez!*
Those were her favorite two words. *Otra vez!*"

"*Es verdad,*" Olaya said, completely serious, but I
could see a glint of amusement in her gold-flecked

eyes. "*Y hoy también.* Do not do this bread correctly and you begin again. *Otra vez.*"

Martina and Consuelo burst into laughter, then chanted, "*Otra vez! Otra vez!*"

Olaya dismissed them with the practiced look of an older sister at her younger, irritating siblings. "*Entonces* . . . my sisters can have their big laugh. We will continue. Knead until the dough is soft and elastic."

Nanette was the first to dig her hands into her bowl of prepared dough.

Olaya rushed over to her. "Turn it onto your floured surface first. We knead here, not in the bowl."

A pink tinge colored Nanette's cheeks. "Oh. Right." She grabbed hold of the soft dough and plopped it on the floured counter. Everyone else followed suit, and a moment later we were each wrist deep in our dough, attacking it, kneading it, and turning it.

"Not too much," Olaya warned. "It should still be a bit rough. The yeast will keep working, allowing the gluten in the bread to develop. If you knead too much, the dough will overdevelop and be difficult to shape in the end. Not too smooth, *pero* not too rough."

I felt my dough, trying to gauge what would be just rough enough but not too smooth. Olaya came up beside me, touched the mound on the counter, and proclaimed it perfect.

One by one she moved to each station, making a determination if more kneading was necessary or if, as was the case with Sally, the person had over-kneaded.

Sally bit her lower lip and stepped back. "Will it be okay?"

"It is not too far gone," Olaya said.

"Oh, *Dios mio*! It will be just fine," Consuelo said. "Olaya, stop tormenting the poor girl. It is just bread."

Olaya turned on her sister, fire in her eyes. "There is no such thing as *just* bread." The blaze in her subsided, and she patted Sally on the shoulder. "I am instructing, not tormenting."

Sally nodded, but the expression on her face was sheepish and hesitant. She eyed her dough, clearly not sure if she could successfully turn it into the baguettes it was meant to become.

Olaya directed us to grease the clear glass bowls she'd placed at each station. "Put the dough in the greased bowl. It will rise for one hour."

Jolie worked two stations down from me. "She wasn't kidding when she said this would be an extended class," she said to Becky.

Becky brushed her hair away from her face with the back of her hand, leaving a trail of flour behind. "Good thing I canceled my dinner plans."

"Oh, give us the details," Mrs. Branford said.

Becky blushed. "It's not that big of a deal."

Mrs. Branford pshawed. "You know, dear, I'm far too old to go out on dates of my own. I must live vicariously through others."

"That's putting it mildly," Nanette said under her breath beside me.

"What?" I had heard her perfectly well but wanted to see if I could get her talking.

She kept her voice low so only I could hear. "That woman is a busybody. Always in other people's business. She's too old to get a life, but she needs one."

"She seems nice to me." It was an understatement, but I was playing a role. My hackles were up, and I wanted to defend Mrs. Branford. From what I'd already seen, Nanette Masterson was the one in everybody's business. In Jackie Makers's, anyway.

"Don't let the sweet old lady performance fool you. It's just that, a performance. She's . . ." She looked around to make sure no one was listening and then dropped her voice a bit more. "She's diabolical. She's turned the Historic Landmark Commission against my husband and me. We are looking out for our entire district. For all the home owners. For everyone! But that's not good enough. No, the HLC has called us out. Like *we're* the bad guys. She's almost as bad as Jackie was. The two of them have been thorns in our sides for as long as I can remember."

I couldn't believe she'd opened the door for me by bringing up Jackie Makers. I feigned disbelief. "Really? That's awful."

"This one?" She held her thumb up like she was hitchhiking and directed it at Mrs. Branford. "She's underhanded."

I had kept tabs on the other women in the class, noting that they had all left their bread to rise and had gone to wash their hands at the sink in the back corner of the kitchen. Nanette Masterson and I were alone.

"But why would she want to get you in trouble with the HLC?"

Nanette threw her flour- and dough-covered hands up. "Good question."

"How do you know it was Mrs. Branford? Maybe it was Ms. Makers?"

She hesitated. "I think it was both of them. My husband? He confronted Jackie the day she died. Told her to back the hell off and leave us alone. Do you know what she said?"

I shook my head, holding my breath, afraid that the slightest move or sound would wake her up and make her realize the extent to which she was spilling the beans.

"That we deserved her wrath. She actually used that word. *Wrath.* Well, someone got wise to her and gave her a dose of their wrath." She blinked, and her eyes suddenly grew wide. Realization had hit, and suddenly she was backtracking. "Not that I'm glad she was murdered," she quickly said. "Oh my, no. And not that we had anything to do with it. Buck—that's my husband—he told me Jackie wasn't feeling too well, so he just up and left. Told her he'd talk to her about their issues some other day."

"So he left her in the car?"

"She was alive when he left—" She stopped, eyeing me sharply. "I didn't say they met in a car."

Shoot. I kicked myself for revealing that tidbit. "Oh, it was just a guess. Jackie said she had been at her own class, then had rushed over here. When you said they talked before she died, I assumed you meant *right* before she died."

She still looked suspicious, but she relaxed slightly. "She was alive when he left her," she repeated, as if saying it enough times would make people believe it was true.

"Did you tell the police? It could help them with the investigation."

She grimaced. "Yeah, by giving them a suspect with motive and opportunity. We're not fools, Ms. Culpepper."

"Don't you think they'll find out?"

"Why? Are you going to tell them? What's any of it to you?" She sounded harsh, but it was an act. I could see the fear in her eyes. She didn't know me from Adam, and yet she'd just handed me a suspect and motive for the murder of Jackie Makers. I couldn't help but rationalize that if Buck Masterson was involved, then my earlier thought that my mother's and Jackie's death were somehow related had simply been a case of my imagination getting the better of me.

"I was just making conversation, Mrs. Masterson. Don't worry about me." It was an outright lie, but what could I say? Emmaline's warning that Buck and Nanette might be the killers, and that if they were, they'd be willing to kill again to stop the truth from coming to light, surfaced front and center in my mind. Diffusing the situation was the only sane thing to do.

"People like her and that Jackie Makers," she

said, glancing once again at Mrs. Branford, "they're the menace."

I bit my tongue, stopping myself from accusing her and her husband of exactly the same type of behavior. "Hmmm," I said, as noncommittal a response as I could muster.

I studied Nanette Masterson. Her dyed red hair was short and in need of a wash. She couldn't be older than fifty—at least that was my guess—but her frumpy clothes gave her an extra ten years. She had thin lips, which she was pursing. Her anger was palpable . . . and from where I sat, it seemed wholly unwarranted.

"They shouldn't get involved in things that don't concern them," she said.

I wanted to set her straight, tell her what Mrs. Branford had said, warn her to mind her own business, but instead I said, "Huh." I waited a moment, watching Olaya lead the other class members to the front lobby of the bakery, and then said, "So you and Jackie weren't friends, I take it."

"Not even close. I didn't wish her dead. Let me be clear about that. But now that she is, let's just say we sleep easier at night knowing we aren't going to wake up to some new terror she decided to inflict on us."

All I could think to say was, "Wow," but I kept that to myself. Nanette Masterson was a piece of work. "I helped Olaya clean out some things in Jackie's kitchen," I said, wanting Nanette to know I'd been on Maple Street.

She pursed her lips tighter. "Is that right?"

"Beautiful kitchen. Beautiful house, actually."

She grimaced. "She ruined it. Painted authentic wood trim inside. White. Why would she destroy something that had been so carefully crafted? That's the problem with the people in the historic district. My husband and I work to preserve our town's history, but people like Jackie Makers, they just destroy it on a whim."

"You mean the moldings? What's wrong with white?"

"Not. Authentic."

"But it's pretty. It makes the house feel so clean and open. And it was her house, right?"

She gave me a withering look that I could translate only as "You're an idiot." "You don't move to the historic district and ruin a landmark house. The people who live there want to preserve history, just like me and Buck. That house . . ." She shook her head, as if she still couldn't believe what Jackie had done to it. "It should not have a green roof. And new windows? What was she thinking? You never replace windows in a historic house. The windows are its soul. That house has lost its soul."

"Because of new windows?" I happened to think the white grids and frames of the windows, edged by brick-red trim, were lovely. And new windows were probably far more energy efficient. If that house were mine, I wouldn't change a thing. In my opinion, it had plenty of soul.

"Clearly, you are *not* a historic home owner."

"No, not yet. Hopefully someday," I said, once

again feeling that my future did include living in a house like Jackie Makers's or Mrs. Branford's.

She eyed me, seeming to take a closer look. "Have we met?"

Not in so many words, I thought, remembering seeing her and her husband the first day I'd met Mrs. Branford, not to mention the stakeout, during which I'd seen Nanette Masterson break into a dead woman's house. "I don't think so," I said.

She wasn't going to let it go. "You look familiar."

I shrugged it off. "I must have one of those faces."

"Red hair, freckles, those green eyes. You definitely do not have one of those faces." She stopped suddenly, and I could see her mind working. "Wait a minute. Six months ago. Maybe longer. I saw you at Jackie Makers's house."

I shook my head. "Um, no."

"Oh yes. I'm sure it was."

"It couldn't have been. Six months ago I lived in Austin. I came back here when my mother died—"

She inhaled sharply. "The woman who died in that hit-and-run?"

I breathed in, bracing myself for the wave of emotion that always came when talking about the tragedy. "Anna Culpepper."

"You look like her, don't you?"

"Most people think so."

"Then it must have been her I saw."

"I think she took cooking classes from Jackie, but I don't think they were friends."

As I said the words, I wondered if they were true. I hadn't lived in Santa Sofia for years; there was no way to know if my mom had become friends with her cooking teacher—and maybe the parent of a former student.

Nanette shrugged, her mouth pulled down in an exaggerated frown. "Perhaps not, but I'm sure I saw her—" She broke off, and a lightbulb seemed to go off in her brain. She pointed at me. "Wait. I know where I saw you. You were on Maple Street."

My nerves stabbed in my gut. Had she seen me in the stakeout car, spying on her? "Um—"

"I saw you on Penny Branford's porch. It must have been a few weeks ago. You *do* know her." She leaned against her workstation, accusation in her voice.

I feigned innocence. "I remember! I was looking at the houses on your street with my father. He's the city manager."

"And Penny—"

This line of questioning felt like the Inquisition. At least she hadn't noticed the stakeout. I resisted filling the empty space with further explanation and just said, "She was outside."

"What? Are you watching the dough rise?" Nanette and I both turned as Sally sashayed into the kitchen. "Come on. Olaya sliced a lavender loaf."

We joined the group and savored a slice of heaven.

Mrs. Branford caught me by the arm as we retreated to the kitchen afterward. "Got anything good? Did she confess, for example?"

"Ha! Not even close." I recounted the conversation as quickly as I could. "She doesn't like you."

She swung her cane and tapped the floor with the rubber-tipped base. She definitely didn't need it. "The feeling's mutual."

I separated from her before Nanette saw us talking, and then I returned to my station. As if by magic, my baguette dough had risen and was full of bubbles.

Olaya came around and punched each of our bubbly loaves, deflating them by releasing the air. "Now, we let them rise again for three hours."

A series of gasps and disbelief circulated in the room.

"Three hours!"

"That's crazy!"

"I have things to do tonight!"

"*Cálmense.* Relax." Olaya smiled, and I knew we wouldn't be here all night long. She disappeared back into her secret corner of the kitchen and returned a minute later with a shiny silver baking tray dotted with perfectly smooth and rounded dough mounds. "I have prepared the dough to this stage for you all."

She made the rounds, stopping once again at all our stations. We each took one of the soft, elastic mounds Following her directions, I divided my dough into three equal pieces. After flattening them into ovals, we let them rest for a few minutes. "So the gluten can relax like you just did," Olaya said.

She modeled the next step at her teacher's station, and we observed by watching her in the angled mirror above her area and followed her lead. First, we shaped one of the ovals into a rectangle. Next, we folded the rectangle in half and sealed the edges with our fingers. We flattened, folded, and sealed it again.

"Now look!" Olaya held her hands together in a prayer-like position. "See how it has stretched from about eight inches to ten? It is magical. It is bread."

It *was* pretty amazing. We laid the seam side down and gently rolled our rectangles with our hands, working from the center to the outer edges.

"Not too hard," Olaya warned. "We don't want to make the dough tough."

After going through the same process with the other two pieces of dough, we placed the three fifteen-inch loaves on the three-welled baguette baking trays Olaya had given us.

"Your loaves will bake on your baguette pans, but I will have to move mine. I use a couche to let the dough rise rather than the baguette pan. It is the French method," Olaya said. She demonstrated with the loaves at her station, first sprinkling flour on a linen towel and then rubbing it in. She laid her three loaves on the towel, cradling them between the folds she created.

We cleaned our stations while the loaves rose for the final time.

"The final step," Olaya said when we were finished and after she'd moved her loaves to a baking sheet, "is to spritz them with water. This will give them their crunchy outside." She then scored each loaf three times at a forty-five-degree angle. "This gives the baguette its signature look."

"I don't care about their signature look anymore," Sally whined. "I'm tired."

"You will care when they come out of the oven."

The loaves were placed in the kitchen's professional-grade ovens.

"Four hundred fifty degrees until they are a golden brown," Olaya told the women.

Before long, the aroma of baking bread filled the space.

"Okay, maybe I do care. When will they be done?" Sally asked, and everyone laughed.

Olaya grinned. "Soon."

"Time to set the table," Consuelo announced. She'd stepped into a closet. When she came back out, her arms were laden with brightly colored place mats, spoons, bowls, and small plates.

We all followed her to a back area of the kitchen. Cream window panels hung on either side of an archway. Martina pushed them aside, letting Consuelo and the other women pass through. I hadn't known this cute room existed. A rectangular walnut table sat in the middle of the space. Twelve chairs were positioned around the table. They were red, turquoise, yellow, and green and were arranged around the table in a pattern.

"It's beautiful!" Jolie walked the perimeter of the room, taking in the delicate lamp in the corner, the story quilt hanging on the wall, the metal sheet with the words *Buen Provecho* cut out in an angled cursive font. A primary-colored Mexican flag banner was strung across the top edge of one wall.

Consuelo and Martina quickly set the table. They did it with an expertise that told me this wasn't their first time doing this particular job. When they were finished, candles flickered across a lace table runner, and each place setting had a sprig of lavender tied to the napkin. I completely agreed with Jolie. It was warm and inviting.

"Did someone order soup?"

I immediately recognized that male voice. Miguel stood in the archway. His mahogany hair was windswept, and his smile was enticing. He met my gaze, and I got the feeling the smile was just for me.

Olaya surged toward him. "Just in time." She took one of the bags he held, set it on the sideboard, and removed two tall containers. "Poblano corn chowder. *Perfecto*, Miguel. *Muchas gracias.*"

"*De nada,*" he said, unloading the second bag.

Martina set two soup tureens on the sideboard, and Olaya carefully poured the soup, one container at a time, into them. Miguel carried them to the table and placed one on either end, between the candles.

Consuelo had disappeared back into the kitchen and soon returned with a wooden tray and three of the freshly baked baguettes.

We sat at the table and broke bread as Miguel ladled soup into our bowls.

Mrs. Branford sat next to me. She took a bite of the bread and breathed in the scent of the chowder. A slow smile spread across her face.

"Olaya Solis, it pains me to admit it, but this is quite spectacular."

Olaya bowed her head once in acknowledgment. I could see the pride on her face. Coming from the woman who had been her archenemy just days before, this was a big deal. "I also hate to admit it, but, Penelope, your approval, it makes me quite happy."

Chapter Sixteen

I brought leftover poblano corn chowder and baguettes home. The hours my dad was working were getting longer and longer—a way to escape his pain—which I understood, but I missed him. And I worried about him. I'd texted him that I was bringing dinner, but he wasn't home when I got there. I set the table and readied the soup and bread so that I could reheat them.

And then I leashed Agatha and headed out for a walk. Instead of taking our normal path to the beach, I stayed on the sidewalk and in the neighborhood. Agatha trotted along, her bug eyes facing forward, her ears flattened back as she walked, her tail curled up tightly in a little loop. She didn't have a care in the world. I was envious.

As I was heading back, I saw my dad's car parked in the driveway. I pushed my worry aside for the time being, and my pace quickened. Agatha's little legs worked double time. A short while later, we were sitting at the kitchen table.

"Good day?" I asked. The small talk seemed so banal and pointless, yet I knew we had to keep moving forward in hopes that one day the unimportant stuff in our day-to-day lives would be worth thinking and talking about again.

"Normal day, I guess," he said. "Soup's good."

Billy, Dad, and I had all had to redefine what ordinary was. Billy was a lone wolf, so I didn't actually know how he was coping. He internalized everything and didn't share what he was feeling. My dad was the same way. He had nothing new to take his mind off things. Work, work, and more work was his only outlet. I, on the other hand, had Olaya Solis and Penelope Branford and my newfound baking classes, not to mention the amateur sleuthing I was becoming slightly obsessed with. It didn't make coping easier, but it did give me something else to think about.

"You'll never guess who made it."

He looked at me, the interest on his face genuine, if clouded by his numbed emotions. "Who?"

"Miguel Baptista. You remember him, right?"

Dad half scoffed, half chuckled. "How could I not? I think you cried for six months after he left Santa Sofia."

I slapped his hand playfully. "No, no. Maybe six weeks. He did break my heart, after all."

We sat in silence for a while. My stomach was in knots, in part because of the emptiness inside me, but the truth was that I couldn't push my thoughts to some remote corner of my mind. They escaped and returned front and center. Nanette Masterson had said that she'd seen my mother talking to Jackie Makers at Jackie's house, but as far as I knew, they hadn't been friends. No matter how I looked at the situation, it didn't feel right. I wanted my dad to tell me that Nanette Masterson had been mistaken. That Mom knew Jackie Makers only from the cooking classes they'd taken. That my mom's death had been an accident.

But deep down I suddenly wasn't sure. My mind whirled around the idea that my mom and Jackie were connected in some way, and that what we thought we knew about my mother's death might not actually be the truth.

I drew in a deep breath and launched into the conversation I'd had with Nanette. "Were they friends?" I asked when I was done.

With his elbows on the table, he folded his hands and propped his chin on them. I took the moment to study him. His hair had always been a sleek dark brown, and while his mustache had been salt and pepper for the past seven or so years, the pepper had all but vanished. New gray hair had sprouted at his sideburns and temples. I hadn't realized it until this moment, but he'd aged ten years in the past six months. My heart broke for him all over again.

"Not that I'm aware. We took the cooking classes, like I told you."

"That's what I thought, but Nanette was sure she saw Mom and Jackie Makers on Maple Street."

His brow furrowed, and I could tell he'd thought of something.

"What is it, Dad?"

Instead of answering, he pushed back from the table and disappeared down the hall. A moment later he came back, sat down again, and slid a cloth-covered journal across the table to me.

I stared, afraid to touch it. "Mom's?"

"It's not a diary. Not exactly, anyway. Your mom jotted down notes and . . . just . . . stuff." He pushed it toward me. "I haven't looked at it. Haven't wanted to. It's too tough for me, Ivy. I hope you understand that. But if you want to know more about your mom, look in there."

I stayed up into the wee hours of the morning reading my mom's journals. Turned out the one my dad gave me at dinner wasn't the only one my mom had. There were eight altogether. I had figured out the order and had lined them up on my bed from the earliest to the most recent. I'd been afraid that starting at the beginning would take me on an emotional journey I wasn't ready to take. Starting with the most recent would be difficult enough, but that was the journal that could potentially tell me about her connection to Jackie Makers. And that was the thing I wanted to know about more than anything.

But once I'd got started, I couldn't stop. Page after page, I read about her students, her passion for everything French, sketches of the Eiffel Tower, and random pictures of birds, which had been her favorite thing to photograph. As I read her poems and snippets of ideas for stories and articles, my

mom seemed to unfold before me. I saw her
thoughts, her desires, her soul . . . all in new ways.
I began to see her not as my mother, but as a
woman.

I'd thought that not reading the early journals
would make it easier somehow, but it hadn't. What
I realized was that while I knew my mother, I knew
only the part of her that she had shared with me.
And she was so much more than that. She'd been a
woman, a mother, a wife, a friend, a teacher, a
writer. . . . She'd been so much more than I'd ever
recognized. I could see why my dad didn't want to
read her journals yet. It was too soon, and seeing on
the page all that we were missing with her not here
was salt in the wound.

I had made it to the last pages of the most recent
journal and had all but given up on finding anything in it about Jackie Makers. Then I turned the
page.

> *Jesus. I* knew *I was right.* Knew. It. *I won't tell
> Owen yet, not until I talk to Jackie. He wouldn't
> want me getting involved. The problem is that she
> doesn't really know me. Will she trust that I want
> to help?*
>
> *How to approach her? Not at cooking class.
> Maybe I'll stop by her house. Yes. That's what
> I'll do. But what about Gus? That's what I still
> don't know.*

I reread the entry, trying to read between the
lines. What was she right about? If she'd ended up

telling my dad whatever had been on her mind, he would have mentioned it, so maybe whatever she'd thought hadn't panned out. I read the entry again, zeroing in on Gus's name. What about him? Could my mother have discovered an affair? It was possible, but my mom was not a gossip. She'd always made a point to steer clear of the riffraff in her school, staying above the fray. I didn't think she'd get involved in an affair that Jackie or Gus had been having. She didn't *know* them, so why get tangled in anything they were doing? Plus, they were divorced, and this journal entry of hers had been written long after Jackie and Gus had called it quits.

I turned to the next page, but it was blank. So this was the last entry. Flipping back, I checked the date of the last thing she'd written, but she hadn't noted it. I turned to the previous page. I read the date. Blinked. Reread it. It couldn't be.

But it was.

My heart caught in my throat.

The last dated entry had been written two days before my mother died.

I tossed and turned the rest of the night, mulling things over, trying to talk myself out of what I now suspected. But I woke up the next morning more sure than I'd been a few hours ago, and I made the call I'd wanted to make at two in the morning. I worried that 6:00 a.m. was still too early, but the bright, clear tone of Emmaline Davis's voice erased that concern. Ever since college, she'd been an early bird. Earlier than me, and that was saying something, since my favorite thing to do, even back then, was to photograph the sunrise. That meant I was often up before the sun. Even so, Emmaline usually beat me.

I launched in the second she answered the phone, and told her about my mother's journals and the entry about Jackie Makers. "Em, she knew something, and that's why she died. I'm sure of it."

"I don't know, Ivy—"

"I know I'm right. I feel it in my gut. I didn't think my mom knew Jackie Makers outside the cooking classes she and my dad were taking—"

"Which is so cute, by the way. I love that they did that."

I had, too. After thirty-seven years of marriage, they'd still loved each other and been sweet with each other. Another nail in the coffin of my dad's misery.

"But maybe she did *know* her," I said. "She learned about something. And she was . . . was . . . killed for it."

I stumbled getting the sentence out. I didn't know why, but I knew in my heart that her death hadn't been accidental. My mother . . . my mom . . . had been murdered.

Chapter Seventeen

I looked for Gus Makers at the antiques mini-mall. I hadn't been in the building in years and years. Under different circumstances, I would be drawn to the vintage treasures. I would be educating my taste, which was all I could do given that I didn't have a house in which to put anything.

For now I walked straight to the front counter, bypassing the nooks and crannies of the shop, each filled with old china, crystal, record albums, bags and purses, vintage clothing, ceramics, reclaimed wood, shutters, old doors, and more. It wasn't Gus I found, however. It was Randy Russell.

My heart seized a tiny bit, his volatile encounter with Miguel that night in the parking lot of Yeast of Eden resurfacing front and center in my mind, quickly followed by his assertion to Miguel and me that someone had been in the car with Jackie Makers the night she died.

Which had proved to be true, according to Nanette Masterson.

He eyed me suspiciously as I approached the U-shaped counter. "You're that girl who was with Baptista the other night, aren't you?"

"Yes, sir. Ivy Culpepper. Good to see you again."

A blondish ring of hair ran like a horseshoe around his head, the top portion completely bald. He ran his hand over it. "Didn't I see you at Jackie's funeral, too? You knew her?"

"No, not really. I'd met her only once," I said, glad for the opening. At least I didn't have to try to come up with some vague story line so I could try to get information. "My mom knew her, though."

He looked skeptical, and his voice was rough, like he'd smoked a pack a day for the past thirty years and it had destroyed his vocal chords. His was a hard life lived, from what I could tell. "Did she, now? And who is your mom?"

"Anna Culpepper. She was a teacher at the high school in town. She, um, she died about six months ago."

His narrowed eyes opened wide as recognition took hold. "I remember that. She was hit by a car in the parking lot." The gravel in his voice loosened. "Darlin', I'm sorry for your loss."

I hadn't expected any compassion from him, and it softened his rough edges in my mind, despite the belligerence I'd witnessed and Gus Makers telling me that his business partner and friend was a bit of a loose cannon. "Thank you."

"What can I do you for? In the market for some antiques?"

"No house to put anything like that in right now. I'm staying with my dad."

"Okay, so what do you need, Ms. Culpepper?"

"I was actually looking for Gus. Is he around?"

Randy's eyes rolled up for a split second, and something in his expression made me think there was a lot of baggage in their friendship that neither one hid very well. "He'll be in later."

I tried to hide my disappointment. "Okay. Thanks. I'll come back."

He hesitated for a second and then seemed to make up his mind about what he was going to say next. "Gus hasn't mentioned you. You're friends?"

"No, no. I've met him only once or twice. It's just, my mom . . . her death. I'm trying to piece together some things that happened before she died, and I thought Gus could help me."

The creases of his weathered face deepened as he frowned. "I've known Gus since we were kids. He didn't know your mother. That I can guarantee."

"Oh." I felt my face fall. "How can you be so sure?"

"We've worked together nearly every day of our adult lives, darlin'. Pretty hard to keep secrets. I've managed to have a few, but Gus? He wears his damn heart on his sleeve. He don't know the meaning of the word *vault*."

I'd intended to try to get information from Gus about his ex-wife and whatever connection she might have had to my mother, but if what Randy said was true, then he might very well have his own information. "My mom talked to Jackie Makers right before she was ki—" I swallowed the emotion clogging my throat. "Right before she died," I amended. "I can't ask Jackie about it, obviously—"

"Obviously," he parroted.

"So I thought I'd ask Gus about it. Since he'd been married to Jackie and all."

"They were divorced."

"I heard they were still friendly, though."

He shrugged. "For Jasmine's sake."

I rested my elbows on the glass counter and leaned in, lowering my voice to a level that suggested conspiracy. "I'm always curious about people. Why'd they get divorced?"

But if I'd thought Randy Russell would just spill the beans and tell me his best friend's dirty secrets, I'd been wrong. "Not my story to tell," he said. "I do know the meaning of the word *vault*, and this, Ms. Culpepper, is locked up tight."

"It's my story, so I guess I can tell it."

I jumped at the voice behind me and turned to see Gus Makers and his affable smile entering the store, the door silently swinging shut behind him. They really needed a bell on that door to announce customers. And owners.

I swallowed my guilt, hoping he hadn't heard our entire conversation. "Hi, Mr. Makers."

"Just Gus, remember?"

I smiled, tamping down the nerves in my gut. For all I knew, Gus Makers could have had something to do with my mother's death. She'd specifically mentioned him in her journal. Maybe she hadn't spoken only with Jackie. Maybe she'd sought out Gus, too. Did he have a secret worth killing for?

"Gus. I was just . . . I stopped by to . . ."

"She wants to know if her mother and Jackie were friends," Randy said, jumping in as I stumbled over my words.

Whereas Randy had a ring of blondish hair that still crowned his head, Gus was completely bald. If he'd had a dark covering of hair, he would have been the spitting image of Denzel Washington, complete with the wide smile and the intelligence emanating from his eyes. He wasn't going to let his lack of hair define him; instead he had taken charge, had shaved it all, and had remained in control. The difference between him and Randy was night and day. Gus was Mr. Cool compared to Randy's curmudgeonly persona. They were both good-looking men, but completely different from one another.

"Your mother?" Gus asked.

This time I was determined to get through my own story without my voice cracking or the words catching in my throat. "My mom died about six months ago. I ran into someone who said she saw her talking to your ex-wife a few days before." I drew in a quick breath to steady my emotions. "I didn't know they knew each other, and I'm just trying to piece together the time before my mom died."

Gus folded his arms over his chest. "And your mother is . . . was who?"

"Anna Culpepper. She was a teacher at the high

school. She and my dad were taking cooking classes from Jackie at Well Done." I studied him, looking for a reaction or a sign of recognition.

He gave me neither.

"So there you go," he said. "They knew each other from the class she was taking, right? Seems logical to me."

I tapped my fingers on the glass. "That's what I thought at first, but they were outside of Jackie's house." I didn't mention that his daughter might have been in my mom's English class. That was something to dig into separately.

Gus and Randy looked at each other. Gus raised his eyebrows, as if he were silently communicating that maybe I was a bit off my rocker. "Ms. Culpepper, maybe they *became* friends. It happens, you know."

That was, of course, a logical conclusion for someone who was not privy to the entry my mom had written in her journal. "Maybe . . ."

"Not maybe. Probably. You seem to be looking for some cryptic explanation. Let me tell you something I've learned over the years. The most obvious reason is usually the correct reason."

I sighed and spoke honestly. "I guess. I just . . . It's been hard, you know, losing my mom. I'm sure you understand. I miss her. I'm just trying to get closer to her—"

"I do understand. I ask myself all the time why my wife—ex-wife—did the things she did, what she thought and felt, her choices and decisions. I can never know these things, and the last year isn't how I want to remember her. I choose to remember her the way she was when we were together. When we were raising our daughter. Before things fell apart for us."

He'd given me an opening, and I jumped. "What happened, if you don't mind me asking?" It was a bold question, but I needed to know if I was right and if my mother was actually murdered, and the only way I knew how to do that was to be bold.

Another look passed between Gus and Randy. Randy made a face, his brow crinkling, as he shrugged at his friend. The message seemed to be that it was Gus's life, so it was up to him if he wanted to share his dirty laundry.

"Let's just say that relationships are complicated. Secrets and lies. Secrets and lies are nothing but destructive," Gus said.

I hadn't expected that level of honesty from him, even though it was cryptic. From that response, I had no idea which one of them, Jackie or Gus, had kept secrets and told lies. Maybe both. I didn't come away with anything that would help me understand what my mom had discovered about Jackie and if that had had anything to do with her death, but I couldn't, in good conscience, pry any more than I already had. I said good-bye and headed across the street to Yeast of Eden to regroup and figure out what to do next.

Chapter Eighteen

Olaya Solis had a style all her own. Loose-fitting dresses and caftans were her go-to apparel. I'd always classified such clothing in the housedress category, but on Olaya, they looked stylish and hip. Today she wore a flowing dress with a colorful symmetrical tribal pattern. The vibrant black, blue, and coral colors made her skin glow. She had bangles on her left wrist and gladiator sandals on her feet. She was a modern-day Aztec goddess—in her early sixties.

We sat down at a little bistro table in front of Yeast of Eden, and I told her about my mom's journal, the last entry, my conversation with Randy Russell and Gus Makers, and the niggling fear I had that my mother's death hadn't been accidental.

Once I'd finished, we sat in silence for a minute.

Only the sudden pallor of Olaya's skin showed she was shaken. "Murder?" She looked stricken, her green eyes wide and clouded. "Do you really think so, Ivy?"

"It makes sense. My mother *knew* something." I recited the words I'd memorized from my mom's journal. "Jesus. I *knew* I was right. *Knew. It.* I won't tell Owen yet, not until I talk to Jackie. He wouldn't want me getting involved. The problem is that she doesn't really know me. How to approach her? Not at cooking class. Maybe I'll stop by her house. Yes. That's what I'll do. But what about Gus? That's what I still don't know."

I went on. "Nanette Masterson said she saw my mom talking to Jackie on Maple Street. It had to be around the same time as the journal entry my mom had written. She knew something . . . *something* . . . and she went to talk to Jackie about it."

"But no, that does not make sense. If someone saw them talking and was worried about some secret coming out into the open, Jackie would have been killed then, too, yes?"

"But she was."

That simple statement hung between us for a minute.

"Maybe my mom told someone else what she knew. Or somehow someone, meaning the killer, found out. He or she killed my mother to keep her quiet."

"And six months later Jackie was killed," Olaya said.

"They *have* to be related."

She took a bite of the chocolate croissant she'd brought out with her, and continued a moment later. "*Entonces*, Jackie died because she knew the same thing your mother did?"

I shrugged helplessly. Truly, I had no idea. I could speculate all I wanted, but as of now, all I had was a feeling. Intuition. A suspicion. And Emmaline was forever telling me that only hard and fast proof was worth anything in the eyes of the law.

"Hola!" Consuelo strode down the sidewalk toward us, waving her hand. Her style was so completely opposite of Olaya's. She wore jeans and a T-shirt that hung loosely on her rounded midsection. She was casual, whereas Olaya had style. Still, it was obvious they were sisters. Same nose. Same lips. Same almond-shaped eyes.

Martina trailed behind Consuelo, her cell phone pressed to her ear. I looked at the three sisters, noticing how different Martina looked. I already knew she was the quiet one, but she also had a much darker complexion, dark eyes instead of the green of her sisters, and almost black hair. Her features were more refined than those of her sisters. An aquiline nose, big round eyes, and defined lips. She was trim and was dressed in white fitted capris and a blue and white tunic. Her style was younger and hipper than her sisters', and she was definitely the one who stood out and didn't look like the others. Still, it was clear that their connection ran deep.

"Buenos días, mis amores," Consuelo bellowed as she reached us. She breathed in. "Ah, *qué rico.* I love the smell of the bread shop, even from outside. Eh, Martina?"

Martina had put her phone away, and now her

eyes were closed and a soft smile graced her lips. "Oh yes. *Delicioso.*"

Consuelo looked from Olaya to me and back. "*Qué pasa?* What is going on with you two this morning?"

With a nod, I gave Olaya my okay to share what we'd been talking about. After Olaya brought her sisters up to speed, Consuelo tapped her finger against her upper lip.

"Many rumors went around about Jackie and Gus's divorce. Jackie never talked about it to us. Not even to Olaya, and they were closer than any of us," she said.

"What kind of rumors?" I asked.

"Some people said Gus had an affair, but I don't believe that," Olaya said. "He loved Jackie. But he never would say what happened. He said it was his business and no one else's. I have to respect the man for that."

"I can't figure out what my mom meant when she said, 'But what about Gus?' To me that means that whatever my mom knew and wanted to talk to Jackie about affected Gus somehow." I'd been thinking about it. Could it have had to do with their house? "Was Gus okay with moving out?"

Olaya answered. "Yes, yes. Jackie bought him out when the divorce was final. He didn't care about that house—"

"It wasn't the house," Martina said. "He hated the politics of that street."

Olaya nodded to me. "Ask Penny Branford about

that. Jackie said Gus got into it a few times with someone on the street."

I'd lay odds that that someone had been Buck Masterson.

Olaya went on. "After the divorce, Gus moved out. After twenty-five years, it was over. It all happened so fast, but now that I look back on it, I think it was actually a long time in the making. She always did her best to be happy, *pero* I know she was not."

Martina swallowed the bite of her sister's croissant she'd taken. "I remember there was a time when I stopped by her kitchen to drop off bread for you, Olaya. When I went to the back office, I found Jackie crying."

"*Yo recuerdo,*" Olaya said. "You called me, and I came over right away. Hugged her and hugged her, but she would not say what had her so upset."

I remembered what Gus had said to me earlier. *Relationships are complicated. Secrets and lies.* "Was she always secretive?"

"No, not at all. That is the strange thing, you know. Jackie and me, we have been friends for many, many years. We told each other everything. But then divorce . . . and even before that . . . something changed."

I remembered what Olaya had said about the falling-out between Jackie and her daughter. "With Jasmine, too, you said?"

"Jasmine was so angry, but I do not know why. Jackie kept it—how do you say?—close to the chest."

I tried to put myself in Emmaline's police shoes. What would she do next? "Maybe we should talk with Jasmine," I suggested. Even if they'd been at odds, she was still Jackie's daughter. Without police resources, it seemed like the logical next step to me.

Without missing a beat, Olaya sauntered inside. We followed and gathered around as she picked up the phone and dialed. A moment later she was talking to Jasmine.

"*Cómo estás, m'ija?*" she said. They talked for a minute, and then Olaya cut to the chase. "*Bueno.* See you then."

I hadn't realized I'd been holding my breath until Olaya hung up the phone. What if the secret my mother had uncovered had to do with Jasmine? What if Jasmine Makers, daughter of Jackie and Gus, had killed my mother, then killed her own mom? It seemed unfathomable, and yet I knew stranger things had happened. Emmaline had told me on more than one occasion that people killed for the most trivial reasons. And as Gus had said, the most obvious reason was usually the right reason. I doubted my mom had somehow become privy to an elaborate corporate embezzling scheme or some political corruption in Santa Sofia. Her discovery had probably been about something so banal that she never could have imagined someone would kill over it.

I released the air trapped in my lungs. But someone *had* killed over it.

"You will come with me," Olaya said to me. "If Jasmine knows anything, we may be able to get it out of her."

"Look at you two," Consuelo said. "You are like two real-life detectives. *Como* Jennifer Lopez in that police show."

Whereas Consuelo looked amused, Martina seemed far more serious. "*Con cuidado.* You must be careful. Remember, someone killed Jackie. And if you are right, Ivy, someone killed your mother, too."

It was sobering, but accurate—and exactly what Emmaline had said to me. Olaya and I had to be very careful. This was no game. This was murder.

Chapter Nineteen

I'd seen Jasmine Makers from the back as she sat in a front pew at Jackie's funeral, but now, at Jackie's house, I had the opportunity to get a closer look and really develop a first impression. I'd seen her father up close more than I'd seen her mother, but there was no doubt that she was a combination of the two. With a white mother and a black father, she'd ended up with blue eyes and skin the color of milky hot chocolate. With her cropped hair, she was refined and stunning from head to toe.

Olaya greeted her at the front door. Jasmine gave her mother's oldest friend a hug, and from where I stood, it seemed genuine.

"*M'ija*," Olaya said. "You look good."

Jasmine smiled wanly. "I guess."

As I watched them, I felt for Jasmine. Beautiful as she was, she looked worn out, with dark circles under her eyes. I wondered if she'd slept a full night since her mother's death.

"I brought you something," Olaya said, leading her into the kitchen.

"Olive loaf?" Jasmine asked. Her eyes remained flat, though, a sign that she was trying, but that her emotions had a strong hold on her.

"Your favorite. You have not been in to the bread shop in a long while."

"I know. I'm sorry. Just busy, I guess."

Olaya gestured at me. "Have you met Ivy Culpepper? She is a wonderful photographer, *pero* now she is my apprentice at the shop."

I was? Her apprentice? That was news to me. I was loving baking bread, but I didn't think I had the inherent talent to be Olaya's apprentice. Nevertheless, I smiled softly and greeted Jasmine. "Nice to meet you. I'm very sorry about your mother."

She gave me the same detached smile, and I suddenly understood the depth of the rift between her and Jackie. It was a deep chasm that, at least for Jasmine, seemed unbridgeable even in death.

"Ivy lost her mother about six months ago," Olaya said, pulling out a chair at the kitchen table. She sat, and then Jasmine and I followed suit. "She was a teacher at Santa Sofia High School."

Understanding crossed Jasmine's face. "That was your mom? The one hit by a car?"

I blinked away the emotion. "Mmm-hmm. It's been difficult. I know just what you're going through."

A hardness settled onto her expression. "No offence, Ivy, but I don't think you do. Your mom . . . the accident. That was tragic, but my mom was killed. Murdered."

"Jasmine!" Olaya pronounced the name as any Spanish speaker would, saying the J like a Y. "They are both tragedies."

I brushed aside Olaya's indignation. "It's okay, really. But, Jasmine, I want to tell you this. The reason I'm here."

She looked at me, a wall still up between us. "Okay . . . ?"

I'd contemplated how to approach the subject. Should I be cagey and subtle and try to pull information from an unwitting suspect, or should I be direct? In the end, I opted for direct. I wasn't trained to investigate anything except a sunrise with my camera and the best light in which to photograph someone. Trying to act like Miss Marple or Jessica Fletcher seemed like a very bad idea. "I've come to believe that my mom was also . . ." I swallowed hard to get the final word out. "Murdered."

Whatever reaction I'd been expecting from Jasmine, it wasn't what she gave me. She scoffed. "So, what? You want to form a murdered daughters' club? Bond over our dead mothers and sing 'Kumbaya'?"

I felt like I'd been slapped, but Olaya reacted for me. "*M'ija*, what is wrong with you?"

Jasmine shoved back from the table, nearly knocking the chair over behind her. "What's wrong with me is that people need to stop thinking they know what I'm feeling. Olaya, I love you. But you don't know what my mom did. She betrayed me. She betrayed my dad. She . . . she . . ."

Olaya reached for her hand, pulled her close

until she could wrap her up in a mama bear hug. "It is okay, *m'ija*. People make mistakes. Holding on to your anger, it is hurting you. Only you."

Jasmine's hard exterior cracked under Olaya's motherly embrace. Her shoulders heaved, and a sob escaped, muffled against Olaya's shoulder. "She lied. All these years, she'd been lying to us."

I held my breath, hardly daring to exhale for fear any sound would snap Jasmine out of her safe zone and back to her protected reality.

Olaya patted her back, comforting her. Encouraging her. She wanted the truth as much as I did. More maybe, since Jackie had been her closest friend. "Lying about what, *m'ija*?"

Jasmine pulled away, wiping away a tear with the back of her hand. So she wasn't the coldhearted young woman she presented herself as. She was hurt. Betrayed. And I felt for her. "She had a baby, Olaya." She sucked in a shaky breath. "A daughter." She shook her head, as if she were clearing cobwebs away, and her voice dropped to a whisper. "I have an older sister somewhere."

Olaya looked taken aback. It was clear she'd never suspected that *this* was the source of discontent between Jackie and Jasmine. "A daughter," she said quietly, as if she were trying to make sense of that bit of information and the fact that she hadn't known about it. How was that even possible? She snapped her head up. "Are you sure?"

"I'm positive. I got a letter in the mail. At first I thought it was a joke, right? I didn't believe it. But

I asked her." Her voice escalated. "I asked her straight out, and she couldn't deny it."

I rewound. "You said you got a letter in the mail?"

She nodded.

"When was that?" I asked.

"I don't know. A year and a half ago?"

So that explained the big falling-out Jackie and Jasmine had had, then.

"Where is she? Your si . . . , Jackie's other dau . . . child?" I said.

Jasmine shrugged and looked at Olaya. "She cheated on my dad, you know. He was in the marines way back before I was born. They hadn't been married that long, but she got pregnant by someone else. She kept it a secret for a few months, and then he was deployed. She had the baby while he was gone, and gave it up for adoption."

"And years and years later your father found out," Olaya said, nodding to herself, as if it all suddenly made sense. "The reason for the divorce."

When I'd first heard of the rift between Jackie and her daughter, I'd thought that Jasmine was selfish and not a very likable person. That was before I'd heard her story and learned about the bombshell dropped on her life. My perception of her had been instantly reshaped, and I felt for her. I still wished, for her sake, that she'd been able to be in a better place with her mom before her death, but I understood now why they'd fallen away.

Gus's words came back to me. *Secrets and lies.* They were hard to overcome. "Your dad must have been devastated."

"That's one way to put it. He always said she was the love of his life, but when he found out, he just couldn't forgive her. It wasn't even that she'd cheated on him and had another baby—okay, well, it was—but it was more that she'd lied about it for so long. He said their entire marriage had been built on this faulty foundation, you know? Everything was a lie."

Olaya looked shell-shocked. "How could I not have known?"

"You were friends back then?" I asked.

Olaya nodded. "Oh yes. She was the first person I met when I moved to Santa Sofia. It has been, oh, thirty years now. *Pero* she was not pregnant—" She broke off, her eyebrows lifting as she realized something. "After Gus, your dad, was deployed, she went away for a few months. I'm trying to remember. . . ." She thought for a minute, then snapped her fingers. "I think it was for a cooking program, but I wonder . . ."

"Maybe it was so she could go off and have the baby?" I asked.

"It is the only thing that makes sense. If she was here, she could not have hidden it."

For more than twenty-five years, Jackie had kept her secret well hidden. She must have felt unhinged when Jasmine confronted her about the child she'd long since forgotten.

The child who had found her birth mother and her sister.

I slipped my cell phone from my back pocket, stepped away from the table, and leaned against the slick cement countertop in Jackie's kitchen. Jasmine's story had created an entirely new possibility for Jackie's murder, and I had to tell Emmaline. I quickly texted her the abridged version of Jasmine's story, ending with:

> Maybe Jackie's daughter was mad enough to kill her mother over being abandoned by her. It's possible. And if my mom figured it out somehow . . . it could all be connected.

I tapped the pads of my fingers on the counter while I awaited her reply. "Come on, Em," I said under my breath. She was taking too long.

Finally, her response came.

> Wow. What a soap opera. Good work, Detective Culpepper. I'll see what I can find out.

Another text came immediately after.

> Could you be careful, though? Statistically, if a person has killed once, it's easier for them to kill again. I prefer you alive.

I told her I'd be on high alert at all times, then smiled to myself. I was proud. I wasn't a detective, but I'd succeeded in finding a new possible motive for Jackie Makers's murder.

What I hadn't done, however, was find a link between that and my own mother's death. But a possibility came to me the next second. "That essay," I said.

Olaya and Jasmine both looked at me.

"What essay?" Jasmine asked.

"Olaya, that day we went through the cookbooks. We found a school essay with Jackie's things. We thought it might have been yours, Jasmine, but what if it wasn't?" My heart was in my throat. Had I just figured out how my mom was involved and why she was killed? I leaned forward. "Olaya, do you still have it?"

Her face clouded for a moment and then cleared as she realized why I was asking. She went to the cookbook shelves we'd sorted through and searched through a stack of papers and books she'd set aside. "Right here," she said, holding out the sheet of paper.

The typed and double-spaced piece of writing felt powerful in my hands. I knew that it held a clue to my mother's death. I reread the prompt, silently at first, then aloud to Jasmine and Olaya. "Write a story about a time when you taught something to someone. What you taught could be a song, an activity, a game, a way of figuring out a homework problem, or something else. Be sure to narrate an event or a series of events and to include specific details so that the reader can follow your story."

Jasmine looked from Olaya to me. "I don't understand. What is that?"

I tried to tamp down my beating heart and the wave of heat that was pooling in my head. "I think this is the reason my mom was killed."

Chapter Twenty

First, I studied the notes in the margin. They were faded and scribbled, but the more I looked at them, the more confident I was that they'd been written by my mother. This prompt had been given to her students. Which, if I was right, meant that Jackie Makers's other daughter had been the one in my mom's class.

What it didn't necessarily mean was that the girl was a killer. It was one thing to write an anonymous letter to your sister saying that you existed, but it was quite another to kill your birth mother over giving you up for adoption. It was a stretch that even I couldn't quite believe.

And it didn't explain a motive for killing my mother, either.

When I'd first read the essay, I'd thought, as my mother had commented on in her margin notes, that it was cryptic and incomplete. Some lesson was alluded to but never stated directly. But now, as I reread it from the lens of it being Jackie's unwanted daughter, I filled in the blanks. It felt more like a threat than anything else. The lesson was that people made their choices and had to live with the consequences. If I read between the lines, the message was that Jackie had chosen to give her child up, and now, years later, she had to face the truth about that decision with her other child and her husband. The secondary message was that the decision to give up her child hadn't affected only her. Decisions, by their very nature, had a long reach, often far beyond what we thought they did. In Jackie's case, the choice to give up her daughter had affected the child's life, of course, but much later it had also had a major impact on Jasmine's and Gus's lives.

The last line of the essay echoed in my mind. "Was it worth it?"

I could answer that quickly and honestly, because another piece of collateral damage to Jackie's choice so long ago was that my mother had died. No, it was not worth it. And it was not fair.

I gasped, rolling over in my bed, my eyes flying open. My sleep had been fitful, one face flashing in my mind over and over. "There was a teacher—Mrs. Culpepper," she'd said when I first met her. She was the right age, in her mid- to late twenties. A few years older than Jasmine Makers.

Could she be the one?

Could Jolie, from the Yeast of Eden baking classes, be Jackie's other daughter?

Chapter Twenty-one

I sat in the restaurant lobby of Baptista's, waiting for Miguel. I didn't know what to do with my dream and what I thought might be the truth about Jolie. I'd scoured my mother's teaching boxes again, looking for some shred of proof that Jolie had been one of her students. I'd found a stack of photo-copied essays with the same writing prompt as the one we'd found among Jackie's cookbooks, but I'd seen nothing with Jolie's name. Which indicated that the one in Jackie's possession could well belong to her.

My cell phone rang.

"You got my message?" I said by way of answering. I had called Olaya to find out Jolie's last name from her Yeast of Eden class registration—Jolie Flemming—then had passed it on to Emmaline.

"Yep," Em replied.

"Are you going to question her?"

"I don't know, Ivy. It's not much to go on. Let me dig around a little more."

"We have class at Yeast of Eden tomorrow," I offered. "Four o'clock."

"I need more, Ivy. I need proof."

"I'll get it for you," I said, more determined than I'd been about anything in my life.

Miguel walked through the dining room of the restaurant just as I hung up with Emmaline. "This is a surprise," he said.

"Sorry for just dropping by, but I had a question, and it couldn't wait." I had to speak over the din of the lunch crowd.

"I'm not sorry," he said, his strong jawline and grin revealing those two deep dimple-like crevices on either side of his mouth. "Want to walk?"

We left Baptista's and headed toward the pier. The restaurant's location had to be the best in town. It was on the right side of the pier, with an expanse of windows facing the ocean. They boasted the freshest seafood dishes in town, all with a Latin American flare. I had had a few minutes to look at the menu while I waited and had noted the house specialties. The bacon and jalapeño-wrapped shrimp tacos, which I'd had and loved, had looked to be a crowd favorite. The crab- and shrimp-stuffed avocados had caught my eye. I'd have to bring Olaya and Mrs. Branford here for dinner one night. Girls' night out, multigenerational-style.

Miguel and I walked in companionable silence for a few minutes.

"See the seals?" he said, breaking into my thoughts. "They sun themselves on those rocks every single day. Watching them is one of my favorite things to do."

I could see why. The salt air, the soft breeze, and the slick black water mammals would make a perfect afternoon for me, too.

I wasn't sure how much to tell him about what I'd learned. We weren't exactly friends anymore, yet I still felt linked to him. Maybe more than I did with any of my other old connections in Santa Sofia, with the exception of Emmaline. I guessed history had a way of erasing the years we'd spent apart.

We leaned against the railing of the pier, the breeze blowing gently, the bright blue sky dotted with puffs of white clouds. I could see why he loved being out here. It was the same reason I loved to walk with Agatha along the beachfront. Being so close to the surf brought me a sense of calm that I couldn't find anywhere else. I'd missed it the years I'd been in Texas, but now that I was back, I didn't think I could ever leave. I breathed in the fresh, damp salt air, and as I exhaled, the tension I'd been holding was released.

Miguel turned to face me, one elbow propped on the railing. "What did you want to ask me?"

I debated simply asking the question, but instead I opted for the full account of what I'd learned, beginning with Jackie Makers's attempt to oust Buck Masterson from the historic district's council,

Nanette Masterson breaking into Jackie's house, Gus Makers's comment about secrets and lies, and Jasmine's confession that Jackie had had another daughter. I ended with my belief that my mom had not died accidentally but had been murdered. "I'm sure they're connected," I said, gauging his reaction. So far, he'd schooled his face, keeping it noncommittal.

"So tell me what you think."

I looked back at the seals, wishing for a moment that life could be as simple as lying on a rock and soaking in the sun. Then I remembered that there were sharks out there just waiting for their next meal, and usually that meant a poor unsuspecting seal. No creature was safe.

"What I think is that my mom realized one of her students was Jackie's daughter. I'm not sure how, but it has something to do with the essay that we found at Jackie's house. I think she met with Jackie and gave her the essay. But somehow, someone found out and wanted to keep my mom quiet. That's why she was killed."

"By someone, you mean the other daughter?"

Did I? I wasn't sure, because I didn't understand that as a motive for murder. "Maybe?"

Miguel's brows pinched together slightly, creases appearing on his forehead. "Let me play devil's advocate."

"Okay." I braced myself for him to discount my theories completely and tell me to leave well enough alone. Why dredge up my mother's death? She was gone, and I should hang on to the best memories I had of her.

"If you're right and this woman, Jolie, is Jackie's daughter, and that's a big if since it's just a guess on your part, right?" I nodded, and he continued. "She wouldn't have had a reason to kill your mom. That is, assuming she's the one who sent the letter to Jasmine telling her about her existence. By the time your mom figured it out, Jasmine knew, Jackie knew Jolie was back, Gus and Jackie had got divorced. Jackie's world had already fallen apart, right?"

I breathed a sigh of relief. On the one hand, Miguel hadn't dismissed my effort to ferret out the truth, like I'd feared he might. But, on the other hand, he had put into words what I'd just thought, and I was back to square one. He was right; the time frame didn't work. I went through what I knew in my head, making a mental list in the order that things had happened:

- Jasmine gets an anonymous letter about the sister she didn't know about.

- Jasmine confronts her mom and presumably tells her dad.

- Jasmine and Jackie have a huge falling-out that lasts until Jackie's death.

- Gus and Jackie get divorced.

- My mom puts two and two together and realizes that Jolie is Jackie's daughter.

- Mom meets with Jackie, possibly gives her the essay Jolie wrote, and what? Warns her? But Jolie's already made herself known, so she has nothing to hold over Jackie.

- My mom dies.

- Six months later, Jackie dies.

"You're right," I said. "It doesn't make any sense."

Miguel started walking again, heading toward the end of the pier. I fell into step beside him. We passed a bait-and-tackle shop; a surf-wear shop that sold swimsuits, touristy T-shirts, boogie boards, and miscellaneous knickknacks; and a glassblowing shop run by a local family of glass artists. The Glassblowing Shop, as it was so creatively named, had been on the pier for as long as I could remember and sold handblown glassware, as well as novelty items and unique gifts. I stopped to gaze in the window. Galileo thermometers were artfully arranged on a table, each cylindrical container filled with liquid and then smaller floating glass vessels, which rose or fell depending on the temperature. I'd always loved the colorful fluid in the small upside-down teardrops inside the thermometers.

My gaze settled on the largest cylinder, and I watched as a blue glass teardrop inside rose to the top, displacing a yellow-filled one. This was how I needed to look at the situation, I realized. I might be wrong about what my mom had discovered and talked with Jackie about, but the fact was, she'd discovered something, and she'd met with Jackie. Nanette had seen her, and my mom had written about it in her journal. Those were the facts.

Like the thermometer, I needed to displace the old theory, push it down, so I could allow a new idea to rise to the surface.

Miguel seemed to read my mind. "You've been focusing on the theory that the big secret Jackie had was about the child she gave up for adoption, making your theory fit the facts rather than letting the facts guide the theory. It wasn't widely known, but Jasmine and Gus knew about it. I don't think anyone would have killed your mom over that in order to keep her quiet."

He was completely right. I picked up the thread, thinking aloud. "So my mom must have discovered some other secret about someone, and she was killed to keep her quiet. Secrets and lies." I remembered a line in her journal. *But what about Gus?* Did she find out something inflammatory about him? Could *he* have killed her?

Deep down I hoped not. Jasmine had already lost her mom. I couldn't imagine the pain she'd experience if her dad turned out to be a murderer.

A horrible thought crossed my mind. "What if . . ."

I trailed off, not wanting to say it aloud, but Miguel pressed. "What if . . . ?"

I walked to the edge of the pier, stared out at a barge anchored offshore. The new idea that had surfaced in my mind was not one I wanted to put into words. It was not one I wanted even to think about. But I had no choice. I turned to face Miguel, drew in a breath, and shared the theory.

"What if my mom discovered something about Jackie that Jackie wanted to keep quiet? I've been thinking all along that she discovered this long-lost daughter and that maybe the daughter was up to no good, blackmailing Jackie or something."

Miguel was six feet tall and stood four inches over me. I looked up at him, meeting his gaze, wishing I were wrong. But deep down I knew I wasn't. I'd been swayed by Olaya's friendship with Jackie, and by the fact that she was a victim, too. But before Jackie was killed, what if she'd *done* the killing?

"I guess I didn't want to think that Jackie could be the bad guy here." I blinked away the moisture gathering in my eyes. "But what if she was?"

Chapter Twenty-two

After Miguel and I walked back to Baptista's, I did the logical thing. I sat in a corner booth, ate chips and *queso*, ordered the crab- and shrimp-stuffed avocado, and called Emmaline again.

"It's a good theory, Ivy," she said when I was done filling her in on my thought process, "but I think you should talk to your dad. He may know something and not even realize it."

"Billy too," I said, thinking aloud. "My mom might have mentioned something to him. Who knows?"

"Um, yeah. Good idea." Emmaline's voice sounded strange. Even the mere mention of Billy sent her reeling. God, love was just ridiculous sometimes. It was unspoken, but I was relieved that Miguel and I had somehow come to the point where we could be friends.

I paused long enough to take a few bites of the avocado, my eyes rolling back in my head at the sublime combination of tastes. Once I'd recovered,

I called my dad, told him that I wanted a family meeting.

"What's going on, Ivy?" He sounded tired.

"It's important, Dad. Please?"

He agreed, and we arranged to meet at the house at seven that night. I called Billy next.

"You have something you want to talk about?" he asked me before I could pose the question.

My intuition flared. His response was almost too quick. Red flag. I'd told Emmaline I wanted to talk to Billy, as well as to my dad. Maybe her strained voice wasn't so much about her angst over not having Billy. Maybe it was because she was keeping her own secret from me, namely, that she and Billy had something going on. "How'd you know?"

"Brotherly intuition."

"Uh-huh." I remembered the other night, when she'd hightailed it out of Baptista's, leaving me to catch a ride back to my car with Miguel. What if it hadn't been a case she'd had to rush off to? What if it had been Billy? It would certainly explain her caginess and the fact that she never called me back that night.

I filed my theory away to a back corner of my mind. I had more pressing matters to think about. Billy and Emmaline could wait.

"Hey, I'm perceptive," he said, his tone playful, but I wasn't buying it.

"If you say so," I said, letting it go. I had bigger fish to fry. Emmaline and Billy were adults. If they chose to pussyfoot around a relationship—or whatever they called it—that was their business, not mine. "Family meeting, Billy. Tonight, okay?"

He nodded and we went our separate ways.

I'd found that baking was becoming a way to clear my mind, so I spent the rest of the afternoon baking bread. I didn't try anything as ambitious as baguettes, not on my own. Instead, I tried dinner rolls to go with the chicken salad and French onion soup I'd decided to make for my dad and Billy. We hadn't had a family meal since my mom died. If I was going to broach a difficult subject tonight, I wanted to offer them a good meal, complete with home-baked bread. It was the least I could do as I tore their worlds apart for the second time in a year.

They arrived at the house at the same time, Billy coming through the front door and Dad coming in through the garage. Billy came straight to the kitchen and leaned down to kiss my cheek.

"Turning into Betty Crocker, huh?"

I swatted him away.

"She's brought some pretty good stuff home to her old man," my dad said. Once again, he was trying to engage, but it was only on the surface.

While our dad went into the backyard to water his garden, Billy stayed with me, stirring the pot of soup I had simmering on the stove. "He's not any better," he commented, stooping to slurp a spoonful of the oniony beef broth. "Mmm, good."

"Wait till I top it with the day-old baguette and broil it to melt the Gruyère."

He reached for a ladle and started to spoon the broth into a bowl. "You could have made boxed mac and cheese and I'd have been happy. I haven't had a home-cooked meal in forever."

I took the ladle and bowl from him and poured the soup back into the pot. "You really should learn your way around a kitchen, you know. Women like a man who can cook. Bobby Flay. Michael Simon. Emeril Lagasse. Ever heard of them?"

He arched an eyebrow. "Miguel Baptista."

"It *is* romantic when a man cooks for a woman—"

"Even if it's his job?"

"Miguel doesn't cook for me."

"But if he did—"

"If he did, I'd enjoy every bite, I'm sure. But that is not the point. You're thirty-three, Billy. You should learn to make something besides scrambled eggs."

"I can. I do. Ask E—"

He stopped, but I filled in the blank. *Ask Emmaline.* So my intuition was right on the money. He and my best friend had finally gotten over whatever hang-ups they had and were seeing each other.

"Aha! I knew it!" I said with a grin. "I'll get the scoop from Em, you know."

"Not *all* of it," he said with a wink.

I resisted throwing a precious dinner roll at him and instead grinned stupidly. "It's about time. That's all I have to say."

Billy just shrugged. I'd already set the table. He tossed the freshly baked dinner rolls into a basket, and I ladled the soup, finishing just as Dad came back in. I placed the chicken salad in the center of the table, and without any fanfare, we began our first meal together since my mom's funeral.

"So what's the occasion, Ivy?" Billy finally asked after we'd exhausted all our small talk.

The thrumming of my heart in my chest echoed in my ears. This was not a conversation I wanted to have, yet I had no choice. I released a shaky breath and plunged right into it. "I think Mom was killed."

They stared at me like I'd lost my mind.

"Uh, yeah, Ivy. We know that."

"That's not what I meant." I closed my eyes and regrouped. "I mean, I think someone killed her on purpose. She was a target. What I mean is, Mom was murdered."

It took an hour to explain my thought process, field questions, and offer explanations. Finally, disbelief gave way to acceptance.

"Knowing mom, she was probably trying to help someone," Billy said with a frustrated shake of his head.

Dad pushed his dinner dishes away and placed his palms flat on the table, but he kept silent.

Billy cupped his hand over his forehead. "You think she discovered something about the woman who was just killed? What was her name?"

"Jackie Makers," I said, tucking my hair behind my ears. "And yeah, I think it's possible."

My dad leaned back in his chair and folded his arms over his chest. It was his typical stance. He was closed off, protecting himself. After a minute, he finally spoke. "It doesn't matter, Ivy. She's gone."

I stared at him. "It does matter, Dad. Someone murdered her."

"And you think Jackie may have done it? Mom discovered something, and she was killed over it, and now that same woman, Jackie, is dead, too. Where will it stop, Ivy? You're going to dig around and try to vindicate your mom, try to make sense of what happened, but why? You'll end up dead, too, if you're not careful. And no matter what you find, it's not going to bring her back."

Billy clasped my hand, then squeezed. "I get what you want to do, Ivy, but Dad's right. It's not going to bring her back. And if you're right and she was killed by Jackie Makers, then it doesn't matter, anyway, because Jackie's already dead. There's no justice to be had here."

Heat crawled up my chest, then spread like tendrils through my body. I wrenched my hand free. "How can you say that? Don't you want to know what happened to her?"

My dad stood and calmly gathered his soup bowl and plate. "Good dinner, Ivy." He rinsed the dishes, stuck them in the dishwasher, and with a quiet good night, he disappeared into the bedroom he'd shared with my mom for nearly forty years.

Chapter Twenty-three

I left Billy to clean up the kitchen. I didn't agree with the two men in my family. I wanted to know what my mom had discovered. I wanted to understand why she had died. I wanted to let go of the unknown and come to peace with it, and the only way I knew how to do that was to find out the truth.

The only thing I could think to do was to start with the most tangible theory I had—that Jolie was Jackie's oldest daughter. I texted Olaya to get Jolie's address. When she didn't reply, I unlocked my phone and dialed her directly.

"Why do you want it?" she asked.

I didn't want to tell Olaya my suspicions about Jackie being behind my mother's death, so I kept my answer vague. "I don't think she had anything to do with her mother's murder, but I want to ask her a question. Please, Olaya."

She hesitated but gave me the address. Ten minutes later I pulled into a guest parking spot at Beachfront Apartments, a midrange complex on

State Street. It wasn't actually beachfront, but it sounded good. According to her registration form at Yeast of Eden, Jolie lived in apartment 232. I tried to open the front door, but without a key fob, there was no entrance. I found her name on the directory and pushed the intercom buzzer.

It took about thirty seconds before she answered with a short "Yes?"

"Jolie? It's Ivy. Culpepper. From baking class?"

"Ivy!"

There was a buzzing sound, followed by a click as the door to the building unlocked. I grabbed the handle and let myself in, then headed up the stairs and down the hall until I reached her apartment.

She was waiting at the door, a huge smile on her face. Her black hair was piled up in a loose top-knot. She had on jogging shorts and a tank top, was barefoot, and had not a stitch of makeup on her beautiful face. She hadn't been expecting company, but if she had, I didn't think she would have changed a thing. She was one of those perfect specimens that made other women crazy with jealousy and men fall at her feet.

"What a surprise!" She grabbed my hand and pulled me into her apartment. I quickly took in the interior. It was sparse, but tasteful. Neat and tidy. A book was open and facedown on the sofa.

"Sorry to barge in on you."

She waved away my apology. "Something to drink? I tried to bake some bread earlier today, but it was a complete bust. I should probably get my money back and give up on the baking classes."

"I tried dinner rolls today. They weren't bad. I'm not sure Olaya would agree, but we ate them."

"It's a lot harder than I thought it would be. Baking, I mean. I figured it would be easy and I'd be able to bake and bake and bake."

I'd thought the very same thing. So far it seemed my success inside and outside class was better than Jolie's.

She poured two glasses of cabernet, and we sat on her white sofa, chatting about baking and Yeast of Eden. After a while I broached the subject I'd been waiting to bring up.

"You went to Santa Sofia High School?"

"Yes! Good school. Good teachers," she said, sympathy in her eyes.

"Did you grow up here?" I'd wondered whom Jackie had given her baby to. Someone in town, if Jolie went to the local high school.

"Born in San Francisco but raised here. I don't know if I could ever leave, actually. I love it here. You must, too, since you came back. You were in Texas, right?"

"Yep. Austin. Now that I'm back, I realize how much I missed it. There's something about the ocean air. It's clean. Fresh."

"I know what you mean!" She said everything with such enthusiasm; it was hard not to smile. "I keep the windows open as much as I can, which is pretty much whenever I'm home."

I leaned forward, elbows on my knees, cupping my wineglass in my hand. "Can I ask you something?"

She drew her lips into a straight line, which I took to be her serious look. "Is something wrong?"

"No. Well, yes. Kind of."

"Ask me anything."

I was fishing and felt completely incompetent as a sleuth, but I kept my focus. If I asked enough questions, and somehow one or two of them were the right ones, I might discover something that would help me get to the truth. I decided not to mince words. "Do you know Jasmine Makers?"

Whatever she thought I'd ask, it wasn't that. Her persona completely changed, the happy-go-lucky Jolie replaced by a reticent, nervous young woman. "Wh-what?"

"Jasmine Makers. She told me about . . . her mom and . . ." I just went for it and dropped the bomb. "You."

Her jaw dropped, and she looked away. Her voice dipped low. "Did she say she wanted to see me?"

That was all the confirmation I needed. I'd been right. Jolie was Jackie's other daughter. But from the raw emotion emanating from Jolie, I didn't feel like it was a victory. The crack in Jolie's optimistic veneer was painful. She was an upbeat person, but the estrangement from her biological family had broken her on some level. She wanted to connect with her sister. The fact that Jackie had gotten pregnant and had given Jolie up wasn't her fault. Jasmine needed to recognize that. I hoped that she would someday and that the two could become real sisters.

"We, uh, didn't talk about that. She told me about you—about her mom's other child. About her mom giving you up for adoption."

"I get it, you know. She was married, and Gus is black." She gave a wry laugh. "Look at me. Not much chance of her trying to hide the truth from him."

"Do you know who your father is?" It was a blunt question, but I didn't know how to ask it subtly. In that instant, a new theory surfaced. It was possible that Jolie's biological father could have been so angry at losing all those years as a parent that he killed Jackie out of anger. It was also possible that my mom had somehow learned who he was, confronted her about it, and was killed by Jackie to protect *that* secret.

But she shook her head. "I wanted to talk to her about it that night at the bread shop. I had it all planned out. I was going to pull her aside during one of our breaks and come right out and ask her."

"But she died before you had the chance."

"Don't get me wrong," she said suddenly. "My parents were great. I don't know how Jackie found them, but they were good to me. They died when I was seventeen, just before I graduated. It was a horrible car accident down in Santa Barbara. I loved them, but eventually, with them gone, I just really wanted to find out where I came from. Who my biological mother was."

"Is Flemming the name you used in school?"

"No. I got married right out of high school. Big

mistake. It lasted only six months, but I kept the name."

I sipped my wine as I thought about what to ask next. "Did Jackie know you were her daughter? You'd met?"

"She knew. I mailed her a letter. God, must have been more than a year ago now. I sent one to Jasmine, too. It took three more letters and four months before Jackie finally replied and agreed to meet me."

"How was that?"

She set her wineglass on the glass coffee table and stood, then folded her arms over her chest and walked to the sliding glass door. "Not what I expected," she said after a moment. "She was distracted. Looking over her shoulder. She kept saying that she had to get back to the kitchen. She definitely didn't want to be meeting me."

"That was it?" I could see why Jolie's naturally exuberant personality was tamed when talking about Jackie. It certainly hadn't been a fairy-tale reunion between a mother and her long-lost daughter.

"Pretty much. She said it was a mistake. That she didn't mean to. Get pregnant, I mean." Jolie's eyes pinched as she remembered. "But you know, even though she said it, I didn't ever feel like she was talking to me. Like she really meant it. But then she never called me. Never tried to meet me again. I tried a few more times, but it was pretty clear she wasn't interested, so finally I gave up. She was really focused on her business, so maybe she just didn't have time for me. The other cooking school in town had just closed. She said something about her being the better chef and now she'd have the chance to prove it.

"She kept looking at her watch and checking the door, like she was expecting someone else. Finally, she just got up. She told me that she couldn't 'do this' right now. *Do what?* I thought. She couldn't make time to meet her daughter? The one she'd given up without a second thought? Before she left, she told me that she'd done things she wasn't proud of, and that other people had paid the price. She said she was sorry and that she'd make things right." Jolie wiped away a tear. "And then she left."

"And did she? Make things right?"

Jolie shook her head sadly. "I waited for her to call. To reach out to me. But she never did."

I didn't want to beat a dead horse, so I redirected the subject. "Did you know she'd be at the baking class? Because you said you were going to ask about your biological father."

"I knew. I love the bread shop, although, as you know, I'm not a natural. Olaya mentioned the classes to me one day when I was in there getting my daily fix. She pulled out the sign-up sheet, in case I was interested, and Jackie's name was right there. I thought, *Maybe it's fate. Maybe this will give us the opportunity to get to know each other.* No pressure, right?" She sighed. "But it didn't quite work out that way. She never even looked at me that night."

We finished our wine, and I got up to leave. "Will you be there tomorrow?" I asked.

"With bells on. I am determined to learn how to bake halfway decent. It's in my genes, after all."

Before I left, I gave her a hug. I didn't know if I was a good judge of character, but I liked her. She'd been dealt a bum hand, what with Jackie giving her up, a sister who wanted nothing to do with her, and her adoptive parents being dead. "See you tomorrow," I said, adding to myself that maybe I'd have some answers by then.

Chapter Twenty-four

My dad was waiting up for me when I got home, Agatha curled up at his side. My pug lifted her head as I walked in, her ears twitching back when she heard my voice.

My dad sounded tired. "Sit down, Ivy."

I perched on the edge of the coffee table opposite him. I knew my dad, and I knew that he had something he wanted to say to me. I couldn't rush it, so I waited.

Finally, he spoke. "You're right. I know it, but that doesn't make it easy."

I leaned forward, reaching for his hand. "I know, Dad. I just want the truth. It may not help at all, but then again, it might."

He didn't look like he thought the truth would bring any peace, but I appreciated the effort he was giving. What he needed and what I needed were two different things. He might not agree with me, but he could respect me. "You're looking for a reason, Ivy. You'll never find one that's good enough. Mom died, and she shouldn't have. But if you're determined to look for answers, then I'll help you."

Heat pricked the skin on my face, and my nostrils flared with emotion. I fought the tears that burned in my eyes. "Thank you, Dad."

"You said you thought Jackie Makers had some sort of secret."

"More than one, I think. She gave up a daughter for adoption before she and Gus had Jasmine, but I think Mom figured out something else."

"You can retrace Mom's steps. Maybe that'll help you."

"What do you mean, retrace her steps?"

"You know your mom. She never went anywhere without her planner."

I felt as if a lightbulb had suddenly gone off in my head. My mom had written down everything, in a million different places. She'd had her lesson plan book. Even though the school district had gone to an online method of tracking and submitting lesson plans, my mom had kept her old-school spiral book. She'd had her journals for her writing and inspirations. And she'd always kept a day planner. The one my dad handed me now was called a Spark Notebook The hard black cover gave it a utilitarian look, but inside it was filled with graphic elements, quotes, spaces to write and doodle, and prompts to make you think about your desires, accomplishments, and goals.

I flipped through it and immediately saw what my

dad had seen. My mom's appointments were noted on the calendar pages, along with a few anecdotal notes here and there. I started at the end—her last entries.

The last few pages were mostly school related. Department meeting, parent-teacher conference, staff meeting. She'd made an appointment to take her car in for service the week before she died. There'd been a community cleanup day she'd noted. But the thing I zeroed in on was a ten o'clock Saturday meeting with someone named Renee at Divine Cuisine. The business's name rang a bell, but I couldn't put my finger on why.

"What's Divine Cuisine?" I asked my dad.

He had been scratching Agatha's head. Now he stopped and let his hand run from her head to her curled-up tail. "One of the cooking schools your mom was looking at for our classes."

"But didn't you start the sessions with Well Done and Jackie Makers?"

"We went to three or four be-before the accident."

That was what I'd thought, which was why it seemed odd that my mom had made an appointment with someone from Divine Cuisine.

"Did Mom like the classes?"

"At Well Done?"

I nodded.

"I think so," he said. "She never said she didn't. She came home pretty inspired. Mostly, though, I think she just liked that I did it with her. Being an empty nester was hard for her. Harder on women than on men. She was always looking for something we could do together. She suggested salsa dancing.

Do you believe that? I said no way in hell was she getting me on a dance floor, but now I wish . . ."

He left the sentence unfinished. I imagined that the what-ifs and the wishes could eat him up alive if he let them.

"Dad . . ."

He swallowed down the emotions bubbling up in him and tensed his jaw. "Why? What do you see in there?"

I pointed to the Divine Cuisine appointment.

He frowned, peering to get a closer look. "You know your mother."

I did. She was a thinker and a doer. "Why would she meet with another cooking school if she was happy with Well Done?" I mused aloud.

"That is definitely a puzzler."

"Right? If she was happy with Well Done, would she want to switch to another school?"

"Maybe she thought the other place had an interesting concept or something. Who knows? Your mom was always looking for new things. But no, that's not what doesn't make sense."

"What is it, then?"

"Divine Cuisine," he said, and at that moment, it came back to me. Olaya had told me about it. It had been the other cooking school in Santa Sofia, but it had closed down. "They shut down. A year ago or so. Maybe a little more."

"Why?"

He looked to the ceiling, thinking. "Something with the owner. An accident, I think."

"Was it bad?"

"I don't remember the details," he said, "but yes. Bad enough that they had to close their doors."

"And they didn't reopen?"

"Ivy, you're asking the wrong person. I've been a little distracted. Haven't kept up with the local cooking schools." He almost said it as a joke, but as always, the undercurrent of pain was evident.

"I know, Dad."

He thought for a second and then shook his head. "Now that I think of it, though, I don't think it reopened."

"So . . ." I trailed off, processing my thoughts before speaking up again. "If Divine Cuisine shut down more than a year ago, then Mom couldn't have scheduled a meeting with this Renee woman to talk about classes."

"No, I don't suppose that's what it was about," he said.

We fell silent because neither of us had any inkling what might have been behind the meeting my mom had scheduled with Renee at Divine Cuisine.

Finally, my dad squeezed my hand, his eyes glassy and his skin cold to the touch. "Be careful, Ivy. I can't stand the thought of losing you, too."

"I will, Dad. I will."

As I climbed into bed a little while later, my cell phone beeped. A text from Mrs. Branford came through.

Community meeting at Mastersons' tomorrow morning. Come with me!

I turned my smartphone sideways and quickly tapped in my response.

What time?
Ten o'clock.

I told her I'd see her there, and then I turned off the light. My head sank into my pillow, as if it were cradling the myriad thoughts ricocheting in my brain. As I drifted off to sleep, I wondered what tomorrow would bring.

Chapter Twenty-five

I parked at Mrs. Branford's, arriving thirty minutes early.

"Step right in," she said, ushering me through the living room and into the kitchen. This room, I'd come to realize, was where Mrs. Branford lived her life.

"What's this meeting about?" I asked. I did not have a stake in the neighborhood, although I wished I did. Regardless, I was happy to tag along—if only to see inside Nanette and Buck's historic house.

She offered me a cup of tea in a dainty floral cup. Mrs. Branford was a tough bird, but she had a soft side underneath it all. She sat down at the kitchen table, and her usually bright smile tempered. "Ivy, I want to talk about something with you."

Worry instantly coursed through me. I took a close look at her. She didn't appear sick. Her cheeks were rosy, and the jovial twinkle was still in her eyes, despite her serious expression.

I sat down across from her. "What is it? Are you okay?"

"I don't think so." She looked around, as if someone might be listening. "Remember the envelope in the freezer?"

"I remember." It had been only a week ago that she'd brought it across the street to Olaya and me.

"I found another one."

"Another envelope in the freezer?"

"An envelope, yes, but not in the freezer. This one was under the cushion of the couch."

Curious. "That's, um, an interesting place to keep an envelope. What's in it?"

"Pictures."

"Pictures?" I realized that I was repeating everything she was saying, but I was stymied by her confession. Mrs. Branford had found an envelope filled with pictures under the couch cushion. It felt like a game of *Clue*. Professor Plum in the library with a candlestick.

She stretched her hand behind the fruit bowl and slid out a five-by-seven manila envelope. Just as she'd said, inside was a stack of photographs.

I slipped them out and quickly scanned them, then slowed my pace to take a closer look at each one. The first was a picture of Buck Masterson in his front yard, hose in hand. He stared across the street, his bad comb-over thready on his forehead. It felt like he was looking right at Penny Branford's house.

"Did you take this picture?" I asked.

"You'd think I did, wouldn't you? But no. You've seen my shaky hands. I couldn't take a good picture to save my life."

"Then who?"

She looked pointedly at me. "That's the winning question, dear."

The next photo was of Nanette Masterson, hand on a door handle, her head turned to the side, as if she were looking over her shoulder.

"Whose house is that?"

"Jackie's." With a bony finger, she pointed to the flowerpot on the front porch, to the left of where Nanette stood. "I helped her plant that pot not two months ago. See how the impatiens have grown? They started as single-stalk flowers."

In the photo, the flowers were full and colorful. The picture, then, had to have been taken fairly recently.

"You think Jackie took these?"

Mrs. Branford threw up her hands, clearly exasperated. "I don't know. Why would she hide in my yard and take a picture of Buck? And how would she be outside, across the street and hidden, in order to take that one of Nanette?" She rubbed her temples. "My dear, my head hurts."

I looked at that picture again, noticing the almost menacing look on Buck's face. It was as if he was staring straight at the camera. "What if she—Jackie, I guess—*was* in your yard to take a picture of Buck?"

Mrs. Branford looked at me like I was short a few

marbles. "It's puzzling, but at the same time it seems fairly obvious, dear."

"No, no. I mean what if she wasn't hiding? What if she stood there, plain as day, and was snapping pictures?"

"Why would she do that?"

I looked at the next photo in the stack. Buck had dropped the hose and was on the edge of his yard, still looking at the camera. His hand was raised, as if he were scolding an errant child, and his mouth was open. I could almost hear the vitriolic words spewing from him. "Leverage?"

"Explain that to me, Ivy."

"We know Jackie was trying to oust Buck from the historic district's council. She gathered all those letters against him, and the petition to remove him from his position."

She nodded. "Correct."

"What if she was trying to intimidate him? Play at his own game?" I slapped my hand on my thigh. "What if she discovered that Buck and Nanette had broken into her house, looking for something? The letters, probably, which is why she'd hidden them in your freezer."

"But why would she stake out her own house and photograph someone trying to break in? Why not confront Nanette? Jackie was not a shrinking violet."

I smiled to myself. Such an old-fashioned expression. "What if she wanted to catch them in the act of breaking in so she could prove it? Hold it over them or show the council?"

"Okay, but why would she put the pictures under my couch cushion?"

I thought about this. If Jackie knew Nanette and Buck were regularly breaking into her house, she'd want them to be safe. "She didn't give them to you to hold for her? Or to hide?"

"If she did, I have absolutely no recollection of that. Maybe I'm losing my marbles. I'm no spring chicken anymore, so it's possible, you know."

Once again, things didn't quite add up. "Mrs. Branford, I think you'd remember if someone gave you an envelope. Two envelopes," I corrected. The first, with the stack of letters against Buck Masterson, had ended up in her freezer somehow. Now she'd found these pictures. "It had to be Jackie, and she's the one who had to have hidden them."

She seemed to breathe a little easier. Realizing you weren't completely losing your faculties would be a relief, I imagined. "It makes sense for the letters. She was the one going after Buck. But these photos, I don't understand them. There's nothing in here worth hiding."

I had to agree. It didn't make sense.

"Would you keep them, dear?" Mrs. Branford said. "I don't want to misplace them again."

I squeezed her hand. "Mrs. Branford, I don't think you misplaced them in the first place."

Mrs. Branford's hand trembled slightly, the tea in her cup sloshing from the movement. She braced her cup with her left hand, controlling the motion. "Will you keep them, anyway?"

"Of course," I said, and I slid the pictures back into the envelope and tucked the envelope in my purse. "For safekeeping."

I took our teacups, rinsed them, and placed them in the drying rack to the left of the sink. "Shall we go?"

"No time like the present."

Mrs. Branford stood, took her cane, and together we crossed the street to the Masterson house. She shook her head as we walked up the crumbling brick pathway.

"If I break a hip—"

"You're not going to break a hip," I said, but I took her by the elbow just in case.

As we climbed the porch steps, Mrs. Branford pulled free of my protective guidance and kept walking, bypassing the door. I hurried after her.

"Where are you going?"

"Odd ducks, the Mastersons. You have to enter over here."

I looked back over my shoulder. The walkway led to the porch, which led to the front door. "They don't use the main entrance? Why?"

She stopped walking and leaned against her cane. "There's no accounting for anything they do," she said. "I used to try to make sense of them, but no more."

The side door was open. We stepped in, and I made the mistake of breathing. I nearly choked and covered my nose and mouth. I moved my hand to whisper, "Cats?"

Mrs. Branford pinched her nose with her thumb and forefinger. "About five million of them. And I think they pee wherever they want to."

I grimaced, trying hard not to breathe and hoping I didn't step on one of the five million tabbies that surely must be lurking in the house. I looked around. We stood in the entryway to the side door. An overstuffed period chair sat in the left corner, and a small round table was in the middle of the space. Jars of jelly were lined up around a bowl of plums. A stack of printed notes was next to the bowl. I picked one up and read it.

Our neighborhood is only as strong as the individual people in it. A weak link jeopardizes us all. Take this plum jam, homemade from our trees, as a symbol of how committed we are to the Maple/Elm Historic District in Santa Sofia.

I handed the note to Mrs. Branford. I'd lay money down that in the Mastersons' world, Jackie had been the weak link.

A low chatter came from a back room.

"They're in the kitchen," Mrs. Branford said. She led the way, walking to the dining room. An embossed silver ceiling, heavy wood moldings and trim, and floral wallpaper made the room feel closed in and dark. Oppressive. It was as if they were trying to recapture every bit of life more than a hundred years ago. They seemed to have succeeded in capturing the look, but then they'd kept going, somehow choking the soul from it in the process.

A few people sat at the rectangular dining table. Mrs. Branford stopped to chat and introduced me to a few of them. I smiled and waved.

"Do you live in the neighborhood?" a middle-aged man asked me.

"No, just friends with Mrs. Branford," I said. "Tagging along."

I followed Mrs. Branford into the kitchen and stopped to take it all in. *Cluttered* was an understatement. There were pots and pans hanging from a makeshift pot rack made from an old pulley system. Flowerpots, some with dying plants, lined the back of the counter, intermixed with container after container of cooking utensils. In one corner, a stack of papers, magazines, and books teetered precariously. It was an odd kitchen space, and despite the food offerings on the island and the cooking paraphernalia all around, I wondered if any cooking actually happened here. My gut was telling me that it didn't.

"Penelope. Good of you to come," Buck Masterson said, hand extended. He had what I could describe only as a smarmy smile on his face. There was something untrustworthy about him, and although his words said otherwise, he seemed absolutely less than happy to actually *see* Mrs. Branford.

"Wouldn't have missed this for anything," she replied, a saccharine smile on her lips. "You remember Ivy Culpepper. Owen's daughter."

His nostrils flared, but he kept up his facade. "Of course. Are you here as Penelope's home health nurse? Getting older is a terrible thing, isn't it, Penny?"

I did a double take. Was he intentionally trying to get Mrs. Branford's goat, or was he inordinately socially awkward? Mrs. Branford rallied, bless her heart.

"It is indeed, Buck, as you know firsthand, but Ivy is not here as my nurse. In fact, she knew Jackie and has been helping finish up a few things the poor woman started."

The color drained from Buck's face. He whipped his head around to look at me more closely. "Is that so? What sort of things, exactly?"

"Oh, Mr. Masterson, I don't want to bore you with city business," I said as coyly as I could.

"Actually, city business fascinates me. I'm the representative of the Maple/Elm Historic District, which I believe you know. Any city business involving our historic designation *must* go through me."

Mrs. Branford cocked her head. She looked like the perfect grandmother, with her fluffy white hair, her velour sweat suit, which was powder blue today, and her sweet face, but underneath, I knew, she was tough as nails and would do whatever it took to bring down Buck Masterson. "Must it? Everything?" she said, quite innocently, but I knew and he knew that she would never answer to Buck.

"You know that, Penny. I'm your representative. I know the ins and outs of the district, the zoning, the city officials and how they are always trying to screw us. No one else is watching out for us. It's me. I take care of everyone in our district."

"Don't forget me," Nanette said, sidling up to her husband. Her dyed red hair hung in two stringy sheets on either side of her head. It was a nice cut, but with her heavy jowls and chin, the straight hair looked plastered to her head in a particularly unflattering way. "There's always a good woman behind a successful man."

I did believe that old expression to be true, but I liked to think more progressively than that. Behind every successful woman was a smart man. That was my belief, and I needed a man who believed it, too. I phrased my response carefully. Specific enough to make them worry, but vague enough not to give anything away. "I'm sure you both do everything you can for your neighbors. I'll let you know if I have any questions as I go through Jackie's papers." I patted my purse for good measure. "Now that I know you're the go-to people."

The skin around Buck's neck reddened and the flush spread upward, coloring his cheeks first and then the entire flat surface of his face. He managed to remain expressionless, despite the fact that he was the color of a tomato. "You have some of her papers?"

I turned to survey the other people in the small kitchen, trying to be nonchalant. Buck's feathers were clearly ruffled. Outside of Mrs. Branford's tales and our surveillance, I didn't know Buck

Masterson at all. Despite that, I was pretty sure that playing coy about what I knew or didn't know was going to drive him nuts. "Papers, some notes, and some letters, I think. Is that right, Mrs. Branford?"

My elderly friend puffed her cheeks and nodded innocently. "And pictures," she said. "Don't forget the pictures."

"Right!" I looked him in the eyes and tilted my head, as if I were puzzled. "I'm surprised you didn't work together on some of your district projects. She was pretty involved in the neighborhood, too, from what I've seen so far."

Nanette choked, then broke into a cough. She patted her chest with her palm. "Sorry. Something caught in my throat." She and Buck shared a look that I couldn't decipher; then she turned to me. "Will you be at the baking class tomorrow? I sure did enjoy my time there the other day." The fake saccharine in her voice revealed the truth behind her innocent words.

I smiled as naturally as I could, although I knew she was fishing. "Oh, I'll be there. Of course! I'm Olaya Solis's apprentice."

"Doesn't your dad work long hours these days, Ivy?" Mrs. Branford was getting in on the game, trying to give the Mastersons an opportunity to do some snooping while I was gone at Yeast of Eden.

"He's hardly ever home. It's easier for him to keep his mind busy at work."

"Poor fellow," Buck said.

I rolled my eyes. As if he actually cared.

Nanette squeezed my arm. "And that's where you're living right now? With your father?"

I had to give her credit. Her attempt at subtly gathering intel about my situation wasn't half bad. If I didn't know that was what she was doing, I might have been snowed.

"Me and Agatha."

She cocked a faded red eyebrow.

"My pug," I explained. "She's my little shadow."

"Ah. We're cat people." Her tone said she thought cat people were far superior to dog people. I'd read the studies. Cat people were smarter, blah, blah, blah. Maybe so, but I'd take Agatha any day of the week. She was loyal, loving, and as warm as a basket full of freshly baked dinner rolls.

"I'm sorry," Mrs. Branford said with an exaggerated sniff.

Nanette's face flamed red, and I stifled a laugh.

Nanette scowled, then turned her body so she had her back partially to Mrs. Branford. "I'm sure it's terribly difficult for your dad to be home alone."

I took the bait. "Oh, it is, Nanette. So tough. I usually call him when I'm on my way home from the bread shop, or wherever I'm at, so we get home about the same time."

She shot her husband a look, and I met Mrs. Branford's eyes. Nanette was like a fly caught in a spider's web, and I was the spider. I knew right then and there that they'd be coming up with some plan to search my dad's house for Jackie's "papers" while I was at Yeast of Eden. All we had to do was set a trap

to catch them in the act of breaking and entering.
They certainly wanted whatever Jackie had had her
hands in. There was no question about that. What
I still didn't know, however, was if they'd killed her
over it.

Chapter Twenty-six

Early the next morning, Olaya phoned and asked me to help her at the front counter at Yeast of Eden. "One of my regular girls called in sick, so we're shorthanded."

I hightailed it over just as soon as I walked Agatha and got her situated with a bowl of food, water, and a chew toy. The weather had taken a turn. The beautiful spring days we were having had become cold and windy. I grabbed a jacket before I left the house, and gave my dad a quick kiss on the cheek.

"I also have baking class," I said, feeling a little like I was back in high school, accounting for my time and outings. "I'll come back to check on Agatha, though."

"You're allowed to have a life, Ivy," he said. "I can take care of myself. I'm going to have to, you know."

I sighed. He was right. We were both going to have to cut the ties and figure out how to move forward, and that meant I'd have to find a place of my own and he'd have to figure out what his life looked like without my mom. "I know, Dad."

"Stay out late. Go on a date. I don't want to be the one holding you back."

"You're not holding me back from anything. I don't want to be doing anything else right now."

"Not while you're playing detective," he said with a frown.

"I'm trying," I said, leaving it at that. I didn't want him to get upset again over the digging I was doing.

The line for bread was ten people deep when I walked in the door of Yeast of Eden.

"Here," Olaya said, calling me over. She handed me a bakery apron and a small order pad. "Write down the orders here, give a receipt if the customer wants one, and put the original here," she said, pointing to a metal base with a long, pointed spike. A stack of order sheets had been speared onto it. "I track everything that we sell at the end of the day. It helps me know how we do with each item and how much I need to bake. I compare the inventory to the receipts. It is how I balance the books, so to speak."

It sounded like a lot of paperwork, but aside from the phenomenal bread, this was definitely why Olaya and her business were so successful. We worked for an hour and a half before the line finally died down and we could breathe again.

"Is it always like this?" I asked. I'd been in at various times of the day, but I'd never seen it so swamped.

"When the temperature drops and the wind picks up, it is always busier."

Outside the wind howled. The heavy breeze from earlier had turned into whistling gusts. I could see why people would want the comfort of freshly baked, warm bread. I went back to check on Agatha. Back at the bread shop, we worked for the rest of the day, closing the door and flipping the OPEN sign over at four o'clock. One of Olaya's afternoon workers came in to help with the day's cleanup, which allowed Olaya and me to set up for the evening's baking class.

One by one, the women in the class trickled in. Becky, Sally, and Jolie came in together, followed by Consuelo and Martina. As usual, Mrs. Branford sauntered in last, swinging her cane, apron on, white hair perfectly coiffed. She looked around.

"No Nanette?" she asked.

I frowned. "Not yet," I said, but at that moment, Nanette Masterson walked into the kitchen. Her thin bright red hair was slicked back, and her heavily drawn eyebrows framed her eyes.

"*Bienvenidos, Señora Masterson*," Olaya said. "Glad to see you back here."

Nanette checked her watch and nodded. "I wouldn't miss it. What are we making today?"

"Seeded pull-apart rolls," Olaya answered.

Sally placed her hand flat on her stomach. "Sounds so good," she said.

Becky grabbed Sally's arm. "Doesn't it? My stomach's growling!"

We all went to our stations and followed Olaya's

directions for making whole-wheat dough. "The pull-apart rolls begin with this," she said. We followed the process of mixing the ingredients and setting our dough aside to rise. Meanwhile, as with the baguettes, Olaya began pulling out dough she had mixed and readied for us the day before. "This is one of those recipes that you can make a day ahead. In the interest of time, I have prepared the dough. Now we will create the seeded rolls."

I glanced at the clock hanging above the door that led to the bread shop lobby. Five on the dot. I peeked at Nanette and caught her looking at her watch. I'd been doubting my intuition, wondering if I was completely off the mark about what I suspected, but seeing her check her watch again two minutes later alleviated my misgivings. Something was definitely up, and if I was right, Buck Masterson was en route to my dad's house at this very minute.

I moved quickly, rolling my dough into a rectangle, then cutting it into twenty-four pieces. The women in the class laughed and chatted, none as focused as I was, because none of them had somewhere to be, like I did. I rolled each piece of dough into a ball, then rolled each of the balls in one of the three bowls of seeds I had set out. Before long, I had twenty-four balls, each coated in either toasted white sesame seeds, untoasted white sesame seeds, or black poppy seeds, laid out on a cookie sheet.

Nanette was at the station next to me, still pressing her ball of dough into a rectangle. "You're fast," she said, eyeing my tray of seeded dough balls.

"Getting better every day. I love it!" I took my

camera out and snapped a few pictures, then left the camera on the counter. "I'll be back in a minute," I whispered to Nanette. "Watch my rolls?"

"Where are you going?"

I held up my cell phone. "Checking on my dad. He's working late tonight."

"What a good daughter," she said. Her smile reached to her eyes, but I suspected it was because it meant clear sailing for her husband's breaking-and-entering gig at the Culpepper house, not because I had compassion for my father.

"I try." I nodded toward my phone and walked out of the kitchen.

Once I was out of sight, I grabbed my purse from behind the counter and hightailed it out of Yeast of Eden. If I was right, Nanette was on her own phone, giving her husband the "all clear" signal. I had only a few minutes to get to the house.

I made it in record time. I parked down the street, just in case Buck Masterson was lurking around somewhere already. I'd grown up on this street, and I knew every nook and cranny. Billy and I had spent our childhoods climbing fences, sneaking through backyards, and being as stealthy as we could to stay out as late as we could. Now, nearly twenty years later, I was reliving those moments on Pacific Grove Street. I tucked my purse under the front seat of my old car, pocketed my keys, and cut through Mr. and Mrs. Buffington's side yard. They lived two houses down from our house. They'd been in their sixties when I was a teenager, so by now they were in their eighties. I hoped me sneaking around their property didn't send them into heart failure. I'd have to explain it to them later.

Sneaking through their yard, I felt like Peter Rabbit hopping around Mr. McGregor's garden. I jumped the fence between the Buffingtons' yard and the Martinezes', dodged the Martinezes' German shepherd, and climbed under their fence to sneak into my childhood backyard. I looked high and low. No sign of Buck Masterson. I let myself into the house through the back door, got to work, and a few minutes later I sat down by Agatha to wait.

Twenty minutes passed. My eyes drooped, and I'd begun to wonder if I'd completely missed the mark. Just as I stood to stretch my legs, Agatha's ears perked. She jumped up and faced my dad's bedroom. She was on full alert. Any second, she'd bark and wreck my plan. I snatched her up, shushing her, and cuddled her like an upset child. Agatha held her bark. We sank back into the shadows just as the bedroom door opened.

Agatha started to growl, but I quickly held her flattened pug muzzle and whispered in her ear. She relaxed and seemed to accept that the stranger in the house was, at least in this instant, okay.

I watched as the figure crept forward. With the fading sun, I couldn't make out any details. The man slunk closer, then quickly closed the blinds in the front windows. My heart beat wildly. My dad's worry and Emmaline's warning that I be careful resurfaced. What was I doing?

But my trepidation couldn't stop me now; I was in it up to my neck, and there was no backing down. I took in his stringy hair, which was slicked back; his narrow eyes; and his thin lips, drawn into a tight line. Buck Masterson stood across the room, just as I'd known he would.

It took him only seconds before he spotted the dining-room table. I held my breath, and he made a beeline for it. He bent over the table and grumbled under his breath. "I knew it."

He acted quickly, gathering up the pictures I'd laid out on the table, the pictures Mrs. Branford had found under her couch cushion. He rifled through them and then tucked them in his jacket pocket. But he didn't turn to leave. Just as I knew he would, he turned to his right. It took a few seconds before he surged forward, staring at the second set of photographs I'd arranged on the kitchen counter.

"Son of a . . . ," he snapped, leaning over to get a closer look. These were the photos I'd taken on my stakeout with Mrs. Branford. They weren't the highest-quality pictures, but they certainly did their job. Buck Masterson's hands shook as he gathered up the pictures. Several fell to the floor. He crouched and collected them, then stood slowly.

His phone buzzed, and he looked at the incoming text. "What the—"

As he raced to the window, cracked the blinds, and peered outside, I realized what the text must have been: Nanette alerting him that I hadn't come back after the phone call to my dad. He was afraid I was on my way to the house.

Too bad for him, I was already here.

Instead of seeing a car pull into the driveway,

though, he heard a siren. I gasped, dropping Agatha. The pug zipped toward Buck Masterson, letting loose the barks she'd been holding back while I'd held her. Agatha was mostly bark and little bite, but she charged him, looking up and down, growling, yapping in her high-pitched way, then backed up, sucking in a raspy breath, and charged forward again.

He whipped around and finally spotted me. "What the—"

I moved into the light but kept my distance. This was the one risk in my plan. I didn't know if Buck Masterson had killed my mom or Jackie Makers, and I had no idea what he'd do if he was backed into a corner. "I see you found the pictures I left for you."

He scowled, waving the prints at me. "You took these?"

"I did. I was pretty surprised to see your wife sneak into Jackie's house. Were you looking for the pictures or for the letters the neighbors wrote against you?"

His face turned beet red. "Wh-what letters?"

Agatha had run back to stand next to me, but her tail was straight and hung down at her back legs, and her tiny teeth were bared.

"Seems to me that the neighborhood is pretty divided. It was Team Buck or Team Jackie."

He scoffed. "She didn't understand that I only want to help the historic district. She was a thorn in my side. She needed to be stopped."

"A thorn in your side," I repeated. They'd been the exact words Nanette had used at Yeast of Eden.

His upper lip curled. "It's like she had a vendetta against me."

The sirens that I'd heard passed, and it was completely quiet outside. Another drawback in my plan was that I hadn't planned for the cavalry to ride in and help wrap things up. No one, aside from Mrs. Branford, actually knew I'd left Yeast of Eden, and no one, except Mrs. Branford, knew I'd planted enough seeds in hopes that Buck Masterson would do just what he did and break into my dad's house. I was on my own, but thankfully, Buck hadn't budged from where he stood near the kitchen counter.

"She must have thought she was doing the right thing," I said.

"The right thing. Pft." The way his upper lip caught on one of his teeth made him look a little like Agatha. "She was messing with my reputation. I asked her to stop. I asked for her *support*," he said, as if asking was all he'd needed to do. "She wouldn't stop."

I'd set this little sting up, thinking he hadn't hurt Jackie, but the way he was talking made me wary. I didn't want to ask, but I had to. "Did you . . . were you the one . . . Did you kill her?"

He recoiled, flinging his hand to his chest. "Me? Are you crazy?"

"No, not crazy," I said. "You just said she needed to be stopped."

"But not by murder!" His voice was shrill. "And definitely not by me. That was just dumb luck."

He charged toward the door, the pictures still clutched in his shaking hand. Just as he reached for the door handle, someone on the outside turned it. My dad!

Buck jumped back, looking shocked and trapped. I'd moved forward, effectively blocking his path back to my dad's bedroom, where he'd managed to break into the house, and to the kitchen, which was the only other way out. He couldn't go anywhere unless he barreled right past me, knocking me over in the process.

It wasn't my dad's voice I heard, but my brother's. He laughed and talked, and then a woman responded. I could almost see the wheels turning in Buck's head. If he made a run for it, there'd be a chase, and it would be three against one. The odds were not in his favor.

I called out to my brother. "Billy! We have a little situation in here."

He stopped short just as he came into view. "I thought you were at your baking class," he said, but then his attention shifted to Buck Masterson, who was standing in the center of the room, looking like a kid who'd gotten caught with his hand in the cookie jar. "Hello. What's this?" He sounded casual, but his body tensed, and I knew he'd gone on high alert.

"This," I said, "is Buck Masterson."

Billy's smile vanished, and he stood light on his feet, ready to break into a run if Buck took off. "Should I know that name, Ivy?"

"He broke into Dad's house—"

I stopped as I caught a glimpse of the woman Billy was with. Her black hair hung in curls around her face, and her cell phone was pressed to her ear. Deputy Sheriff Emmaline Davis. She wore civilian clothes—a flirty floral dress with coral flats. She looked beautiful, but at the moment, she did not look relaxed. *Of course not*, I thought. I'd interrupted their long overdue date.

She shot me a look that said, "What in the hell are you doing, Ivy?"

"I'm stopping him from stealing something that doesn't belong to him," I said, answering the question she didn't actually ask me.

Buck spun around, looked from Billy to Emmaline to me. The color had drained from his face, taking it from tomato to ghostly white. "It's just a misunderstanding."

"Oh yeah? How'd you get in?" Billy asked, folding his arms over his chest.

Buck glanced toward the bedroom.

"Well now. Let's try this again. If my sister didn't let you in the front door, did you break in?"

"It's a mistake—"

"It's a yes-or-no answer," Billy snapped. "Either you broke in or you didn't. Which is it?"

Buck's eyes bugged. He was busted, and there wasn't any way he could talk his way out of it. "Y-yes, but—" He flung his hand out, pointing at me. "It doesn't belong to her."

Emmaline stepped past Billy, her phone in her hand, her purse slung over her shoulder. She patted the air with her hands to calm him down. "What doesn't belong to Ivy?"

He crumpled the photographs in his hand.

Emmaline's gaze dropped to his fist. "What do you have there, Mr. Masterson?"

He tightened his fist. "Nothing."

Outside the front door, tires squealed and doors slammed. Two uniformed police officers rushed in, then stopped to take in the scene and confer with Emmaline. She directed one of them to the bedroom.

"Check the window," she ordered.

The officer returned a minute later with the report that the window had been jimmied from the outside.

Emmaline looked at Buck. "Breaking and entering? Mr. Masterson, you have the right to remain silent." She proceeded to read him his rights, and her officers took him into custody. "Bag the photographs," she told them. The officers gathered up all the photos and slipped them into a clear plastic bag. "Did he take anything else, Ivy?" she asked as the officers led Buck to their cruiser.

"That's it. That's what he was after."

"I don't think he's the one who killed your mother, Ivy. There's no motive. No connection."

I hung my head. What had any of this accomplished, other than payback for him making Mrs. Branford's life miserable? "I know, Em. I know."

Chapter Twenty-seven

Emmaline's words invaded my sleep. "I don't think he's the one who killed your mother, Ivy."

I felt as if I were an airplane circling the landing strip, but there was no chance of ever getting clearance to touch down. I might not have had an ounce of proof—yet—but I knew in my gut that my mom had been murdered. I had theories, sure, but in reality, I was no closer to figuring out why and by whom than I'd been a week ago. All I'd succeeded in doing was getting Buck arrested for breaking and entering. It was a minor win for Jackie Makers, but not for my mom. I ran through the possibilities in my head, along with the hows and the whys, jotting down my own notes in the back of my mom's journal.

Buck Masterson. He'd said he'd had nothing to do with any killing, and I believed him. I didn't think he was guilty of killing the two women, but could his wife, Nanette, be? Maybe she'd been so angry with Jackie over her vendetta against Buck that she'd taken matters into her own hands.

Jasmine Makers. She and Jackie had been at odds because of Jolie and the lies. Could she have felt so betrayed by her mother that she'd kill her?

Jolie Flemming. The daughter Jackie gave up could certainly have been hurt and angry enough to have killed her mother for revenge.

Gus Makers. He and Jackie had ended up divorced, according to Jasmine, at least in part because of the affair Jackie had had years and years ago, and the daughter she had had and had given up. Maybe he'd killed his ex-wife over her betrayal of him. In his eyes, their entire marriage might have been nothing but a giant lie.

Jolie's father, whoever that was. He'd been deprived of being a father for twentysomething years. Was that enough for him to kill Jackie over? Of course this theory hinged on some assumptions, namely, that Jolie's father had discovered that Jackie had had a child that she'd given up for adoption, and that he'd actually been upset that he'd not had the opportunity to be a father to her. An added complication was that, with Jackie gone, there was literally no way to know who the father was.

I breathed out a frustrated sigh. Any of these could have been a motive for killing Jackie; I had no way of knowing which was most likely or which was the truth. And none of these scenarios helped me figure out my own mother's connection.

Everything, I realized, came down to what my mom knew . . . and who she told. If I was operating under the notion that my mom's and Jackie's deaths were connected, then my mom was collateral damage. Which of the scenarios was bad enough that my mom was killed to keep her quiet?

I had one last thought. It was more of a Hail Mary than a fleshed-out concept, but I wrote it down, anyway. According to my mom's calendar, she'd been planning to meet with the owner of Divine Cuisine. Renee. Meeting with her was now on my list of things to do.

The more I thought of all of this, the more I knew I needed someone to bounce ideas off of. I considered whom I wanted to call to talk this all through with. Olaya? I was beginning to think of her as an aunt. I worried that I was using her to fill the void in my heart from my mom. I wanted to turn to her, to confide in her, to tell her everything, but I also wanted to pull back, not to overstep, to be cautious.

Mrs. Branford? I wanted to *be* Penelope Branford when I was in my eighties. She was spritely, feisty, and still quick-witted. But I didn't want to burden her with all the different scenarios. I'd seen what Buck Masterson had done to her, and I didn't want to add to her load.

I considered waking up my dad or calling Billy. I even considered Miguel, but in the end I went with my oldest friend. We'd always told each other everything. Or at least we had . . . until she'd stopped.

"You and Billy," I blurted when she picked up.

Her voice was groggy. "It's two in the morning, Ivy."

"Sorry," I grumbled. "But Billy?"

"What do you mean, 'but Billy'? You've been wanting me and Billy to get together for years and years. We finally are."

"Together?" I squealed. "You're together?"

"We are." I could hear the smile in her voice.

I grinned. This *was* exactly what I wanted. What needed to happen. And I was so happy about it. "How?"

"It *is* the twenty-first century, as you have reminded me so often. I called him up and asked him out."

"That night at Baptista's when you left me there with Miguel, was it a case like you said or were you going to meet Billy?"

She hesitated for a split second and then admitted it. "Billy."

I slapped the bed. "I knew it!"

We broke into a fit of laughter. In the background, I heard the low rumble of a man's voice. Billy was there. My heart filled with warmth. Emmaline and Billy. Billy and Emmaline.

"Sorry to wake you," I said. "Can I run something by you? Real quick."

She gave me a sleepy okay and then listened while I told her all my theories. "You missed your calling," she said, not for the first time.

"You really think so?"

I could almost see her nodding. "Absolutely."

"If only I could figure out what actually happened."

"You will!" Billy shouted into the phone. And then his voice grew more somber. "You will, Ivy. But tomorrow. Go to bed."

After what felt like a million fitful hours, I finally fell asleep, but I woke up with a start sometime later. *Josephine Jeffries! Of course!*

Josephine was my mom's best friend and taught social studies at Santa Sofia High School. Just like Emmaline and me, she and my mom had told each other everything. Why hadn't I thought about talking to her before? My mom might have kept her suspicions from my dad, not wanting to upset him, but from Josephine? Not likely.

I drifted back to sleep, relieved to have a plan for the morning.

Chapter Twenty-eight

Like clockwork, I awoke just before sunrise. I threw on a pair of black leggings, a Santa Sofia sweatshirt, brushed my teeth, and harnessed Agatha. Five minutes after I'd climbed out of bed, my sweet pug and I were in the fresh air and heading toward the beachfront. I stopped at the highest point of the small hill my parents' house was on, readied my camera, and captured the layered colors as the sun made its entrance for the day.

We made quick work of our walk; it was a school day, and I needed to get to Santa Sofia High School to meet Josephine before her first class. She'd always been Aunt Josie to me outside of school, and when we were within the walls of Santa Sofia High School, she'd been Mrs. Jeffries, but at some point she'd insisted I transition to her first name. Not an easy thing to do; even being around her made me feel as if I was back in high school and just sixteen years old.

I held my breath as I walked through the hallways

of the school, a wave of nausea rolling through me. It was too familiar, but not because of my own years there. My unease was because of the connection to my mother. This had been her home away from home. Everywhere I turned, I remembered something about her. I could picture a bulletin board she'd created for the journalism club. I had a vision of the time we'd gone to the school musical and she'd brought a bouquet of roses for one of her students who'd had a supporting role. The girl had been overwhelmed. Her own family hadn't come to a single performance, but my mom had been there for her. I remembered the academic decathlon teams she'd led to victory.

Maybe it was a mistake to come here. It was too soon. I stopped, ready to turn around and high-tail it out of the there, but Josephine called my name from the doorway of her classroom. "Right here, Ivy."

I felt as if I'd been caught red-handed. Slowly, I turned back around. Josephine looked just like she had the last time I'd seen her. Her short auburn hair was streaked blond in the front, framing her face with soft waves. She had never looked like a stereotypical teacher. No slacks or clogs or vests for Josephine Jeffries. She had on skinny jeans, ankle boots, and a draped top that flattered her soft-around-the-edges body. She was a few years older than my mom had been, but even at sixty, Josephine looked hipper than many of her teenage students.

I met her gaze, and I felt as if an opera singer had just hit the highest soprano note and shattered every bit of glass in sight. I crumpled, my nose pricking with emotion, tears pooling in my eyes. I stumbled forward, and we fell into each other's arms. She wrapped me up, her hand on the back of my head, calming me with her touch.

"It's okay, baby," she said. "I know. It's okay."

I hadn't seen Josephine since my mom's funeral, and now I knew exactly why I'd been avoiding her. Just seeing her brought out every last shred of emotion I had so carefully packed away. I felt myself cracking, my grief just as real in this moment as it had been when I'd gotten the phone call from Billy, when I'd rushed back to Santa Sofia on the first flight out of Texas and seen my dad, when we'd buried my mom, the three of us each tossing white rose petals into her grave, tears streaming down our faces.

I pulled away and ran my fingers under my eyes to clear away my tears. "I'm sorry, Josephine. I'm not normally so . . . so . . ."

She held up a hand to stop me. "There's no normal anymore, sweetheart," she said. "It's fine."

She led me into her classroom. It was like the calm before the storm. Her handwriting scrawled across the whiteboard, posing questions about *The Sun Also Rises*. I realized I didn't know anything about Josephine's life since my mom died. She'd been the conduit to my previous life in Santa Sofia.

"You still teach tenth grade?"

"Still. Always. They'll have to take me out of here kicking and screaming."

"I don't know how you and Mom did it," I said. "Do it," I added, correcting myself.

She laughed. "Some people say it's a calling. Some people say it's craziness."

"And you? What do you say?"

She shrugged. "I guess it's a little of both." She checked her watch—a leather strap that wound around her wrist three times. "Class starts in a few minutes, Ivy. What did you want to talk about?"

I sat down at one of the student desks and leaned my chin on my fisted hands. I had only a few minutes, so I launched into my tale, trying to keep my emotions at bay. "I think my mom was killed because she knew something," I summed up. The more I said it, the more normal it was sounding.

I couldn't remember ever seeing Josephine at a loss for words, but she certainly was now. She stared at me.

"She was killed, Josephine. *Purposely killed*," I said, driving my point home.

Finally, she found her voice. "It was an accident, Ivy. She was in the wrong place at the wrong time."

"No. No! Josephine, I'm right about this. She knew something."

"She was a teacher, Ivy. What could she know?"

"That's what I wanted to ask you about. She and my dad were taking cooking classes at Well Done with Jackie Makers, the woman who was just killed. But she had an appointment with someone from Divine Cuisine."

"So?"

"So it doesn't make sense to me. She was happy

with the classes at Well Done. You know Mom. Once she finds something she likes, that's it. I don't know if it was a secret, but she didn't tell my dad about it."

Josephine looked at me with her sympathetic brown eyes. "I think you're trying to find an explanation for what happened, Ivy, but there isn't one. It was a horrible accident."

My dad had said basically the same thing. Maybe they were right. Maybe I was reaching, but deep down I didn't think so. Focusing on discovering the truth kept my emotions at bay. I rallied, asking the questions I'd come to ask. "She never seemed strange to you in the days before she died?"

"Strange?"

"You know, distracted or preoccupied?"

Josephine shook her head. "Not really—" She stopped, her eyes clouding. "Well, there was this one thing."

I leaned forward. "What thing?"

"She was concerned about one of her students. She thought the girl was in trouble or something. Of course, that was nothing new. The concern, not the girl in trouble."

"In trouble how?"

Josephine cupped her hand over her forehead, thinking. Finally, she shook her head. "Something about an essay she wrote raised a red flag for your mom. She was afraid the girl might *do* something."

"What does that mean, *do* something?"

Josephine ran her index finger under the band

of her watch. "I can't quite remember, Ivy. It was a while ago."

I put my hand on hers. "Please, Josie."

She pressed her fingertips to her temples, nodding. "I remember when she mentioned it to me the first time. She stopped by my classroom after school one day with this essay in her hand." She closed her eyes, as if she were reliving the memory. "She's going to hurt someone."

"What? Who?"

"That's what she said. 'She's going to hurt someone.'"

I stared. "Like who? Who was she going to hurt? Who was the student?"

"I don't know."

"You didn't ask?"

Josephine shook her head. "I did, but then we started talking about something else, and she never said." She paused, then added, "That had to have been a few months before the accident, though, Ivy. You don't think—"

"I don't know. Maybe." I looked at her, wishing she felt what I did, wishing she was as convinced as I was that something about my mother's death wasn't right. "I think it might be. Related, I mean."

"I don't have the essay."

And just like that, a lightbulb when off above my head. The essay I'd found in Jackie's kitchen. "Did my mom have a student . . . Jasmine Makers?" I asked.

Josephine nodded. "Yeah, of course. Jasmine

graduated in May. Why? You think she might have been the student your mom was worried about?"

"Maybe," I said. But inside I was more convinced than I let on. It made sense. I didn't know how it might factor into my mom's death. Maybe it didn't. But it felt like progress, nonetheless.

I'd read the essay, and I hadn't gotten any red flags about the state of mind of the author, but then again, I wasn't a teacher with years of experience dealing with hormonal and emotional teenagers. I grabbed my cell phone and texted Olaya, asking her to bring the essay we'd found to Yeast of Eden. I wanted to have another look.

The first bell rang. The storm came as a group of students careened into the room.

"Thank you, Aunt Josie." I fell back on the name I'd grown up calling her. She wasn't related by blood, but she was as close to an aunt as I had, and suddenly I wanted to have that connection with her.

"I miss her, too, Ivy." She stood and began greeting her students. "This place isn't the same without her."

Chapter Twenty-nine

What I lacked in a plan, I oozed in determination. I left Santa Sofia High School and headed east to Divine Cuisine. I'd Googled and read about the car accident that had befallen Renee Ranson, the owner of Divine Cuisine. It had forced her to close shop, but now she was reopening her cooking school/catering business, and I hoped to find her there.

My mind was swirling with a million thoughts. Jackie Makers. The cooking schools. My mom's planner. The student she was worried about. The historic district and Buck Masterson. It felt like all the ingredients to a complex bread dough that I just had to mix together and let rest.

The whole Divine Cuisine lead could be a big, fat dead end, but I felt I needed to talk to Renee. If nothing else, it would help me understand what was going through my mom's mind before she died. I parked on the street in front of the building. It was in a warehouse area, so it didn't have the quaintness of so many businesses in Santa Sofia. Next to it was an embroidery and uniform shop, and on the other side was a cheerleading and tumbling studio.

The front door was unlocked. I let myself in and called out, "Hello? Ms. Ranson?"

I heard a noise to my right and turned as a woman in a wheelchair rolled out. She leaned forward, her hands on the wheels, propelling herself forward. She looked up at me. "We aren't open yet. Can I help you?"

"I hope so. My name is Ivy Culpepper."

She angled her head slightly. "Culpepper?"

"My mother was Anna Culpepper."

Her expression didn't change, but she said, "I remember. A car accident."

"Yes. At the high school."

She gestured to her wheelchair. "I know a little something about hit-and-runs."

"Is that what happened?"

She grimaced. "That's what happened. It was like some bad scene from a movie. One minute I was standing there, and the next I was flattened. I woke up without the use of my legs. This," she said with a sweeping gesture, "is my lovely future."

"I'm so sorry."

"Yeah, me, too." Bitterness spilled from every syllable.

I had the impression that she wanted to talk about it. People who were wronged often did, I'd realized over the years. I waited, giving her the space and permission to speak, and in another few seconds, she continued.

"I was unloading my catering van. Minding my own business. My shop—this shop—was doing great. A full calendar of catering gigs, cooking classes. I worked damn hard for this place, then *bam*!" She slapped her hands together. "Just like that, it was over. A car came out of nowhere. All I saw was a white blur, then nothing. It hit me head-on, and then it backed up and ran right over my legs as it backed away."

I tried to hide the shudder that rolled through my body. In the blink of an eye, her life had completely changed. In a similar flash, my mom's life had ended. It wasn't fair.

"Do you know who did it?" I asked, knowing full well that the driver had never been caught.

"Oh yes. I know exactly who it was."

A flare of excitement shot through me. "Really?"

She lowered her voice, as if she were imparting some deep, dark secret. "The owner of Well Done. It's a cooking school and catering business in town. Her name is—well, was—Jackie Makers. She's the one who ran me over."

My mouth gaped, and I was speechless for a minute. "Are you sure?" I asked once I found my voice.

She hesitated. "Well, I didn't see her behind the wheel, but it was pretty obvious after a while. She came around to check on me at the hospital, trying to be a"—she made air quotation marks with her fingers—"Good Samaritan. Right. As if I couldn't see right through that. She was my competition, and suddenly I was out of the way. Her cooking school started to take off. Since I was out of commission, the catering jobs that had been on my schedule moved over to her. Guilt must have gotten the better of her. She wouldn't freaking leave me alone. *Always* bothering me, calling to see if I needed anything. Finally, I told her like it was. That if she couldn't rewind time and stop herself from mowing me down in my own parking lot, then leave me the hell alone."

I was flabbergasted, but I managed to ask another question. "And did she?"

"She had the gall to deny it. 'I didn't run you over, Renee.' Yeah, right. And I have a million-dollar piece of swampland for sale."

"Did you tell the police?"

She pinched her nose and closed her eyes for a beat. "What do you think? Of course I did. But there was"—more air quotes—"no evidence. No witnesses. No reason for them to believe me." She tapped the tires of her wheelchair. "Put me in this thing for life, and she got off scot-free."

"Well, she did meet her own tragic death, so not scot-free." I couldn't believe that Jackie had been behind the hit-and-run. It wasn't at all what I'd expected, and it didn't help me figure out who, then, had killed *her*. Maybe one of Renee Ranson's family? Revenge for the accident that had stolen their wife and mother? And once again, it didn't help figure out what had happened to my mom.

The face Renee made indicated that she didn't seem to think Jackie's murder was enough pay-back for what had happened to her, but she said, "Whatever. I'm moving on. My business has reopened. My family and I are working round the clock to get back to where we were. My son is the new chef. My daughter is talented in the kitchen, too, but she's a numbers girl. She's doing the books. My husband is the driver and all-around muscle. I'm contract-ing some things out. Hiring temp workers for service, getting bread from a local bakery, and keeping one full-time employee on staff for every-thing else. Dishwashing, loading, prep. And me, I'm the delegator. Because—ha!—that's all I can do. Raise my voice and yell at people."

Her bitterness was understandable, but it was wearing. I hoped she could come to terms with what had happened and let her anger go, otherwise it would eat her up, bit by bit by bit.

"They never caught who killed my mom, either," I said, turning the conversation back to the reason for my visit. "That's kind of why I'm here."

"Sit," she said, indicating a low stool at the stainless-steel counter.

The seat of the stool was shaped like a bike seat, only without the cushion. It was oddly comfortable.

"My mother came to see you the week before she died."

She nodded, and from her expression, I knew that she remembered my mom. "That's right. She thought she might know something about my accident, but she wasn't sure. She'd wanted to ask me a few questions."

My heart thrummed. Finally, I might get some answers. "You mean about Jackie?"

Renee tucked a mass of hair behind her ears. Her cheeks were flushed, small red splotches marking the angles of her face. "No. I told her what I thought, but she wouldn't say if that's what she *knew.* Said she couldn't, in good conscience, until she was certain. Those were her words exactly."

That sounded just like my mom. "Err on the side of caution," she'd always said. She would never throw someone under the proverbial bus if she wasn't 100 percent positive about the situation. Still, I was disappointed not to get some nugget that might help.

"When I heard she'd died, I thought, *That's it. There goes my last chance at finding out the truth.*"

"So you thought she really did know something?"

Renee tapped her fingers absently on her wheels. "Hard to know. I thought maybe she'd somehow pony up the evidence against Jackie Makers that I needed."

"What did she ask you?"

"Same as the police. Did I see the driver? Description of the car. License plate. Anything else I remembered. It all happened too fast. I've racked my brain. I've gone to therapy. Hell, I even tried hypnosis. I never saw it coming."

"Can I ask you one more thing?"

"Ask me anything. Like I said, if it might lead to proof, then I'm there. I don't care that the woman already died. I want her crucified for what she did to me."

"Do you think it was intentional?"

"I've asked myself that over and over. I'm basically a good person. I don't have enemies. I haven't done anything to warrant . . . this. But how could it *not* be? Isn't it too much of a coincidence that my one competitor in town is the person who ran me over?"

Allegedly ran you over, I thought. She was ready to convict without a shred of proof, but I wasn't so sure. I couldn't say why, but I felt there was something missing from the story. If Renee Ranson was right and Jackie had run her over, how did my mom know? What did any of it have to do with her? And why would my mom even get involved? Then again, she did go see Jackie, and shortly after that, she was run over. Coincidence?

I couldn't think of anything else to ask, so I stood, ready to leave. Renee stopped me.

"You know . . ."

I sat back down. "Yes?"

"About a month ago I got a strange e-mail. It had a list of people and e-mail addresses. Some of them were city e-mail addresses, a few were school district, and there were others that were just Gmail or Yahoo or whatnot. Your mom was on there."

I let this information sink in. A list of random e-mails, including my mom's. "You don't know who sent it?"

"No idea. I responded, but it bounced, saying the e-mail was not valid."

"Did you share this with the authorities?"

"Not at all. Until this moment, I didn't think there was a connection to anything, but now I'm wondering."

"There was no message?"

"Nothing. Just the list."

"Could Jackie have sent it? A list of clients for you to—I don't know—add to your mailing list?"

"More retribution." She nodded circumspectly. "Could be."

"Thank you for talking to me," I said.

"Ivy, right?"

I nodded.

"The not knowing is hard. It's always in the back of my mind. Why me? I'm sure you feel the same about your mother. I hope you find what you're looking for."

So did I.

Chapter Thirty

Next stop, Yeast of Eden. I barreled in, anxious to reread the essay Olaya and I had found among Jackie's cookbooks and piles of papers, the one I thought was written by Jasmine Makers.

Olaya greeted me with a smile, her eyes crinkling at the corners. She took one look at my face, reached under the counter for the single paper, and said, "It's right here."

"Thank you!" I took it and sat at a little bistro table, not even taking the time to ask for a luscious popover or croissant. My mother and Jackie were both dead, and nothing I did was going to change that, but discovering the truth felt urgent, nonetheless.

I read the essay through once, then again, more slowly, looking for any clues or evidence that the content might relate to Renee Ranson and what happened to her. If I worked under the assumption that this was, in fact, the essay my mom had taken to share with Josephine Jeffries, and then later with

Jackie Makers, then it also made sense that it was also this essay that had led her to Renee Ranson.

But if it was, I couldn't find the obvious clues. There were parts that said things like *I've always been hotheaded. I'm like my dad in that way. I react first, think later. It may be my greatest fault.* And *Sometimes my actions have horrible consequences. It's like that butterfly effect. Something happens here, and then way down the line, somewhere else, something happens that you could never have predicted.*

The prompt had been about a lesson taught. I skipped to the last paragraph of the essay and stopped cold. *I meant to teach a lesson, but really all I did was hurt everyone. Collateral damage. If I could take it back, I would. If only I could.*

This had to have been what alerted my mom. I went back to my assumption that Jasmine Makers had written the essay, and worked through a hypothesis. I tried to think like my mom would have. She had read it and got concerned that her student had done something, so she'd gone to Josephine first. There was no name on the essay, though, so my mom had been piecing things together, maybe through the process of elimination. If she'd scored all the other essays in the class and made her typical photocopies, she would have known which student the essay with no name belonged to. Assuming it was Jasmine's, she would have met with her first to talk about it. If that hadn't gone well, she would have met with Jasmine's mother. She'd been taking the cooking classes, so she already had a relationship of sorts with Jackie. Knowing my mom, she wouldn't have wanted to talk to Jackie at Well Done, with other people around. It was a private matter. So she'd gone over to Maple Street, expressed her concern about Jasmine, and given Jackie the essay.

Then what? It seemed logical that Jasmine had reacted to the news of a half sister, but what then? What had she done? I racked my brain, trying to piece things together.

Before I could make sense of anything, my cell phone rang.

"Hi, Mrs. Branford," I answered after I saw her name pop up on the screen.

"Interesting things going on over here on Maple Street, my dear," she said, skipping the greeting. "As always."

"Like what?"

"Jasmine is holed up in her mother's house, and Nanette and Buck Masterson are pounding on the door there."

I thought of my mother's English lessons, her teaching about rising action and resolution and, most of all, turning points. This was it. It was all coming together. I could feel it. The climax of the story! Without a second thought, I grabbed my stuff, waved to Olaya, and raced to my car.

"I'm on my way," I said to Mrs. Branford before I ended the call.

I made it to Maple Street in record time and parked down the street, a few houses from Jackie Makers's Tudor. I was afraid whatever was going on would be resolved by the time I arrived, but I needn't have worried. The Mastersons were right where Penny Branford had said they were, standing on the front porch, arms folded, sour expressions on their faces. Mrs. Branford waved at me from her front porch. I quickly crossed the street to meet her.

"How long has the standoff been going on?"

She frowned, the lines of her face deepening the farther her lips were pulled down. "At least thirty minutes. Maybe a smidgen more."

"What do they want with Jasmine?"

"I wish I knew, dear."

I was done being subtle. I knew Jasmine had something to with this entire situation. Whatever Nanette and Buck Masterson's game was didn't concern me. I had bigger fish to fry. I slung my purse over my shoulder and marched across the street, determination coursing through me.

"Out on bail?" I asked Buck, shouldering between the two of them and raising my fist to the door.

"What the—" Buck tried to edge in front of me, but I blocked him.

"Jasmine? It's Ivy Culpepper."

I didn't really expect her to open the door to me, but that was what she did. It was just a crack, and suddenly an arm shot out, grabbed my wrist, and pulled me in. I felt like Alice slipping through the looking glass. From behind me, Buck and Nanette tried to push their way in, but I was barely through the door when Jasmine slammed it shut and turned the dead bolt.

"What do they want?" I asked, practically out of breath, but feeling kind of tough.

She threw up her hands. "Hell if I know. They did this to my mom, too. Harassed her until she could hardly take it anymore."

The pounding started on the door again, so she dragged me away from the entryway and into the kitchen.

"What did they do to your mom?"

She opened her mouth, ready to say something, but then she seemed to think better of it and closed her lips tight. The pounding started again, but this time it came from the other side of the house. "God, what is wrong with them?" Jasmine cursed under her breath. "Leave me alone!" she yelled.

"We just need to talk, Jasmine. Come on. Let us in!" Buck yelled and their pounding grew stronger and more persistent.

Jasmine's nostrils flared, and she yanked at the short strands of her black hair. Finally, she marched to a door off the kitchen, flung it open, and disappeared into the darkness. A few seconds later, there was a clicking sound, and then I heard the automatic garage door kick into gear. The chain rattled, and I wondered if the whole thing might collapse, but it managed to open all the way. A triangle of light came in through the slightly ajar door. I opened it a little more to spy on Jasmine and the Mastersons.

They were behind the white Toyota Camry parked in the garage, but I could see the top of Jasmine's head, Nanette Masterson's brightly dyed red hair, and Buck Masterson's stringy hair. Buck was wagging his finger at Jasmine, while Nanette nodded vehemently. Jasmine shook her head just as intensely, saying something I couldn't hear.

It was all extremely suspicious, but I had no idea what it was about. I edged into the garage and stood next to the hood of the car. I crouched down slightly. I didn't want to broadcast my presence for fear they'd stop their heated argument. My hand rested in a small dent on the cool metal of the car. I craned my neck to listen, but before I could hear anything, Jasmine threw up her hands, turned around, and stormed back into the house.

Buck Masterson looked at me with his dark, beady eyes but made no move to actually set foot inside the garage. Instead, I left the safety of the car and walked out of the garage.

"What was that about?" I asked, cutting to the chase.

His lips twisted in a muted sneer. "God Almighty, she's stubborn, just like her mother was."

Nanette scoffed. "That's not the word I'd use."

I swung my attention to her. "What word *would* you use?"

"I could name several. *Vindictive. Vengeful. Vile.*" She had a corner on words beginning with the letter *V*.

"Jackie? She seemed nice enough to me," I said.

"You didn't know her like we did," Nanette said.

I didn't know her at all, I thought, but I didn't say so.

Buck blew an exasperated raspberry. "She didn't have anything against *you*. She wanted to destroy me."

"Right. With the letters and pictures," I said, more snarkily than I'd planned, but he deserved it.

"Us," Nanette corrected again. "We could have destroyed her, you know. If she hadn't died, we'd have crushed her." The anger oozing from Nanette was palpable.

"Crushed her?"

"Destroyed. Ruined. Ended."

"Why was there such bad blood between you?"

"Some people think they're so much better than you."

"Why did Jackie think that?"

"Because she was messed up in the head," Buck snarled. "Let he who is without sin cast the first stone. Right? She thought . . . Well, I don't know what she thought, but let me tell you, she wasn't an innocent."

"But what did she *do*?"

Buck flapped his hand and turned on his heel. "I'm done. Ask Jasmine, why don't you?"

I looked over my shoulder, back toward the door to the kitchen. "I will—" I started to say, but as I turned back around, I stopped. All I could see were the backs of Buck and Nanette Masterson as they walked down the driveway and turned onto the sidewalk.

Back inside the house, I searched everywhere, but Jasmine was gone. The Mastersons must have completely spooked her with their accusations about her mother. I didn't know Jackie Makers, but I had gotten to know Olaya Solis over the past few weeks, and I found it hard to believe she could so dramatically misjudge a person. Mrs. Branford had thought Jackie was a good person, too.

If I trusted my gut, which I did, then something wasn't adding up. Renee Ranson and the Mastersons had to be missing something.

But what was it?

I hated leaving the house unlocked, but I had no choice. I turned the dead bolt on the front door and then went out the back. It was my first good look at the backyard. Whatever her faults might have been, Jackie Makers had had a knack for landscaping. Or she'd paid someone well. There was a flagstone patio right off the kitchen. A redwood trellis climbing with bright fuchsia bougainvillea shaded the area. A stone path crossed a small grassy area and led to raised flower beds and a small greenhouse tucked in a back corner. The blooming flowers created a kaleidoscope of color everywhere I looked.

"Beautiful," I murmured, taking a moment to look around. The beds were free flowing and looked like those in an English cottage garden. I was no expert, but I recognized lavender, sage, phlox, and purple coneflowers. Butterflies fluttered about and rested on the blooms.

My cell phone rang. I grabbed for it, the sound loud and intrusive in the peacefulness of the garden.

"Hey, Ivy." It was Emmaline. "We know the cause of death for Jackie Makers."

"You said it was poison." They'd suspected that almost from the beginning.

"I mean specifically. It's called ricin. Administered through cupcakes she had in her kitchen."

I remembered the pink bakery box, but there hadn't been an identifying sticker on the box or a business noted on it.

"It's odorless and tasteless, and it can be concocted at home, in any ordinary kitchen, from castor beans."

My throat turned dry. "So someone really planned this."

"Looks like it. It affects the immune system and can take days before it actually kills, but it will. The cupcakes in Jackie's kitchen were infused with ricin."

I went cold. "So she ate a cupcake, and it was just coincidence that she died at Yeast of Eden?" I asked, half to myself.

"Looks that way," Emmaline said before we ended the call.

The peacefulness of the yard suddenly felt stifling. Reluctantly, I veered to the right, followed the flagstone pavers to the side gate, and let myself out. I went across the street to Mrs. Branford's house, filled Mrs. Branford in on what Emmaline had told me, then drove back home to walk Agatha and shower.

And to process.

I was at a standstill. In my gut, I didn't believe Jackie Makers could have run over Renee Ranson or my mom, because that didn't answer the question of who had killed Jackie herself. But if it wasn't her, then who had?

Before I knew it, it was time to head back to

Yeast of Eden. As I walked into the lobby, I noticed the fresh glass vases and sprigs of fresh flowers on the bistro tables; the fiesta Mexican garlands draped in the windows, each intricate, lacy rectangle in a different primary color; the sparkling floor; and the crystal clear display cases filled with the scattered crumbs of the day's bread. I breathed in and instantly relaxed. This was like home away from home. I'd come to love the bread shop.

I walked through the front and into the *cocina*. Everyone else was already there. Everyone except Nanette, that is. I wasn't surprised. I couldn't imagine her showing up after the combative confrontation at Jackie's house.

I waved to Mrs. Branford.

"Long time, no see, my dear," she said, her snowy hair perfect, as usual, her lips rimmed with a bright pink lipstick. On anyone else, that color would have been too much; on Penelope Branford, with her fuchsia velour sweat suit and bright white sneakers, the lipstick was perfect.

The chalkboard had today's baking plan: Gruyère and black pepper popovers. I'd never actually had a popover, but if the illustration, with its muffin-shaped base and the billowy, full top, looked anything like it would taste, I knew it would become a favorite.

"You don't usually make popovers for the bread shop, do you?" I asked Olaya as I tied on my ruffled apron.

"Popovers are a quick delight but are best when

they are served warm. So no, I do not carry them normally. Cold popovers, not so good."

"Terrible, in fact," Consuelo commented.

We got right to work, mixing the eggs and milk, then whisking in the flour mixture in three separate stages. Olaya had given us each a popover pan.

"It is special for popovers," she said, pointing to the six individual nonstick popover cups. "The air can circulate around each cup, forcing the batter up, up, up until it pops over the top of the pan. Now, the trick is to fill to nearly the top. None of this 'fill it halfway' stuff."

She demonstrated at her own station, filling each of her six prepared cups to within a quarter inch of the top with the heavily peppered, thin batter. "Take the cubes of Gruyère and plop them in the center." She fanned her hand across her pan like a game show host. "That is all. Now we bake."

While the popovers were in the high-heat oven, we washed our dirtied dishes. The women chattered on about life after college, baking successes and failures, and the spring weather at the beach.

"Tourists are coming," Consuelo said. "We get more and more each year. Does nobody stay home anymore?"

"I need the tourists," Olaya said. "They make my business."

After a few minutes, the conversation turned to Jackie Makers. "The police, they have found nothing about Jackie's murder?" Martina asked her sister.

Olaya shook her head. "Not that I know of."

I looked at the three sisters, and my thoughts turned to my first conversation with Emmaline after Jackie's death. She'd said they were all suspects. They all knew how to cook and could have easily given Jackie a box of ricin-infused cupcakes. I dismissed the idea the very next second. The truth was, I was no closer to knowing the truth and anyone could have killed both Jackie and my mom.

The bell in the lobby tinkled, and Olaya disappeared for a moment, then returned a moment later. "Ladies, you must excuse me for a few minutes. I have business to discuss." She turned and waited as a young man pushed a wheelchair into the kitchen. In the wheelchair was Renee Ranson.

Chapter Thirty-one

Several things happened all at once.

Olaya introduced Renee as the owner of Divine Cuisine. "I'll be providing bread for Divine Cuisine's catering jobs," she said.

As I thought about what a small world it was and how strange it was that only this morning I'd met with Renee Ranson and heard about her theory that Jackie was behind her injuries, I saw Renee's face contort. She was staring at the women in our Yeast of Eden baking class, an inexplicable expression on her face.

"Becky?" she said.

At the same moment, the young man behind the wheelchair said, "Becks! What are you doing here?"

Becky . . . Ranson? The talented daughter who was good with numbers?

I whipped my head around to see Sally and Jolie both staring at Becky, who'd gone completely pale.

"I'm, um, taking a baking class."

"Why?" the young man asked. "You don't need a class."

"Tía Olaya!" The back door to the kitchen slammed open, and Jasmine burst in. She dropped her purse, so her eyes were on the floor in front of her. When she looked up, she froze, staring at the group of people in the kitchen. Slowly, she scanned the faces, growing paler and paler with each passing second.

Becky stared at Jasmine, made a choking sound, and took a step backward. She looked as if she'd been caught with her hand in the cookie jar, which I didn't understand. Her mom ran a catering business, not a bakery. There was no conflict here, so I couldn't understand her reaction.

Until suddenly I did.

The images around me became fixed in my mind like a tableau. My brain processed everything I knew at lightning speed. My mom, the teacher, the essay she'd found and then presumably given to Jackie. The one written by Jasmine. I thought about what Renee Ranson had told me just this morning. Jackie had been the one to hit her with her car. She'd been filled with guilt, showing up at the hospital, asking after Renee's well-being, wanting to make amends. But it wasn't because *she'd* been the one to hit her.

Renee had said she'd seen a blur of white. My mind went to the white car housed in Jackie's garage. The one with the dent in front. The one Olaya had told me belonged to Jasmine. The hit-and-run vehicle.

Jasmine had hit Renee Ranson. That had to be why Jackie had felt guilty and why she'd tried to help Renee. She'd been protecting her daughter, but also trying to make things right . . . in her own way.

Had the Mastersons figured it out?

When I looked at Jasmine now, I knew I was right. Her face seemed to crumple into complete guilt and misery when she looked at Renee Ranson. All at once, my body went cold. My mom had figured it out, and she'd died because of it.

I surged forward toward the girl. "You." Needles pricked under my skin. "You did this?" I pointed to Renee, but then I wheeled back around and put my hand over my mouth, trying to hold in the bubbling emotions. "You killed my mom?"

Jasmine reached for the wall, trying to grab hold and keep herself upright, but she couldn't. She slid down, fell onto her knees. Her sobs were painful and tortured, like a wounded animal's. "I couldn't . . . I didn't know. . . ." She moaned. "I'm sorry."

"You're sorry?" I felt my face turn hot, imagined the rage climbing from my broken heart to my brain. Somewhere in the back recesses of my mind, I heard Olaya's voice, but I couldn't make out what she was saying. I heard the word *now. Now. Now. Now.* Over and over again, it echoed in my mind. "You killed my mother, and you're sorry?"

In my peripheral vision, I saw Jolie move toward me. Felt her arm slip around my shoulder. "Shhh."

She tried to soothe me, but it was too late for that. I shrugged free.

"Why? Why would you kill her? She wanted to help you!"

Jasmine's howls had reduced her to a puddle on the floor. If I hadn't been so hurt, so stunned, so overwhelmed by my grief, I might have felt sorry for the wreck she'd become. But I didn't. Anger bubbled inside of me like a volcano on the verge of erupting.

"I'm sorry," she said again, but this time it was directed to Renee Ranson. Becky gasped, stumbling back against her baking station. "I didn't mean to. I—I was so . . . my mom had—" She looked at Jolie, and I knew what she was trying to say.

I spoke for her. "You found out about Jolie—"

She nodded.

"What does that have to do with me?" Renee's voice held its own degree of confusion. Of shock.

"I . . . nothing," Jasmine managed to say. "I was so mad. I wanted her to pay, so I was going to *help* you. It was a mistake. It was an accident. Please believe me. I never meant to hurt you."

Renee let out a cruel laugh. "Help me? You ruined my life."

Jasmine broke down again, half nodding, half shaking her head. "I—" She sobbed. "Know."

Renee wasn't about to let Jasmine sink into her own self-preserving grief. "And Anna Culpepper, she figured it out, so you mowed her down just like you did me? Figured it worked once, might work again, right?"

Jasmine dipped her chin in a fractured nod. "I wasn't thinking."

Olaya had moved next to me, pale and stunned. "And Jackie? Did you kill your mother, too?"

"No." We all turned to see Mrs. Branford with her cane outstretched like a weapon. "She didn't kill her mother. This one did."

Becky, with her brown hair falling around her pale face, her eyes wide and scared, tried to shrink back. She turned and clutched the stainless-steel counter. Her gaze found her mother. "You said it was Jackie Makers," she said, pointing at Renee. "Every day you said how she ruined your life. How she'd done this to you."

Renee let out a leaden cry. "You . . . ?"

Jolie, Sally, and the Solis sisters stood dumb-struck. I felt my legs go rubbery. I couldn't keep myself upright. Couldn't make sense of what was happening. What had happened. How Jackie's in-discretion so many years ago had ended up impacting so many lives. As Jasmine had said in her essay, it was the butterfly effect.

My gaze found Jasmine again, and rage filled me. "You took my mother." Tears streamed down my face. "You did this."

I somehow stiffened my body and tried to move forward. I didn't know what I was going to do, but I wanted to touch her, to hurt her, to make her pay. But just as I started to propel myself forward, out of my mind, an arm snaked around my shoulder, stronger this time, holding me back.

"Ivy, it won't change anything." Miguel's voice in

my ear was like a lifeline. My body trembled with six months of grief, but he held on to me, grounding me, holding me back. "I'm here, Ivy. I'm not letting you go," he said.

"But she killed—"

"It won't change anything," he said again, and in that instant, I knew he was right. My mother was gone. And nothing I did could bring her back. Like I'd wished for Renee, I had to let go of my anger and move forward. I had to accept what had happened and make the choice to live my life.

Suddenly Emmaline was flanking me on the other side. She directed her officers to detain both Jasmine and Becky. Mrs. Branford finally lowered her cane, her arm shaking with the effort of having held it up for so long.

"You figured out the truth," Em whispered, squeezing my hand. "Like I said, you missed your calling, Ivy."

I managed a small smile through my tears. I had figured out the truth. It was the only thing I could hang on to at the moment, but it was enough.

Chapter Thirty-two

Two months later, I parked my mother's pearl-white Fiat on Maple Street. "It belongs to you," my dad had said, handing me the keys, a few days ago. "She would have wanted that. And so do I."

Now Agatha and I stood in front of 615 Maple Street, the brick Tudor I'd fallen in love with the first moment I'd laid eyes on it. The house I'd just bought. Every detail was emblazoned in my mind, from the tall pine tree to the right of the front door, to the dark brick facade, to the steeply gabled green roof and the tall chimney.

Penny Branford swung her cane as she walked across the street, spritely as ever. "Hello, neighbors!"

Her snowy curls looked freshly done, and her Nike sneakers were brand new. This pair was sparkling white. *To match her hair*, I thought with a grin. Today she wore a coral velour sweat suit. I hoped I could be half the woman she was when I was eighty-five, with a fraction of the energy. She was a force to be reckoned with, and I was proud to call her my friend.

I stooped to give her a hug. "Can you believe it?"

We stood side by side in front of Jackie Makers's former home.

"Actually, I can. You were meant for this street. For this house," Mrs. Branford said.

"Meant for? I don't know about that. I definitely love the house, though."

"Meant for, most definitely. I believe in fate, Ivy Culpepper. Your mother's death brought you back to Santa Sofia. It was a tragedy, to be sure, but it also brought you to me, and to Olaya," she said, adding the last part a little reluctantly. "And that is our good fortune. This is where you're supposed to be. Of that, I'm sure."

When I thought about everything that had happened, I still couldn't believe that I'd been the one to realize that my mother had unwittingly wandered into a situation that had cost her her life. I missed her so much, I could almost taste the sorrow, but knowing why she died and bringing her killer to justice went a long way toward making me feel like I'd let her rest in peace. She was still with me, and always would be, and like my mother, I knew I'd always try to do my best to help the people around me.

Mrs. Branford linked her arm with mine and tugged me forward. "Ready?"

I smiled. "Ready." We walked up the front path-way to the porch. A little table, the top a mosaic made from broken glass and tiles, sat in one corner.

On it was the beautiful Galileo thermometer from the glass shop on the pier. The blue glass bubble inside was at the top, and the yellow-filled one hovered slightly below it. A little note was tucked under the base. I slipped it out and smiled.

> *There's a bottomless bowl of queso for you at Baptista's. But stay balanced, like Galileo. Eat your veggies, too.*
>   *Miguel*

The front door opened. Olaya Solis stood there, a tray of *pan dulce* in her hands. "*Bienvenida,* Ivy. Welcome home."

Gruyère and Black Pepper Popovers

This recipe was inspired by Jodi Elliott, a former co-owner and chef of Foreign & Domestic Food and Drink and the owner of Bribery Bakery, both in Austin, Texas.

Butter for greasing the popover pans or
    muffin tins
2 cups whole milk
4 large eggs
1½ teaspoons salt
½ teaspoon freshly ground black pepper
2 cups all-purpose flour
Nonstick cooking spray
¾ cup Gruyère cheese (5 ounces), cut into
    small cubes, plus grated Gruyère cheese
    for garnishing (optional)

1. Place the oven rack in the bottom third of the oven and preheat the oven to 450°F.
2. Prepare the popover pans or muffin tins (with enough wells to make 16 popovers) by placing a dot of butter in the bottom of each of the 16 wells. Heat the pans or tins in the oven while you make the popover batter.
3. Warm the milk in a small saucepan over medium heat. It should be hot, but do not bring it to a boil. Remove from the heat.
4. In a large bowl, whisk the eggs with the salt and black pepper until smooth. Stir in the reserved warm milk.

5. Add the flour to the egg mixture and combine.
   The batter should have the consistency of
   cream. A few lumps are okay!
6. Remove the popover pans or muffin tins
   from the oven. Spray the 16 wells generously
   with nonstick cooking spray. Pour about
   1/3 cup of the batter into each well. Place
   several cubes of cheese on top of the batter
   in each well.
7. Reduce the oven temperature to 350°F. Bake
   the popovers until the tops puff up and are
   golden brown, about 40 minutes. Remember
   not to open the oven door while baking. You
   don't want the popovers to collapse!
8. Remove the popovers from the oven and
   turn them onto a wire cooling rack right
   away to preserve their crispy edges. Using a
   sharp knife, pierce the base of each popover
   to release the steam. Sprinkle grated Gruyère
   over the finished popovers, if desired, and
   serve immediately.

Makes 16 popovers

Conchas

Conchas Dough

3 teaspoons active dry yeast
½ cup warm water
½ cup lukewarm milk
⅓ cup granulated sugar
⅓ cup unsalted butter, softened
1 egg
1 teaspoon salt
3½–4 cups all-purpose flour
Nonstick cooking spray for greasing the
   cookie sheet

Cinnamon and Vanilla Topping

⅓ cup granulated sugar
¼ cup salted butter
½ cup all-purpose flour
1½ teaspoons ground cinnamon
½ teaspoon vanilla extract

1. Prepare the *conchas* dough by dissolving the
   yeast in the warm water in a large bowl. Add
   the milk, sugar, butter, egg, and salt. Next,
   stir in 2 cups of the flour and mix until
   smooth. Add more flour, a little at a time,
   until the dough is easy to handle and forms
   a ball.
2. Turn the dough out onto a lightly floured
   surface and knead it until it is smooth and
   elastic, about 5 minutes.

3. Place the dough in a large greased bowl, and then turn it so that it is greased side up. Cover the bowl, place it in a warm place, and let the dough rise until it has doubled in size, about 1½ hours. You'll know the dough is ready if an indentation remains after you press on it.

4. While the *conchas* dough is rising, prepare the topping. Beat together the sugar and butter in a medium bowl until light and fluffy. Stir in the flour and mix until a dough with the consistency of a thick paste forms.

5. Divide the topping dough into 2 equal portions. Mix the cinnamon into the first portion and the vanilla extract into the second portion. Divide each portion of topping dough into 6 equal pieces, and then pat each piece into a 3-inch circle. Set the circles aside.

6. Next, grease a cookie sheet with nonstick cooking spray. Punch the *conchas* dough down and divide it into 12 equal pieces. Shape the pieces into balls and place the balls on the prepared cookie sheet.

7. Place 1 topping circle on each ball of *conchas* dough. Shape the circle so that it fits over the ball. Make about 5 cuts across each topping circle to create a shell pattern.

8. Cover the dough balls and let them rise until doubled, about 40 minutes. When 15 minutes of rising remain, preheat the oven to 375°F.

9. Bake the *conchas* for 20 minutes, or until lightly browned.

Makes 12 *conchas*